BOUND BY LOVE

SINNERS SERIES — BOOK 2

SUSAN LIBERTY

DIVA MOUNTAIN BOOKS

COPYRIGHT

First edition March 2021
Print ISBN: 978-0-578-85640-7
Digital ISBN: 978-0-578-85135-8

Book cover designer: Valory Waligoski

Published by Diva Mountain Books
www.susanliberty.com

- *Bound by Love* is dedicated to my dad. He cultivated my love for music. Dad, I know you're rockin' out in Heaven on your electric guitar. Miss you, love you, and I'll be singing with you when we meet again.

CHAPTER 1

ENDLESS ABYSS OF MISERY – HIGH

A warm body cuddles up against my back. Soft, rhythmic breaths caress my spine. I smile. My timid little wildcat has come to her senses. Cookie must have crawled in with me while I was sleeping.

"Hmmm, baby," I hum, keeping my eyes closed, and turn over. It has been a long time coming, but I'm ready to tell Cookie I want to go to the next level—living together. I slither my hand around a *thick waist*. Then, I move my hand up, cupping a *hard as hell fake tit*. A loud snore, followed by two halting snorts, reverberates in my ears—the noxious odor of BO mixed with cheap perfume assaults my nose. I snap my eyes open, jolting back, cracking my head against the headboard.

"Aaah, shit!" I bellow, grabbing my skull. No-no-no, it can't be Trudy, the topless dancer from Ace of Diamonds. She must be a goddamn illusion.

I chance another glance and moan. Nope, the bitch isn't a figment of my imagination; she's here, in my bed. I groan; the woman has had the clap more times than I can count.

What the hell happened last night? *Think, dammit!* It was Sunday night. General, our club's president, sent me to Ace of Diamonds to pick up the take and pay the staff. I did that, and then I had a few drinks at the bar. After that, I'm blank…nothing…nada…goddamn zip. I don't recall bringing Trudy back with me.

"High, wake the fuck up, brother! There's a woman in the game room to see you," yells Sly as he passes by my door.

"Jesus, I'm up," I yell back.

I glance at the alarm clock on my nightstand—8:00 a.m. Who in the hell could be looking for me this early in the morning? Christ, I missed working out with the brothers. We spar for two hours and then cool down with an hour of couples' yoga. Flame's wife, Princess, and Mafia Man's wife, Maggie, run it. Cookie and I used to team up and participate. We'd laugh our asses off, learning new fuck positions.

I reach out my arm, nudging Trudy. "Get your ass up. You need to leave."

Trudy moans, and then she bolts straight up in the bed. "SHIT, I FELL ASLEEP! Shit-shit-shit, this can't be happenin'." She leaps out of bed and digs around on the floor for her clothes. "Oh, g-g-god! He's gonna kill me."

I don't know what the hell she's blabbering on about. She's the intruder…the goddamn bed crasher.

"I need a ride back to Ace, ASAP," mutters Trudy.

I swing my legs over the side of the bed; my bare foot hits something sticky on the floor. I lift my foot; two used condoms are dangling off its sole.

"Dammit!" I peel them off, toss them into the wastepaper basket, and glance over my shoulder. Lord almighty, Trudy's a hot mess: black mascara is running down both cheeks, her red lipstick is smeared over her mouth, and her bleached blonde hair is sticking up in all directions. I cringe. She's naked; her fake tits are on full display.

Lord, I miss Cookie: her long, blonde, daisy-scented hair. The way her body yields to mine. Her tits…she has the most beautiful globes. They're large for her five-foot-three frame. And they have these perfect dusty rose areolas. I miss her giggles and the way she used to speak to me in French when we'd do the dirty. I even miss couples' yoga with her.

You've sunk to an all-time low. Save the "let's be roomies" speech. If Cookie hears about your little sleepover with Trudy, she'll be done with you for good.

Three months ago, the sweet butts ended. Cookie, Jewel, Marshmallow, and Honeypot wanted "real jobs." I lost Cookie as a bed buddy. She needed to work out some shit in her head, and she couldn't do it with me in the picture.

I have no idea what she needs to "work out." It seemed to me we were in a good place. The Sinners had ended all threats: we took out the Diamondbacks, Italian Mafia, South American Cartel, Heaven's Portal, and Landen Logging Company.

The goddamn wrecking ball struck again. Elizabeth Wheeler. I run a hand down my face. Cookie knows about her because of the texts Elizabeth loves to send me. If I don't text back, she blows up my phone. Cookie never said anything; she believes people have their own path to follow in life. If Elizabeth was my chosen path, she would choose another route. But Cookie didn't say that. My best friend, Joker, surmised it: "The woman seems as if she has a lot of baggage, brother. Cookie doesn't need Elizabeth screwing with her head, too."

Elizabeth Wheeler was my high school girlfriend. She was the cliché popular chick all the boys wanted to screw. I was wired over starting college. Elizabeth had a "friend" who was a small-time drug dealer. She said, "Christian, you need to mellow out. Just try weed. I promise you'll like it." I was an athlete and wasn't into drugs. But, for a civilian kid brought up with societal norms, peer pressure is a bitch. I bought a dime bag; that's all it took. Elizabeth and I started getting high together, and then we'd screw like rabbits. I was nicknamed High because I smoked so much of the shit with her. That is, until I took a twenty-foot fall off a bluff, saving her drugged-out ass. That fall ended my college martial arts scholarship. A person can't snap kick repeatedly without a decent knee. After surgery, I got hooked on hillbilly heroin—oxycodone. Me being a stupid kid, I dropped out of college in my second semester and demanded my parents hand over my college fund so I could marry Elizabeth.

My parents told me to end it with Elizabeth Wheeler; she was a troubled girl who needed a meal ticket. Elizabeth's father, Mr. Wheeler, was a community college professor until he got his ass fired for taking bribes from his students.

Mr. Wheeler has what my mom refers to as "champagne taste" on a "beer budget." His thing was gambling on speculative companies. As all dreamers do, he thought his ship would come in and take care of the debt he accrued. Mr. Wheeler has always needed to appear a high roller. Elizabeth drove around in a Lexus SUV and wore only the latest designer clothes. She had her own credit card when her father had the green to pay the bill—hence the five-hundred-dollar A's for his students. The problem: only his students who could afford it received an A, which sent up red flags to the Dean. When pressured, the kids ratted him out.

Dana and Rene Fontaine are the complete opposite of the Wheelers. They don't have an ostentatious bone in either of their bodies. My mom is a retired elementary school teacher. My dad is an ex-Canadian Security Intelligence agent. When he married Mom, he left Canada and planted roots in Butte. Then, he started his own business, Fontaine Commodities. Dad brokers products between foreign countries and the US. My parents worked their asses off to give us a good life. We were well-off compared to most families in Butte, but my parents weren't spendy people. Mom's motto: "You need to save for a rainy day."

My dad made his life all about Mom and me. He taught me everything I know about outdoor life: hunting, fishing, tracking, and camping. Dad was the one who turned me on to mixed martial arts. He was the ultimate badass weekend warrior. He loved his Harley and passed his passion for bikes on to me.

I disrespected my parents when they refused to hand over my college fund. I told them to keep their fucking money and walked out of their house. I haven't spoken to either of them since. Not because I'm still pissed at them. Nope, I love and miss my parents. I'm pissed at how I treated them. I shit on their love and everything they gave me. I doubt they'll ever want to speak to me again. If I had a son like me, I'd kick his ass to the fucking curb.

I was a cocky eighteen-year-old who thought he had the world by the balls. I didn't need college or my parents, so I jumped onto my Harley and headed to Pony. I'd work for Landen Logging Company if it meant I could make enough money to marry Elizabeth.

Yeah, right. Landen Logging Company was where the devil took his dumps. I lived in a tent, without health insurance or money. But nearly starving and freezing to death helped me kick hillbilly heroin damn quick. I was in way over my head. Faith's husband, River, took one look at me and said, "Boy, you have a lot to learn about life." Then he took me to the Reservation and set up a teepee on the side of his tiny two-bedroom house. River took me under his wing, and we became friends. I remember him as always being happy, no matter what the universe was throwing at him. Christ, back then, the Native Americans struggled to put food on the table, clothes on their backs, and heat in their homes. It didn't matter; he loved his people, his wife, and his baby boy.

Two months later, I received the Dear John call from Elizabeth—she'd fallen in love with one of our high school classmates. Jason Cooper was the new love of her life. Elizabeth's newfound *love* probably had something to do with his parents being worth millions. Mr. Cooper owned the meatpacking plant in Butte.

I was devastated and drank myself into oblivion. I took Fawn, a Native American woman five years older than me, to bed, and had unprotected sex with her. Fawn and I found out she was pregnant a month later, and I married her out of duty. We had Megan eight months later. During that time, I met General. He was Running Bear's son-in-law, revered by the Native Americans, and president of Sinners MC. General invited me to the club, and I loved it. *Ride free, die free, in brotherhood.* It was all about badass bikers living by their own set of rules—family, God, country, with distrust for the government. I was all in wanting to become a prospect.

Fawn wasn't happy with my decision. She disliked General and the

Sinners—bossy bikers who had a thumb hold on Running Bear. But if it weren't for General and the Sinners, the Native Americans would have starved and frozen to death, so I didn't give a shit what she thought; I didn't bring her to the club.

Two years later, I became a full brother and received a significant bump in my pay. I bought a fifty-acre chunk of land on Diva Mountain. It had a rundown three-bedroom, one bath hunting cabin on it. I moved my family into the shack with the aspiration of tearing it down and building a large house.

But the universe decided to screw with me again. After three years of not hearing one word from Elizabeth, she called me out of the blue. She said Jason Cooper was killed in a car accident and he'd left her penniless with a three-year-old child to support. There wasn't any life insurance or money in the bank. Her parents were broke, and the Coopers refused to help her. Elizabeth asked me if we could meet for a drink at our old stomping ground, Butte Diner, to discuss her situation.

My marriage was a turbulent cesspool, sucking me under, threatening to drown me. Megan was the only reason Fawn and I were together. Me being a dumbass, I met Elizabeth, not realizing I'd be sucked down into yet another endless abyss of misery.

Turned out, Mr. Wheeler talked Jason into several bad business ventures, and he blew over a mil. Jason's parents refused to give Elizabeth a dime.

That started a seven-year affair between Elizabeth and me. She would call me, and, like a goddamn fool, I would race to her, leaving Megan with her mother. Hindsight being twenty-twenty, that was a stupid move. I was providing the ammo Fawn needed to take Megan and turn her against me. I didn't give a shit if Fawn left me; our relationship was never about love. I was happy to see the backside of her. But I loved my daughter. Megan was mine until I came home to an empty cabin. Devastated and guilt-ridden over losing my kid, I immediately cut all physical contact with Elizabeth.

For the last seventeen years, I've been the one paying for Elizabeth's three-bedroom apartment with the spectacular view of the

Rockies. Along with her cable bill, electric bill, heating bill, cell phone bill, and a cool grand per month for miscellaneous items.

Only the best for Elizabeth and her son.

Over the years, I've asked myself a million times why I continue to support her. Her son isn't mine. It's true; age does bring wisdom. I've come to realize that Elizabeth was just an infatuation. Paying Elizabeth's bills is a habit. Every time I threaten to cut her off, she comes up with a sob story. Elizabeth is relentless; she'll call me multiple times a day, crying. It's easier to pay for the shit.

Bang...bang...bang! "Goddamnit, High! I told you ten minutes ago you had a girl waiting for you in the game room. She needs to leave, but she wants to give you a box," yells Sly through the door.

"Shit," I murmur, trying to figure out who the girl could be.

I glance over my shoulder; Trudy wiggles into her micro lime green miniskirt, then plops her ass down on the floor and buckles her multicolored platform sandals.

"Hey, did you know you have a bag of Hershey's Kisses, a bag of Cheetos, and cans of orange pop under your bed?"

"Leave them fucking there!" JJ, Keeley, JT, and Anna hide their junk food under my bed. It's their "stash."

Christ, the kids crawl around on my floor. I need to sanitize my room after this bitch leaves. I snort. *You need to disinfect yourself.* Trudy screws anything that moves.

I hold the door open. Trudy swipes her faux fur off my dresser and hustles out the door. I retch from the trail of stench she's leaving in her wake: cheap perfume, stale cigarettes, and old grease. *Jesus, never again. You're goddamn thirty-nine years old; you don't need this shit in your life.*

I follow Trudy down the hall and out into the game room. Sly and Cue Ball are at the bar, talking to a woman with long black wavy hair.

"Cue Ball, can you do me a solid and give Trudy a ride to Ace?" I ask, my eyes pinned to the woman's back.

All three heads turn our way. The girl's sky-blue eyes meet my same sky-blue eyes.

I furrow my brow, not trusting who I'm seeing. "Megan?"

"Hello, High. It's nice to see some things never change," says my daughter sarcastically.

Sly and Cue Ball stare at me, then back at Megan.

"Oh, shit," mutters Sly.

Megan turns to Sly, giving him a smile. "Thank you for keeping me company. I need to run." She starts moving toward the door.

JJ and JT come running into the game room; Anna and Keeley are on their heels.

"Uncle High," yells JJ, running toward me.

"JJ, stop," yells Sly. "Don't touch Uncle High!"

"What the fuck, brother?" I ask, irritated as hell.

"It isn't my business where you stick your dick, brother. That said, the kids *are* my business. You slept with the human petri dish and haven't showered," retorts Sly.

Trudy is smart enough not to open her mouth. She's aware Sly would end her.

Sly looks down at JJ. "Anything you four hid in Uncle High's room needs to go into the garbage. Hit the kitchen, Merrill will make you something to eat."

JT's eyes go to me and then to Trudy. He firms his little lips, nodding. "We need to hide our stash in Aunt Cookie's room. She doesn't have a human petri dish."

"What is that?" asks Keeley, moving toward the kitchen behind JT.

JJ shrugs. "I think it has something to do with the dirty. I need to ask my dad." He tosses his arm over Keeley's shoulders. "Aunt Cookie doesn't do the dirty, so her room will be safe."

"Nope, Aunt Cookie never does the dirty," agrees Anna, following them. "Tell us what Uncle Flame says about the petri dish."

Sly chuckles, "Flame is going to kick my ass when JJ asks him about the human petri dish."

I don't miss my daughter's judgmental eye roll aimed at Sly and me. I ignore it; Megan's been raised in the mainstream culture.

"Sly, text Flame. Give him the intel," I order.

Flame won't lie to JJ, but a text will give him time to choose words fit for a four-year-old. Explaining STDs is a hell of a lot different than explaining how babies are made.

"Right," says Sly, pulling out his phone.

General comes through the front door. "Megan, Aunt Raven told me you were thinking of coming to Pony. Did you let your old man know?"

He knows damn well Megan and I haven't spoken in ten years. It wasn't my choice; it was Megan and Fawn's decision to cut me out. General's calling her out on it.

"Hi, Uncle Sean." Megan leans into him, giving his arm a hug. "No, High didn't know I was coming. Things have been a bit crazy."

"Next time give your old man a heads-up," orders General, in his badass tone of voice.

"I'm just here to give High a box from my mom." Megan laughs nervously, "Mom and Ed are downsizing. I need to settle in at Aunt Faith's before I meet Aunt Raven and Aaron Donnelly for lunch. I'm doing a three-month internship at the Reservation's school."

"Fawn is downsizing," repeats General. He looks at me. "Did you know, brother?"

I rub two fingers along my forehead. *Christ, this is goddamn bad.* "No," I breathe out.

"That's something Fawn should have discussed with you, seeing's how you've been flipping her bills for the last twenty-one years. Fucking disrespectful on Fawn's part."

Megan bites her bottom lip.

There is a standing joke among the Sinners: General is more Cherokee than he is Irish. The man was born and raised in Dublin, Ireland, but General's father-in-law is Running Bear, Chief of the Cherokee. General has been his go-to person on all matters for the last forty years. I'm sure he'd dealt with Fawn's shit more than once before I hit the scene and moved her off the Reservation. Fawn is not his favorite person. In fact, if he had his way, the bitch wouldn't be breathing.

Out of a sense of obligation, I decide I need to father up and offer the cabin. It was Megan's home for the first ten years of her life.

"Megan, you could live with me in the cabin. We can get to know each other again."

She slowly turns her eyes to mine and snorts. "Yeah, High, that sounds like a blast. I can get up close and personal with all your floozies. It'd be wonderful to catch an STD from the toilet seat. Thanks, but I think I'll pass."

Everyone in the room goes stiff. I ball my fists at my daughter's disrespect. Yeah, as far as I'm concerned, she can haul her ass right back to Denver.

Megan hugs General, which he doesn't return. We're a brotherhood; disrespecting me is unacceptable to all Sinners.

"Lass, don't spew your goddamn venom in my club," growls General. "If it happens again, you won't be welcome here."

Megan just got an up-front, in-your-face refresher on Sinners' culture.

"Sorry, Uncle Sean," apologizes Megan, rushing out the door.

"The lass has her mother's mouth," growls General. "If she gives that shit to Running Bear, she'll feel my palm on her ass." Pissed off, he walks out of the room.

"Cue Ball, can I have that ride?" asks Trudy anxiously.

"Why in the hell are you tweaking, Trudy?" growls Cue Ball, equally pissed at Megan's disrespect.

"I'm not, Cue Ball. I'm just late, is all," says Trudy from the door. Then she zooms out like the hounds of hell are nipping at her ass.

I head back down the hall toward my room. On the way, I call Patriot, letting him know I'm slipping into the clinic through the back door. I need an STD test, and I don't want Cookie to know I had sex with Trudy.

I'm thirty-nine; I've screwed around long enough. I need to get my life on the same path as Cookie's before it's too late.

CHAPTER 2

INTAKE SPECIALIST – COOKIE

A twenty-something cowboy steps forward, smiling a white-toothy smile down at me. I move my eyes to his right hand; he has his arm bent at the elbow. His fist is cradled to his heart, wrapped in what should be a white towel. The guy's makeshift bandage is saturated crimson—his blood.

"Hey, beautiful," he grins brightly. "I had a fight with my chainsaw and lost."

I inhale, fighting back my lightheadedness. Passing out is not part of the criteria on your first day at Sinners Urgent Care. *Buck up and remember the steps Patriot taught you if an emergency case comes through the door.*

The guy furrows his brow. "You're not going to faint on me, are you, darlin'?"

I push back my chair, leap up, and grab the desk so I don't fall flat on my face.

"Whoa there, little lady." He quickly rounds the desk. "Sit down and put your beautiful head between your knees."

11

What are you doing here? You're a singer; you hate hospitals. But you're here now, and the guy will bleed to death unless you move your butt.

I inhale, filling my lungs with much-needed oxygen. Shoring up my body, I put my arm around the guy's waist as I was taught. *Patients who are in shock faint, Cookie. One minute they will tell you they're fine, the next they're doing a face-plant,* warned Patriot.

The cowboy looks down at me, chuckling. "New on the job." His eyes go to my nameplate. "Chéri. That's French. Right?"

I stupidly nod and keep us moving.

Oui, that's me, Chéri Fayette, ex-singer and ex-sweet butt. Now, I'm the intake specialist for Sinners Urgent Care. I needed a job, and Patriot was desperate.

I snort. *Patriot would have to be in dire need to hire you; the smell of antiseptic makes you woozy. You need to exude confidence. Assure the patient, everything is going to be okay. Escort the patient to an empty stretcher, call for Patriot, Doc, Polly, or one of the nurses. Take the patient's vital signs and fill out a history form.*

"Cook, we're a small clinic. We all wear multiple hats," said Polly as she taught me all the essentials of being a patient care assistant—a job title I don't want. It's one thing to ask for an insurance card; it's a whole different story to do patient care.

I clear my throat and hold my breath. Getting a whiff of the antiseptic will undo me. "Please sit on the stretcher. I'll help you put your legs up. Dr. Kincaid?" I squeak. *Good god, help me.* I clear my throat. "Dr. Kincaid," I say in a stronger voice. "We have a patient in bay two."

A guy yells from bay one: "Aaah, fuck!"

I furrow my brow; I know that voice. It's High's.

Patriot growls, "If you didn't bump uglies with a dancer, you wouldn't need a goddamn Q-tip up your dick. One of the nurses will draw your blood."

My hands shake at hearing Patriot's words. *Non,* High doesn't fool around with dancers. He's picky about his women. He's a Sinner...a badass biker. *You were a sweet butt; you're not allowed to care...you're not allowed to love him.*

I force a smile onto my face and look down at the cowboy.

His eyes go to the curtain and then to me. He chuckles.

I refrain from rolling my eyes and take the guy's vitals.

You have enough crap on your plate. You're climbing the mountain, on your own path to a better life. Keep your eyes forward, and don't look back. Oui, but he's High, and you're going to help him because you love him. Call Jewel ASAP!

CHAPTER 3

RETRIEVING THE GREEN — HIGH

Christ, my cock feels like it's on fire. A Q-tip up your piss hole is no joke. I pound my fist against the steering wheel. How the hell did this shit happen? I don't sleep with goddamn dancers. I haven't slept with anyone except for Cookie in the last two damn years.

My cell buzzes. I yank it from my pocket and look at the caller ID —Patriot. I jab the answer button. "What?"

"Where are you, brother?"

Patriot doesn't sound himself. Christ, my test results must have come back positive.

I blow out a long breath. *Congratulations, you got some messed-up disease from Trudy.*

"I'm on MT-69—fifteen minutes outside of Helena. I need to meet with William Bull about the two new buildings for Sinners Beauty Salon and Sinners Biker Babe Boutique."

"Right," says Patriot. "I forgot. Hey, brother, pull to the side of the highway. I need to discuss something with you."

Jesus, it's fucking bad! I swerve my truck over to the right side of the road. My hands shake; my nerves are buzzing with the pending news.

You're fucked. I lower the window, letting the cold air cool my skin. Inhaling deeply, I fill my lungs with the sweet scent of pine. Then, I look up into the cloud-covered sky. There's no doubt it's going to snow like a bitch.

"High?"

I white-knuckle the steering wheel, steeling myself. "Yeah, Patriot, I'm here. What in the hell did the bitch give me?"

"You need to keep your shit tight, brother. My intake specialist took it upon herself to add a drug screen to your labs."

Intake specialist? I moan. *God no.*

I growl, "How did Cookie find out I slept with Trudy?"

"It's complicated, High. All I know for sure is Cookie called Jewel and asked her to pull up the security footage from last night."

I pound the console. "What...the...fuck?!"

"Brother, you need to calm your ass down and listen."

"Talk!"

"When I confronted Cookie, she said you would never sleep with a dancer willingly." Patriot chuckles, "You're picky about your women. Dancers don't make the list. The security footage showed Trudy helping you out of your truck in front of the club. You were staggering and shit. That tweaked Cookie the hell out, which in turn spurred Jewel to keep searching. Jewel pulled up the security footage at Ace of Diamonds. It shows a guy in his thirties helping you into the passenger seat of your truck."

I furrow my brow. "I don't remember a guy helping me into my truck."

"Nope, you wouldn't. Let me finish. Trudy handed the fucker a black duffel bag."

"The take from Ace?"

"Yeah. Jewel tried to call Beau, but he's hunting. Then the girls decided to call Maggie—"

"Maggie! Why in the hell would Cookie call Maggie and not me?!"

"Brother, Cookie and Jewel were scared. Cookie secretly added bloodwork to your labs, which came back positive for methamphetamine. They knew the duffel contained the take from Ace."

"I'm turning around now. Trudy is fucking dead!"

"Wait, brother, there's more."

For Christ's sake, how much more can there be?

"Maggie, Princess, Jillian, and Raine went to the club and reviewed the footage. You know how they are, brother. The five of them decided they needed concrete evidence."

I groan, "Jesus Christ, what did they do?"

Patriot chuckles, "According to Merrill, the five of them dressed in hazmat suits and entered your room to look for evidence."

I grab the steering wheel, practically ripping it from the column. "Fucking Merrill!"

"Yup. Merrill called General. He didn't want the girls' asses reddened by their husbands. That's when the shit hit the fan." He starts guffawing. "The...girls..." He takes a breath. "The girls held up your used..."

"Aaah, Christ!" I yank the cell away from my ear; pain shoots through my eardrum from his loud as hell guffawing. "My what?!" I yell. "Quit goddamn laughing and tell me!"

Patriot takes a deep breath. "Your used man balloons as proof you couldn't have had sex." He breaks out laughing hysterically. "They... weren't...stretched   out...and...you...didn't...   fucking...come! Concrete motherfucking evidence you were set up by two assholes."

I groan, dropping my head on the wheel. This shit can't be real; I'm a goddamn Sinner.

"Where are Trudy and the asshole?" I growl into the cell.

"In the wind. General called Roxy at Ace. Trudy didn't show for her shift."

I look out the side window—an old white Ford station wagon whizzes by me. I put my truck into gear and peel out onto the highway.

"I just found fucking Trudy," I bark, weaving through the traffic. I jab the end call button, lean over, and grab my Glock from the glove box.

Motherfuckers! I let down the passenger window and step on the gas, pulling up beside the station wagon.

"Pull over," I shout, pointing my pistol at the dude driving.

The asshole looks at me; he pales, his eyes widen. Trudy is screaming at the shithead to speed up. A van coming at me lays on the horn. *Goddamnit!* I swerve behind the station wagon.

"Screw this," I say through gritted teeth. I jam my foot down on the gas and ram the back end of the Ford. It jolts to the right. The asshole yanks the wheel, overcorrects, and the wagon crosses the lane into oncoming traffic. A deafening horn blasts, ear-piercing tires screech, *crash!* Metal against metal reverberates my ears—an eighteen-wheeler smashes head-on with Trudy's vehicle. The semi pushes the station wagon five hundred feet down the highway before it comes to a stop. I hit the brakes, throw my Ford into reverse, and back up. Then, I leap out and run over to the truck driver.

"Hey, bud, are you all right?" I yell up to him. The truck driver is pale. Beads of sweat are forming on his brow—he appears to be in shock. "Stay here, I'll check it out."

The smell of gasoline and burnt rubber is pungent in the air. Smoke from the station wagon is billowing up toward the sky. The car is an accordion; the front seats have been pushed to the back. The entire inside of the vehicle is bathed in blood. Trudy and the asshole are mangled beyond recognition. Christ, the windshield wiper skewered the guy's neck. I reach into the blown-out rear window and grab the duffel.

I glance over at the trucker; another trucker has stopped and is checking him out. They're not paying attention to me. In the distance, sirens are blaring, and red lights are flashing.

Shit! I sprint back to my Ford and toss the duffel bag into the back. Cars are pulling off to the side of the road. I glance at the front end of my truck, clocking the white paint on the bull bars. *Goddamnit!* Getting questioned by the cops isn't an option. I leap into the driver's seat and take off slowly, so I don't draw attention. Emergency vehicles fly by me, going in the opposite direction.

I grab my cell and jab the number for General.

The cell rings once. "High, where the hell are you?"

"Trudy and the asshole had a car accident on MT-69," I yell to be heard over the noise. "They're goddamn toast. I retrieved the green and got the hell out."

"Any blowback?" shouts General, trying to be heard.

"Nope, it was mostly clean. I have a small amount of paint on my bull bars. I need to hang low for a couple of hours. Later." I hit the end call button.

Christ, what a fucked up day!

CHAPTER 4

HE RUINED ME FOR ALL OTHER MEN — COOKIE

It became crystal clear why High was at the clinic. A large part of me was hoping he was being tested for us. High's come to me several times, wanting to talk about our "relationship." I'll admit I miss him. Over the last month, I've been wishy-washy about my decision to break it off. I tried to convince myself my decision had been validated. Isn't it enough High *thought* he slept with Trudy? I battled with myself to stay out of it. But, still, it niggled at me; I knew High wouldn't have sex with a dancer willingly. He dislikes them more than he dislikes Honeypot and Marshmallow. And that's saying something, because he loathes the two ex-sweet butts. The love I have for High won out: I intervened on his behalf.

Patriot questioned me about the added bloodwork. I was scared shitless; my knee was bouncing up a storm beneath my desk. Patriot is a doctor, but he's also a badass biker, part of the brotherhood. I steeled my voice and told him the truth: High would never sleep with a dancer willingly. He's picky about his women. Patriot then asked me about Jewel, Merrill, and the girl posse's involvement. Patriot's knowledge of Jewel, Merrill, and the girl posse's involvement only meant one thing: someone narked me out. Merrill! The Frenchwoman, Chéri Fayette, came out all pissed off. I held my head high, my back ramrod straight, and I told him the truth again. I called Jewel and asked for her help. I took full responsibility; I didn't want any blame placed on my friends. Patriot just tossed an envelope onto my desk. "Give that to High. I need to beat feet." That was it, and he was out the door. Doc, Polly, and the nurses were gone by seven, leaving me to lock up.

I sigh, swipe the envelope off my desk, and tuck it into my hobo bag. I doubt High has an STD. Still, for good measure, I cross myself, saying a prayer for the results to be negative. As much as I hate it, Elizabeth is a factor in High's life. Just as I'm powerless to prevent Sylvie from using drugs, I'm powerless to stop my tears from falling at the thought of High making love to Elizabeth.

Freakin' love. There's no help for it and no getting over High. He ruined me for all other men.

I slide my nameplate out of the holder and place my resignation letter in front of the computer. I was never a quitter, but I don't belong here. From ages seven to seventeen, I sat in waiting rooms to hear if my mother would wake up from her overdose. Or to hear what disease she had received compliments of her johns.

My mind wanders to all the doctors, their faces full of pity for me. Sylvie was like a cockroach; she always survived the poison she shot into her veins. Or whatever new disease she had caught—chlamydia, gonorrhea, herpes, crabs, or vaginal warts.

On our last trip to the hospital, Sylvie was diagnosed with HIV. "It's not a death sentence," said the doctor, fake sympathy laced in his voice. "We have medications to control the virus. Your mother can live a long and healthy life."

The doctor didn't know my love for Sylvie died the night she tried to sell my virginity to one of her pedophile johns for a hit of smack. I was twelve. I threatened to quit paying the rent and feeding her if she tried it again. She never did.

I gave that doctor an eye roll and thought, *Great, a lifetime sentence of Sylvie to look forward to.* I didn't have time for the doctor's insincere sympathy. I needed to get my butt to a gig or busk on the streets of

Quebec. I needed to earn money to pay for Sylvie's medication, the rent, the utilities, and food to put in her belly.

I push the memory away and think of High. I was elated when Jewel called me at 5:00. Trudy had been dealt with: High put her to ground, and the money had been recovered. It may be a sin to want someone dead, but Trudy bit the hand that fed her. Like any rabid dog, she needed to be put down. It's the law of one percent bikers: they protect what is theirs. It wasn't a surprise Merrill narked me out to General. Merrill claims he's loyal to the sisterhood, but in reality, he's loyal to the brotherhood. I don't blame him; that's the way it should be. I just need to take care and not tell him anything I don't want to be spread wide.

I glance out the window. The sky is pitch black; the snow is coming down heavily. Cringing, I kick off my Crocs and tuck them into a plastic bag. Then, I pull on my secondhand Timberland boots. It's 10:00 p.m. I needed to finish the insurance claims. Just because I'm quitting doesn't mean I should leave work for my replacement.

I glance around one last time. The clinic is overwhelmingly busy. Polly wasn't kidding when she said we needed to wear multiple hats. I became excellent at taking the patient's history and doing their vital signs. I even cleaned and dressed a few wounds after Patriot showed me how.

Yup, and you only needed to puke five times.

I shrug into the parka Brainiac gave to me and trudge out the door. Putting my eye to the scanner, I listen for the deadbolt to slide home. Then I look over at the Cayenne, which is covered by two feet of snow. Princess gave me the Porsche after Brainiac taught me how to drive. I cried so hard Flame needed to leave. He doesn't do "emotional bitches." I couldn't help it; the good in life rarely comes my way. Princess hugged me. "It's no big deal, Cookie. The Cayenne is ten years old; it's not worth much." To me, it's worth the world.

I don't have a driver's license or a green card. The Sinners are a one percent motorcycle club: those things are trivial to them. "We live in Pony, Cookie. No one gives a shit if you don't have a driver's license. I'll pay you off the books, in cash, every Friday," said General.

General is like the father I never had—a badass, handsome, older biker who puts his family first.

I inhale the fresh, crisp, pine-scented air. I love everything about Pony, Montana. The people are friendly, the town is a little piece of heaven. Though I'm betting it will change when Diva Mountain Native American Village opens next year. It will still be better than Quebec. The public housing I lived in from ages seven to eighteen was dirty, smelled of rank garbage and cat pee.

Tears brim my eyes. If I'm going to stay in Pony, I need a job. I sniff, wiping my nose on my forearm. The only thing I know how to do is sing. Tomorrow, I need to scope out the more prominent cities surrounding Pony. I need an under-the-table coffeehouse or bar gig. If I don't land one, I'll need to take my chances and busk on the street. It's dangerous without a permit; if I get caught, I'll be sent back to Canada.

Canada isn't the worst thing that can happen to you—Stratton Records could tell the authorities you killed Brian. I exhale, reassuring myself, *you've stayed under the radar all your life; you can do it again.*

I'm just about to clean off the Porsche when bright lights beam me in the eyes. A truck is pulling into the parking lot.

Merde-merde-merde, it's late, you're alone, speed it up. My heart starts pounding as I do double time with my snowbrush. The memory of me being held down, fighting helplessly, hits my chest like a sledgehammer. Adrenaline rushes through my veins. *Hurry, get into the SUV!* I fight for breath, fumbling to find the door handle covered in snow.

The person parks beside me and lets down the passenger window.

I slump heavily against the Cayenne. *Breathe, it's just High.*

"Cook, get in," he yells over the wind.

Every part of me wants to jump into his vehicle. *For god's sake, don't look at him, or you'll cave.* High is a beautiful French American with longish dark wavy hair, gorgeous sky-blue eyes, and six-foot-two inches of pure muscle. And he has a magnificent smile that starts my lady parts dancing. His voice is deep; it rumbles right through me like a train bound for glory. I'm twenty-two, and High is thirty-nine, but age doesn't matter to me. *He's the kind of candy you need to resist.*

Unlike most of the Sinners, High didn't hide his past from me. I know he's divorced and has a daughter a year younger than me. I'm aware Elizabeth was the cause of his failed marriage. She still has her hooks in him; High always answers her multiple phone calls per day. He claims they're not together. That's difficult for me to believe, given he pays all her bills. But, still, the heart wants what it wants, and my heart wants High.

I wish I could lay all the details of my challenging day onto High's strong shoulders. I want to tell him about the twenty-something cowboy who just about severed his hand. And about the lady with the gangrene toe Patriot cut off. And about the kid who stuck a Lego in his ear. I want him to hold me while I tell him I puked five times. I want to hear him laugh over the lady who stripped naked for an infected hangnail on her pinky. She was all pissed off when Polly walked into her bay. The woman wanted Doc or Patriot to take care of her. I want him to commiserate with me over the stupid insurance forms. I want to tell him how sad I am at needing to resign because I'm weak—I can't let go of the things that haunt me.

None of that matters now. It's over, pull your big girl panties up and drive yourself home.

I shake my head and keep brushing. "I need my SUV for tomorrow. Thanks, but I'll be okay; I'll go slow."

High leaps out of his truck and jogs over to me. He takes the brush out of my hand, lifts me up, and plunks me into the passenger seat of his Ford. "Buckle up," he growls. "I'll drive you back in the morning." He slams my door and tosses my snowbrush into the bed. He slides behind the wheel, bitching about Doc and Patriot leaving me at the clinic all alone in a goddamn snowstorm. Then he puts the Ford into gear, and we're pulling onto Diva Mountain Road.

I'm about to open my mouth when High's phone rings. He jabs the answer button and listens for a second. "Yeah, I found her, brother. Cookie was still at the goddamn clinic."

I'm deflated. High didn't come on his own accord; one of the guys told him to look for me.

"It's not happening again, Patriot," barks High. "Cookie leaves with everyone else, or she won't *be* working at the clinic!" He jabs the end call button and tosses his cell onto the dash.

No worries there, I quit.

I chance a look at him. His jaw is granite, and he has an iron grip on the wheel. I turn my gaze to the windshield. The snow is falling more rapidly; the truck's back end is fishtailing with every bump in the road.

High breaks the silence: "Your ass was supposed to be home by eight."

Ignoring him, I dig through my hobo bag and pull out his envelope. Then I slide it onto the dash. "Patriot asked me to give you that."

High glances at it. Then he clears his throat. "Thanks for helping me out today."

My eyes start to brim with tears, and my nose is prickling. I blink back my tears and yank a tissue from my bag. I dab my nose. *You're just emotional and tired from your day. A warm shower and a glass of cab will set your mind straight.*

"It was no big deal," I mumble, keeping my eyes straight ahead.

High blows out a long breath. He glances at me. "You're upset. What happened?"

"I'm not upset," I try to say airily. *Darn it, it came out too high-pitched to be believable. Oh, who gives a fig.*

High pounds his fist against the steering wheel. "My daughter showed up at the club this morning and witnessed the entire screwed up mess with Trudy. I'm tired, and I'm not fucking around. You're upset. Why?"

I shake my head, unable to speak without crying.

High sighs, turning onto Sinners Road. "Cook…"

"High, you have a woman, Elizabeth, and a daughter, Megan. I'm sure Megan will come around when she hears the truth from you. I'm not your responsibility."

"Cookie," growls High, pulling up to Sinners' clubhouse.

I leap out of the truck. "Thanks for the ride. I'll get someone to give me a lift in the morning."

I slam the door and run for the clubhouse. Tears are streaming down my cheeks. I wipe them away and inhale deeply, gathering myself. *No one needs to see you crying over High or the stupid job.* I swing open the door and head inside.

"Hey, Cookie," smiles Joker from behind the bar. "How was your first day at work?"

I plaster a fake smile onto my face. "Really good, Joker," I lie.

He holds up a manila envelope. "I picked up the mail. This came for you."

I stare at it as if it's filled with anthrax. There is only one person it could be from. When I first came to Pony, I had written to my mother, explaining things didn't go as planned with the record label, and I couldn't send her any money.

I move to the bar on jelly legs and take the envelope with a shaky hand. I examine the return address. The hair on the back of my neck stands up; my heart starts pounding. A cold sweat breaks out all over my body. *Wrong. So freakin' wrong.*

Stratton Records found me.

Sylvie Fayette is only concerned about herself and what I can do for her. I'm sure she noticed where I posted the letter and contacted Stratton Records. I'm her cash cow she won't allow to dry up.

I snort, staring at my name. The saying is correct: a person can't hide forever. The devil is at my door.

"Hey, are you all right?" asks Joker, staring at me. "You're pale."

"*Oui*, thanks." I run for my room, wanting to forget Chéri Fayette and Cookie ever existed.

CHAPTER 5

EAR STALKER — HIGH

For the last fifteen minutes, I've been pacing outside, in the freezing cold, trying to get my temper under control. Elizabeth has ruined my life for the last time. In the morning, I'm cutting her ass loose. I don't give a shit if she needs to live in a cardboard box. The bitch can get a damn job. I snort. Flame, Mafia Man, and I are three fucking peas in a pod. All three of us were taken for a ride by bitches. But they smartened up, and so can I.

And Megan, she's *been* a goddamn adult. She could have looked me up years ago. I love my kid, but screw her judgmental attitude. "Glad some things never change, High," I mock, waving my test results in the air like a lunatic. *If she doesn't want a relationship with you, it's okay. You've lived without her for ten goddamn years...while paying alimony and child support.* I'm the one who forked over the dough for Megan's Stanford University education. She got a full ride, on me—housing, books, spending money, and a goddamn meal card. Did I get a thank you card or a fucking phone call? Nope! "Ed and Mom are downsizing," I mock again. Ed and Fawn have been sucking me dry for the last ten years.

Fawn had the nerve to send me pictures of Megan—goddamn holidays, dance recitals, birthdays, and graduations. For years I'd begged the bitch for them. I'm done with the fucking guilt trip.

I storm through the door and clock Joker at the bar. "Did Cookie go to her room?"

Joker stares at me. "Brother, now probably isn't the time to fight with Cookie. She received an envelope from Stratton Records. I thought it was junk mail, but she took one look at it and became pale and sweaty. I thought she was going to fucking faint. Jewel is with her."

"What the hell is Stratton Records?"

Joker turns his computer, showing me a website. "Was Cookie a singer? Stratton manages singers and bands."

Christ, I know nothing about Cookie other than she's French Canadian, she likes wine, and she's excellent in the sack. Oh, and she loves to cuddle up close at night. I was her personal heater.

"I don't know," I confess, rubbing my forehead. "You said Jewel is with her?"

Joker nods. "Yeah, brother. I went up to check on her. She was crying, but Jewel was calming her down." He chuckles, "If Cookie's a singer, we could use her at Callaghan's Bar. Marshmallow got booed off the stage again. General had to give everyone a free round. He was pissed as hell."

"He needs to put that bitch on a bus."

I've heard Marshmallow sing. The lazy bitch sounds like a blue jay screeching. I grab the box of Megan's pictures. They might work as an icebreaker with Cookie.

I round the bar, grabbing two wineglasses. Wine isn't my thing, but I can drink it. "Joke, grab a bottle of cab."

Joker pulls a bottle from the wine rack, pops the cork, and hands it to me. "What are you going to do, brother?"

"I need to get Cookie to talk."

"Good luck with that. I don't think the girl has said more than a dozen words since we've known her."

I nod and head for the stairs armed with the wine and Megan's pictures.

It's past time I learn Chéri Fayette's history and set her straight on Elizabeth.

I raise my hand to knock on Cookie's door and stop. I'm taking a page out of Mafia Man's book—an ear stalker.

"Cookie, you know who I am," murmurs Jewel. "I'll have Beau access my account, and we'll just pay Stratton Records off."

Who the hell is Jewel? And what does Beau have to do with her? I knew Jewel wasn't the typical sweet butt. She's beautiful and intelligent. But even if I wanted Jewel—which I don't—she's untouchable. Joker won't admit it, but all his actions indicate he has a thing for her.

Honeypot is a big-boobed girl with an agenda. The ditzy Valley girl act is just that, an act. She reminds me of Elizabeth. For me, that made her a no-go zone.

Marshmallow is a hot mess. She packs on the makeup and has a boob job that rivals Farrah Abraham's. Her tits have the appearance of blow-up floatation devices. I snort. *If you stick her with a pin, maybe she'll whiz off into the atmosphere.* Marshmallow's a devious, lying, lazy bitch without an ounce of loyalty. Josie and Dyson were toxic to the club and needed to be put to ground. Marshmallow was their friend; she's just as toxic. She lurks around the brothers, trying to gain intel into club business. In church, I've voted multiple times to put her on a bus to nowhere. But the bitch always manages to pull a rabbit out of a hat to save her ass: Marshmallow gave up Dyson to Mafia Man. It was a good thing, done for the wrong reason. Then she helped out with the Diamondbacks. It wasn't to benefit the Sinners; it was to save herself. The bitch knew she was bound for the bus.

I sigh, turning my attention back to Jewel and Cookie.

"*Non*, it's too dangerous for you, Jewel. Besides, the authorities will ask questions about Brian Stratton. I can't get Pick, Beau, you, or the club involved. Stratton died in the freakin' motel, Jewel." Cookie starts crying. "I don't want anyone to know."

"Cookie, you didn't kill Stratton; the evil man had a heart attack.

After what he did to you, I'm glad he's dead. You didn't tell your mother you're living in Pony or about the Sinners. Right?"

"*Non*, I didn't tell Sylvie," sniffles Cookie.

The sound of papers shuffling comes through the door.

"Stratton Records doesn't know you're here. They're fishing, Cookie. Look at the address; it only says Chéri Fayette, Pony, Montana, with the zip code. We're going to send this back to Stratton Records as undeliverable. If they come looking, we'll tell Beau. He'll know what to do. No more worrying."

There is a squeak of the bed, and then the glug of liquid hitting glass. Cookie says something. Christ, I can't make it out; she's sobbing.

"Cookie, I love you—no more crying. Patriot, Doc, and Polly were wrong to leave you at the clinic. Anything could have happened to you. We came here for protection. If the Sinners aren't going to look out for us, we're moving on. We have options."

Marshmallow knocks me in the shoulder. "Didn't anyone ever tell you eavesdropping is rude?"

Jesus! All my attention was on Cookie and Jewel; I didn't hear the bitch come up the stairs.

"Fuck you, Marshmallow," I growl. "Mind your own goddamn business, or I'll snap your fucking neck."

She runs past me, squealing like a pig. *Christ, I hate that lazy bitch.*

Cookie's door flies open. Jewel stares at me and then looks at the wine. "High."

"Jewel," I growl, pushing past her. "Leave and close the door behind you."

I set the wine and box onto the nightstand. Then I drop to my knees in front of Cookie. "Hey," I murmur, wiping her tears away with my thumbs.

Cookie takes one look at me and bursts into hysterical, heart-wrenching sobs.

"Oh, shit." I lift her into my arms. "Shh, everything is going to be okay." I sit on the bed, scoot back, and lie down with Cookie. She's crying into my chest, her body shuddering. Cocooning her within my body, I repeatedly coo, "You're safe."

After a half hour, she's cried herself to sleep. I blow out a breath, not daring to move in fear we'll have a repeat. I'll get no answers tonight; something or someone majorly rattled my woman today.

I sigh, looking around her room. She has a keyboard set up in the east corner, a guitar to its left. There are papers and pencils strewn across the floor next to a fuzzy white beanbag chair. Colorful scarves are draped off the corners of the kids' framed artwork they gave her as gifts. There is a rickety cherry table in the west corner of the room; she uses it as a makeup vanity. Silver, wooden, and glass picture frames cover every available surface. She has all the brothers and the brothers' women. Numerous photos are of Jewel, Maggie, Princess, Jillian, Raine, and the kids. Multiple pictures are of Brainiac. My eyes dart to the nightstand; it's covered with candid shots of me.

"Baby," I murmur, kissing her crown. "We're going to make it through this shitstorm."

CHAPTER 6

DREAM OF ALL DREAMS — COOKIE

I snuggle into High, burying my nose into his pit. I love his warmth, his unique smell of spice and maleness, and the way his large, muscled body engulfs me. Squeezing my eyes shut, I breathe High in. Just for a few minutes, I pretend High loves me, and he's mine to love back. It's a silly illusion.

I furrow my brow, mulling that over. Maybe it's not a pipe dream; High came to me last night. He slept, holding and comforting me. Over the past three months, he's wanted to talk about our "relationship." I'm the one who pushed him away because of Elizabeth.

I say a silent "I love you" and untangle myself from High's limbs. Then, I scoot off the bed, go over to the window, and stare at the full moon illuminating the snowcapped mountaintops. A tear runs down my cheek—some girls dream of meeting Mr. Wonderful, having the house with the white picket fence, and babies. I look up into the dusky sky. Girls like me wish for a safe haven. Now, I find myself dreaming of having it all with High. *Even if you received the dream of all dreams, a life with High, you'd still need a job. Move your butt. You're no leeching loafer.*

I turn away, swipe my makeup off the vanity, and tiptoe over to my dresser. I inch the top drawer open and grab a pink thong, matching bra, and pink socks. Then I head to the closet. Looking over my multitude of clothes, I choose a pair of Racer low-rise dark skinny jeans, a white tee ripped in all the right places, and black Balmain three-inch-heeled over-the-knee boots.

I found a flea market just outside of Butte. Rich people are frivolous: they need the newest styles in season. I learned at a young age how to get items with very little money. The trick is to hit the flea markets and farmers' markets late in the day. The vendors are tired, and they hate to pack up their wares and haul them back home. The key is not to have your heart set on anything and never, ever get into a bidding war. It helps to be a size one and wear a size five-and-a-half shoe: there isn't much competition. The other important component is to look poor: if the vendor thinks you have money, you're done. My entire outfit cost me seven dollars. The picture frames and vanity I got for free. I bought the scarves in bulk for two dollars, and, lucky me, there was a Canon digital camera with the cords at the bottom of the box.

Raven giggled at me when I offered to do General's, Tristen's, and her laundry to use a printer. "Just use the printer, Cookie. Sean can afford the ink." I looked for a unique gift for General. Ink isn't cheap. I found a set of Harley Davidson bookends from 1940 at a garage sale on my way home from the flea market. The old guy said, "Take them, sweetheart. Everything left is going to the dump."

I brought the bookends home and cleaned them up. Then, I wrapped them in the pretty pink paper I'd saved from one of the kids' birthday parties—waste not, want not. General chuckled when I handed him his gift and thanked him for the use of his printer. I didn't stick around to watch him open it. Gifts—giving or receiving—make me uncomfortable.

Later that night, General, Tristen, and Raven came to my room and gave me a gift basket of wine and cheese. They kissed me on the cheek and thanked me for the bookends. Tristen told me they were a collector's item worth more than a little ink. Raven said she put them on General's desk in their home. General just stared down at me; I'm not sure what he was thinking. General knows how Pick found me... beaten, and more than half dead, lying on an alley grate. Maybe the Callaghans were nice because they felt sorry for me.

I tiptoe out of the closet and look over at High. He's lying on his side, hugging my pillow. His wavy black hair has flopped over his face —he's the most beautiful man on earth.

I hit the bathroom and brush my teeth. I can't take a shower; it'll wake High. I wash the essential bits and put my hair into a ponytail. Then I quickly apply my makeup, get dressed, and put on all the silver jewelry I own. I look myself over in the mirror—a blonde-haired, blue-eyed, tiny rocker girl. *You'll do.* I soundlessly slip out of the bathroom, grab my guitar, and swipe my coat, hobo bag, and wool scarf off the chair. I carefully sneak out the door and head for the stairs. With luck, Merrill will give me a ride for an IOU.

I run down the stairs, making sure my heels don't click. A low whistle comes from the back corner of the game room. I look over. *Merde-merde-merde.* It's Joker.

"Where are you going so early in the morning dressed like that, Cook?"

I ignore his comment on how I'm dressed. "I need to get my butt to Sinners Urgent Care," I say, not stopping to chat. I'm praying the kitchen is empty except for Merrill.

"Merrill," I call, pushing open the swinging door. "Are you up?"

Merrill chuckles, coming out of his bedroom. He looks over at me, his eyes widen. "Sweetheart, what are you up to?"

"I just need a ride to Sinners Urgent Care. Will you take an IOU?"

"Cookie, I know you were upset last night. How about you tell me what happened?" says Merrill, leaning against the counter.

"Nothing happened, Merrill. I was just tired from my first day. Can I have a ride?" I ask, tossing a banana and an apple into my hobo bag.

He runs a hand down his face. "Yeah, sweetheart." He grabs his coat off the hook. "Cookie, you can come to me with anything. I won't say a word to anyone."

I refrain from rolling my eyes; he's the one who narked me out to General about High.

I nod, slipping garbage bags over my boots: the snow and salt will ruin the leather. I slide my guitar into another. Then, I head out the back door to wait by Merrill's truck.

Thank god it has stopped snowing. I hope the weather holds, driving in wintery weather is freakin' frightening. A frigid wind whips around me, making me shiver. The whopping fifteen degrees feels more like fifteen below.

Shoot, I forgot to make a travel mug of tea. Go without or break my rule? I never, ever buy food or drinks from restaurants or convenience stores. They're a rip-off. I'll decide on the road.

Merrill jabs the fob to unlock the doors. I hop into his Ford and carefully place my guitar next to my leg.

He slides into the driver's seat and starts the truck. Then he says, "What's the guitar for?"

"I thought I'd try a little music therapy on the patients," I lie.

"Hmm," he hums, driving down to Sinners' gate. He waves to the prospect, who waves back and opens the gate.

I stare out the window, trying to formulate a plan. Tears sting the backs of my eyes; I'm scared.

Come on, you've needed to do this all your life. You were seven years old singing in a darn coffee shop and busking on the streets. At fourteen, you were singing in friggin' dive bars.

I inhale, then blow out a breath. Butte is a big city; that's the best place to find a gig or busk. Parks are best for busking in the summer. *It's winter—find a food truck. People hang by food trucks. They'll give you their change.*

Merrill glances at me. "Cookie, please talk to me."

I watch him make the left-hand turn into Sinners Urgent Care parking lot. He pulls up in front of the building.

"I need to open up. Thanks for the ride, Merrill," I say, grabbing my guitar and hopping out.

"Okay, sweetheart. I'll see you back at the compound when you're done."

I nod and run up the steps. Merrill waves, driving off. I wait for his truck to disappear from view. Only then do I run back down the steps and over to my Cayenne.

Shoot! High threw my snow brush into the bed of his truck.

I use my hand and arm to brush away the snow. Then, I open the back door, lying my guitar onto the back seat. I clean off the driver's side door and hop in. I'm a popsicle; my entire body is trembling. My hand is shaking so badly, it takes me four tries to get the key into the ignition. Cold air comes blasting out of the vents, chilling me to the bone.

I bang my forehead against the steering wheel. *God, please help me. I'm tired of being scared.* A Maggie saying enters my mind: what doesn't kill you makes you stronger.

I sit up and wipe away my tears. Then I put the Cayenne into drive, and head for Butte.

CHAPTER 7

COMMON-LAW MARRIAGE — HIGH

I take a deep inhale, filling my lungs with the scent of Cookie. "Hmm," I hum, reaching over to get a cuddle. My arm comes up empty—cold sheets. I listen for the shower; I get nothing but the birds chirping and the squirrels chittering outside the window. Stretching, I reach for my cell on Cookie's nightstand—8:00. Shit, I missed working out with the brothers again.

I roll out of bed—my plan is piss, Cookie, coffee, shower. I roll my eyes; then I'll call my ex-wife, Fawn, and the "other woman," Elizabeth. That will be as fun as taking the Q-tip up my cock. The women are archenemies. It's laughable: Elizabeth calls Fawn the curse. Fawn calls Elizabeth the gangrenous appendage. They're two of a kind—moneygrubbing women looking for a free ride.

On my way to the bathroom, I catch sight of the Stratton Records envelope lying on top of Cookie's vanity. I take a quick piss, wash, and strut back out of the bathroom. Snatching the envelope off the vanity, I head back to the bed. I drop down, pulling out the papers. The letter is threatening to sue Cookie for breach of contract. It's no wonder she was tweaked, the goddamn bastard! My eyes focus on who signed the letter: Brian Stratton. But Cookie told Jewel Brian Stratton died in a motel room, and dead men don't sign letters.

The twenty-five-page contract is filled with legal language that only Princess or Pick could decipher. After reviewing it three times, I get the gist—Stratton Records owns Chéri Fayette.

I blow out a breath and tuck the papers back into the envelope. According to the document, all expenses would come out of Cookie's cut, and there is an exorbitant management fee. I need to convince Cookie to let Pick review the contract and break it. Cookie was eighteen when she signed the damn thing; I doubt she had a lawyer.

I toss the envelope back onto the vanity and yank on my jeans. Then, I make the crazy decision to move into Cookie's room. I look around, deciding where to put my dresser. Chuckling, I shove Cookie's dresser four feet to the right, careful not to knock off her baubles. I eyeball the area—it'll fit. I leave *our room* and jog down the stairs to find Cookie. The game room is void of people, and there aren't any voices coming from the war room. That's unusual; there is always someone around. I walk into the kitchen. "Cookie!" I shout, darting my eyes around the room. The brothers are at the tables, eating breakfast.

Christ, Megan is here. I roll my eyes, childishly pissed at the way she treated me yesterday. I ignore her sitting with Raven and General.

Merrill turns away from the stove. "I dropped Cookie off at Sinners Urgent Care two-and-a-half hours ago."

My phone vibrates. I yank it from my pocket and hit the message icon.

> Patriot: Brother, I'm looking for Cookie. I need to talk with her ASAP.

> Me: She's at Sinners Urgent Care.

> Patriot: I'm at Sinners Urgent Care. She left me her goddamn resignation letter!

"Merrill, when you dropped Cookie off, was she upset?" I ask while texting Patriot.

> Me: I'll call you in a few, brother.

Merrill furrows his brow and tries to look at my phone. "Why are you asking me that?"

"Just answer my fucking question!"

"High, what the hell is going on?" asks General. "Where is Cookie?"

I run a hand through my hair. "I don't know. Merrill just said he dropped her off at Urgent Care. But Patriot texted she left him her resignation letter, and she's not there."

"No," says Jewel, pulling out her phone. She looks at Beau. "I told you Cookie was distraught last night. The clinic messed with her head. Patriot, Doc, and Polly left her alone. She's afraid to be alone."

Beau takes the cell from Jewel. "Calm down, we'll find her." He jabs a button on Jewel's phone and waits for a few beats. "Hey, sweetheart, it's Beau. Call Jewel back ASAP. We're all worried."

"She didn't answer?" I bite out, knowing she didn't. Beau left her a goddamn message.

Beau shakes his head. "Nope."

I swing my glare to Merrill. "You were the last one to see her…."

"Cookie wasn't herself this morning. I asked her to talk to me. She wouldn't," says Merrill, pinching his forehead. "She was decked out in rocker clothes and had her guitar. She said she was going to do music therapy with the patients."

"Rocker clothes?" I ask, glaring at Merrill.

What in the hell are you up to, Cook?

"Yeah, dark skinny jeans, ripped tee, high-heeled over-the-knee boots…they were killer. Makeup and jewelry…the full shebang. Cookie was off-the-charts, gorgeously hot. Not that I was looking in that way—"

"And you didn't fucking think to come and get me?!" I bellow, banging my fist down on the counter.

"Cookie's in Butte," says Flame, his eyes on his cell. "She just turned onto Grand Street."

"Butte? Grand Street? How in the fuck do you know that?" I growl, irritated as hell.

"I put a tracker in the Cayenne. I worried about Corrie driving in the snow," he explains, holding up his phone.

Grand Street is where the working class hang out. The bars aren't clubs, therefore, they don't charge an arm and a leg for drinks. The cover charges are five bucks instead of the twenty-five bucks the clubs get for hosting bands on Friday and Saturday nights.

"Beau, look," says Jewel, holding out Flame's phone. "She's looking for a gig!" Jewel starts crying. "She's alone; anything can happen to her. Cookie doesn't have a driver's license, a visa, or immigration approval to live here. Stratton Records will find her."

Raven stares at me. "Is Cookie a musician?"

"Quebec's next Celine Dion until she blew it," laughs Marshmallow.

"Shut your mouth, Marshmallow," I growl. "You're a dumb shit. Celine Dion is from Charlemagne."

Beau rubs Jewel's back. "No worries, Pick can sort out her immigration status and Stratton Records."

"Sean," says Raven, "you need to talk to Cookie. Something upset her. She trusts you."

"Nope." General takes a sip of his coffee. "High will handle Cookie. She slept with him…she trusts him."

Megan harrumphs, opening her mouth.

I point to her. "Shut it. You're in my home. I won't tolerate you disrespecting me. I love you, but you can go right back to your mother with that attitude." I turn away, then decide I need to lay it out. I swivel back to Megan. "Your mother won't be getting any more support checks from me. If you need money, come and see me."

Joker chuckles low. "It's past time your father handed you your ass."

I glare at Megan, letting her know talking back to Joker won't be tolerated. Then, I look over at Flame. "Text me the app and password, brother. I'll log in and keep track of her. Joke, I need some help moving my dresser into Cookie's room."

"You're not going after her?" asks Jewel incredulously.

Joker stands and kisses Jewel on her crown. "Babe, we have eyes on her. Grand Street is safe during the day. Give High time to straighten out Cookie's head."

I storm down the hall and hit the button for Fawn. The phone rings three times. "Hello, High."

"Fawn, thanks for the goddamn heads-up on Megan coming to Pony," I say sarcastically, walking into my room.

"High, Megan is an adult. If she wanted you to know she was interning at the Reservation, she would have called you," says Fawn snippily.

Fucking bitch!

"You're right. Meg is a goddamn adult," I bark into the phone. "My support and alimony checks are done, Fawn."

"High, you can't do that. The hundred grand is gone."

I gave Fawn a hundred grand, essentially buying her out of my property on Diva Mountain. I didn't want her coming back, claiming she owned half of it.

"I depend on my monthly check to live, High. Running Bear has refused my request for a cut of the Native American businesses. Corinne Hunter has blocked all my attempts. The court won't even hear my case."

I roll my eyes. Many Native Americans who left the Reservation have tried to get a piece of the pie from Running Bear. It doesn't surprise me Fawn is among them.

"The alimony and support checks weren't court-ordered, Fawn," I remind her. "You've been living with Ed for the past ten years and siphoning off me. Tell Ed to get a goddamn job; the money train has hit the end of the line."

With Fawn screeching at me, I hit the end call button. *Bye, bitch.*

My ex-wife was never a meek Native American woman. Fawn has a big mouth and is never afraid to use it. Our sex life was mediocre at best. Wham, bam, thank you, ma'am, and I was out of there. We slept with Megan tucked between us: the cabin was drafty, and I was worried she'd freeze to death. Therefore, sex was something we rarely had.

Ed Munson worked at Pony Market as a butcher. Faith told me Fawn had fallen in love with Munson before she ever met me. "Ed was married, High. It took him years, but he finally left his wife." Faith is a good woman; she tried to alleviate my guilt for stepping out on Fawn. She believed Fawn was the first to have an affair.

My mind goes to the worst day of my life. It was Christmas Eve. Elizabeth asked me to come and celebrate with her and Jason Jr. Elizabeth's parents were out of town, and she didn't want to spend the holidays alone. We'd been seeing each other for seven years, but I had become tired of Elizabeth, the demands she made for money, and the sneaking around. I was twenty-nine and had a ten-year-old daughter. We were still living in a shack because I was paying Elizabeth's bills. Elizabeth's and my sex life had gone to shit years earlier. I wanted Elizabeth, her son, and her financial problems out of my life. But, in honor of our friendship, I acquiesced and went to Butte.

I had every intention of leaving that night; I wanted to spend Christmas Day with Megan. Elizabeth put Jason to bed, and then she poured us drinks—one turned into two, and then three. I was exhausted from working the nightshift at Ace; I fell asleep on Elizabeth's couch. The next day, Elizabeth talked me into staying for an early Christmas dinner. Stupidly, rather than fight about it, I agreed. I left Butte at 5:00 that evening. It was snowing like a bitch; it took me over two hours to get home. When I got there, Megan and Fawn were gone. Ed Munson had packed them up on Christmas Eve and drove them to Denver, Colorado. Fawn left the Dear John letter on the kitchen table.

A month later, I received the divorce papers. Megan refused to talk to me, let alone see me. I made a verbal agreement with Fawn: I'd buy her out of the Diva Mountain property, give her four thousand dollars per month, and I wouldn't petition the court for visitation. General thought I was crazy. "High, you weren't the only one stepping out on the marriage." Yup, but I lost my daughter because of it. I wasn't going to allow my kid to be used as a weapon.

I threw out most of the shit, locked up the cabin, and moved into Sinners' clubhouse. I cut ties with Elizabeth except for paying her bills. It was a "friendship" thing; I felt sorry for her. Elizabeth had shitty parents and a dead husband. The Coopers didn't want anything to do with their grandson. The years rolled on; I kept writing the checks and taking her whiny-ass calls.

I remember exactly when Cookie decided she needed a break. We were in the heat of things: Cookie was blowing me, and I looked at my goddamn phone. Elizabeth needed a "loan" for Jason's tuition.

Game over! The next day, Cookie told me she needed to get her head on straight.

"High, where did you go, brother?" chuckles Joker. "You've been staring out the window for the last fifteen minutes."

I smirk and download the app Flame sent me. Cookie is still on Grand Street.

Joker looks over my shoulder. "Do you love Cookie?"

"Yup," I affirm, pulling the dresser away from the wall. "Let's get it done. I need to cut another bitch loose and hit Verizon for a new phone."

"Elizabeth," chuckles Joker. "She won't take to that without a fight. Make the call, I'll wait."

Joker is my best friend—supportive, nonjudgmental, and always has my back.

I jab the button for Elizabeth and put it on speaker. *I need a goddamn witness.*

She picks up on the second ring. "Hey, Chris, I was just thinking about calling you. I'm planning Jason's graduation party. Butte Country Club wants a two-thousand-dollar deposit."

Joker rolls his eyes, giving my phone double middle fingers.

"Liz, I'm not going to bankroll Jason's goddamn graduation party from business school."

Christ, the kid flunked out of college more times than I can count. Jason eventually enrolled in some offbeat, online, nonaccredited business school. It was a six-month program, and his mother wants to throw him an extravagant party for finishing. It's bullshit!

Elizabeth blabbers all the reasons why the party is essential: rewarding an achievement, a self-esteem booster, and being supportive parents.

"Liz, stop. Jason isn't my kid, therefore, I don't need to be a supportive parent. And that brings me to why I'm calling you. I need to pull all my support money. I have a woman in my life—"

"A woman!" sneers Elizabeth, cutting me off. "Christian, I'm not sure you're aware Montana has common-law marriages. According to the law, we're married. *So, darling, you can't have another woman in your life unless you want me to get half of everything in our divorce!*"

"*WE ARE NOT FUCKING MARRIED!*" The bitch is one card short of a full deck.

"The apartment, the SUV's lease, the insurance, and the utilities are all in your name, Christian. People know we've been together for the past seventeen years. We're both over eighteen and of sound mind. Husband, we're married. I want my support check and the deposit by Friday. Ta-ta, darling." The line goes dead.

I bellow my rage to the ceiling, whipping my phone at the wall. The cell makes a loud crack and bounces off, spinning like a top on the hardwood floor. The screen is spiderwebbed.

Joker walks over and snatches my cell off the floor. "Calm your ass, brother. We'll cut off the utilities, end the lease, and give notice to the apartment manager. Then we'll sick Princess on her ass."

"Fuck that, I'll snap the bitch's goddamn neck!" I take my phone, moaning. "Now I can't keep track of Cookie."

CHAPTER 8

FINDING A GIG – COOKIE

Horns blare. Other drivers are shouting at me out their windows and tossing me the bird. *I'm going as fast as I can!* I shake, grip the wheel tighter, and push lightly down on the gas. It's been like this since I left Pony—drivers with road rage. They have no consideration for new people behind the wheel. I check the clock on the dash—8:15. Google said the trip was only supposed to take fifty-seven minutes. I've been driving for over two hours.

Another horn blows. "Lady, learn how to fucking drive!" the guy shouts out his window.

I swallow, then blow out a breath, checking my speed—fifteen mph. There's too much traffic. Tears well up in my eyes. *I want High!*

I've thought about High the entire ride. Then, I got mad as a hornet. Why should I step aside for Elizabeth? If High wanted her, he would have moved her to Pony. Then, I decided the only reason High answers Elizabeth's texts and phone calls is because she blows up his cell—the witch has him on autodial. He's always annoyed with her and never texts or says "I love you." And, as far as I know, he never agrees to meet her when she asks.

I made the decision to give us a go. What do I have to lose? I already love High. If he loves me and leaves me, *oui*, it will hurt. But, I miss how he makes love to me as if I'm someone special God made just for him. High's not a gentle lover; he growls, curses, and snaps his pleasure into my ear. High devourers my breasts in such a way, it makes my toes curl. Every nerve in my body lights up when he goes downtown for dinner. And just before he climaxes, his cock becomes enormously thick, long, and hard, stretching me, filling me to my fullest capacity. It's glorious! Non, I need to take a chance and fight for High.

I clock Grand Street and cringe at the roundabout. *Oh, God, help me!* More horns blare as I eye the road. *Stay to the right in the friggin' circle.* I creep around it at a whopping five mph and turn right onto Grand.

Non-non-non, there's no parking lot. *You can't parallel park; you failed every time you tried.* My tears threaten to come again—*I want High.*

There is an empty space straight ahead; maybe I can just pull in. I turn on my blinker. More horns blare, more drivers curse at me as I crawl into the spot. I turn off the ignition, lay my forehead onto the steering wheel, and blow out a long breath. *You did it; you're here.*

I lift my head and look at Blue Heaven Bar. Three sets of male eyes are staring out the picture window, looking at me!

It's now or never. I open my door and check the back end of my SUV. It's hanging out in the road a bit; it'll need to do. I say a quick prayer no one hits my Cayenne. Then, I throw my hobo bag over my shoulder, grab my guitar, and hope I can talk the owner into giving me an audition. I'll deal with the under-the-table crap if he agrees to hire me.

I steel myself, push back my shoulders, and make my way to the door. Exhaling, I pull it open and walk inside. It's decorated with memorabilia of famous bands—The Beatles, Rolling Stones, Pink Floyd, among other legends. The back has a large stage with a piano, drum set, and multiple guitars. Below it is a huge dance floor. To the right is a glossy oak bar that probably seats thirty people. The middle of the room is filled with polished oak tables and chairs. The place is dimly lit; Nirvana—*The Man Who Sold the World*—is playing softly.

Good lord, you chose the wrong bar. This one isn't a dive.

"Hey, Little Bit, toss me your keys," orders a thirty-something man.

I blink, staring up at him. He has to be over six-foot-four, and he's good-looking—long blond hair, dark brown eyes, and a smile that goes on forever. *Non*, the dude isn't my type; he's too skinny for my liking, but still, he's handsome.

"My keys?"

"Yeah, Little Bit, your keys. The ass end of your SUV is going to get taken off if I don't move it," chuckles Mr. Handsome. "Judging from the horns blowing, and your park job, you're a newbie driver."

I hand him my keys. "Thanks. I'm terrible at parallel parking. Do you know if the owner of the bar is available?"

"Benny, get your ass out here," he shouts, jogging out the door.

An older man with shaggy gray hair and a long, plaited beard comes through a set of swinging doors. His weathered, tanned skin, tatts, and jewelry make me think the guy might be a biker. Weirdly, that is comforting.

The man's gray eyes are homed in on me. He looks me up and down, smirking. "What can I do for you, Tinkerbell?"

"I'm looking for a gig."

"A gig," he chuckles. "How old are you?"

"Twenty-two. I've been in the music industry all my life. I'm just asking for a shot. One song, your choice. If you don't like it, I'll be on my way."

Mr. Handsome comes jogging back into the bar. "Benny, give Little Bit a shot."

Benny rolls his gray eyes and then smirks. "Pick the goddamn song, Cam."

"Let's see," drawls Cam. "You're a rocker chick."

"I can sing anything but opera."

Cam chuckles, "We have no use for opera around here. How about a little Journey? 'Open Arms?'"

I smile. "Great." I've got this in the bag: I've sung "Open Arms" over a thousand times.

"The boys and I will be your band," says Cam, lifting me up onto the stage. "Woody is on the drums, Max is at the piano, Lex is on the bass guitar, and I'll play lead guitar. Let us know when you're ready."

I wave to the guys, wishing I had stopped for hot tea to loosen up my vocal cords. I should have broken my rule and paid the three dollars, but geez, it's highway robbery.

"What key, Little Bit?" asks Cam.

"Play it the same as Steve Perry did back in the day," I say, positioning the mic.

Cam eyes me skeptically.

Woody taps his sticks together. "One and a two and a three," and the band starts the intro.

I start the song, letting loose on the hook. Raising my arms in the air, I bounce and twirl, letting the music take me on a ride. High's image is surrounding me, and my voice soars to the heavens.

When the song ends, loud clapping and stomping vibrate the walls. I look out into the bar. *Where did all these people come from?*

Cam yells, "Fuck yeah! Where in the hell did you get those pipes?!"

"Holy shit," laughs Woody. "What in the hell just happened?"

"Scorpions, 'When You Came into My Life,'" yells a young guy from the front of the stage.

Cam laughs. "That's Rod, Benny's grandson. The kids are his college friends."

After hours of singing rock songs for Rod's college friends, my throat is done.

"Come over to the bar, Tinkerbell. We'll discuss terms," says Benny.

"Not happening, Benny," says Cam. "Little Bit is our new lead singer."

"My bar," yells Benny.

"My band," grins Cam.

"Jesus Christ, Cameron. I need to make a goddamn living," bitches Benny.

Cam chuckles, leading me to the bar.

"Want a drink, Tinkerbell?" asks Benny. Looking miffed at Cam, he announces, "Shithead is buying."

I giggle, digging into my hobo bag. My stomach tightens at the thought of needing to shell out a ten-spot for a glass of wine, but I'm not letting Cam pay for it. I look at the time—3:00. I can still find a place to busk and make up the money. I'll need it for gas.

I put the ten-dollar bill onto the bartop. "I'll have a glass of bottom-shelf cab, please."

Benny snickers, "Bottom-shelf." He pushes my money back to me. "It's on me, sweetheart. Where are you from, anyway? I catch a bit of a French accent."

I nod. "I'm originally from Canada." I leave it at that. I don't want to tell my business.

"Hmm," snorts Benny. "You're an allusive one." He pours my wine, then moves down the bar to another customer.

Cam glances at me. Then he takes a few swallows of his beer. "You're gorgeous, and you have a set of pipes that any record label would die to hitch their wagon to. There's a Sinners' patch plastered to the window of your Porsche, but I'm guessing the brothers aren't aware you're here."

"You know the Sinners?" I ask, my heart beating out of my chest. *Good lord, what are the freakin' odds?*

"I know General and Tristen. I went to school with High. The boys and I have played at Callaghan's Bar many times."

I nod, knowing I need to give Cam something. I take a gulp of my wine. "I needed a gig. Celia sings at Callaghan's Bar."

Cam rolls his eyes. "I know the woman. She can't sing worth shit. How much trouble am I going to get into with the Sinners if I hire you?"

I laugh. "There won't be any trouble."

"Yeah, right," he says under his breath. "Here's the deal: I'll pay you a fifth of everything we make, usually five hundred a gig plus door money. Be here every morning at eight for practice. We have a gig on Friday night." Cam downs his beer and slides off the stool. "Beep when you get here. I'll come out and park your car. And one more thing, Little Bit: if the Sinners get pissed off, you're taking the heat. I have a wife and kid at home. They like me breathing."

"Okay, Cam. Hey, do you know where I can find a food truck?"

Cam turns, looking at me. "Are you hungry? Benny will—"

"*Non...* I mean, no. I would just like to know where I can find a food truck."

Cam blows out a breath, running a hand down his face. "I don't know what you're up to, and I don't want to know. Most of the food trucks park over on Lexington. It's the business district." He points out the window. "Four blocks to the east."

"Thanks," I say, sliding off the stool. I grab my guitar and head for the door.

"Little Bit, what is your name?"

"Cookie," I say, pushing open the door. I take a big inhale, smiling up to the clear blue sky. *I did it; I've got a band, and I stayed under the wire!*

I hit the fob; the doors unlock. Now all I need to do is make it over to Lexington without getting into a fender bender.

Lexington Avenue is the busiest street in Butte. Happy Hot Dog food truck is straight ahead. Several businesspeople are waiting in line. I'll ask the vendor if I can busk by him. I inch my way along with traffic and clock a public parking lot. After making the right-hand turn, I park far in the back—easy in, easy out.

I leap out of my SUV. The wind whips around me, making me shiver. Busking in twenty-degree weather isn't fun, but it has its advantages. People feel sorry for you and tend to drop more money into your tin can. I grab my guitar and coffee can, then head in the direction of Happy Hot Dog.

When I step up to the window, the older man looks down at me and then to my guitar. "Sweetheart, it's mighty cold for you to be singin' out here. But if you're game, do your thing. You won't bother me none."

"Thanks. I'm Cookie," I say, taking my guitar out of the plastic bag.

"Al," says the old guy, chuckling.

"Okay, Al, what's your pleasure?"

"I like that Alicia Keys girl. She sings real pretty."

I would have never guessed that in a million years.

"Then it's 'Girl on Fire,'" I giggle and start playing.

It takes a few minutes until Al and I get a medium-sized crowd. At 6:00, Al turns off the lights; it's time to shut down.

He chuckles, shaking his head at me. "Cookie, you're great for business. I made twice as much as I usually do."

I pick up my coffee can and look inside. Then, I grin up at Al. "My can is full. It's been a good day for both of us."

"Cookie, let me shut down. It's too dark for you to be walking the streets alone." He looks over to the empty parking lot. "That's your vehicle over yonder?"

"*Oui*," I say, sliding my guitar back into the plastic bag. Then, I help Al close down his food truck, thanking God for letting me meet Al, Benny, and the band.

Somehow, I need to find a way to tell High I'm in a band.

CHAPTER 9

COOKIE'S MAN — HIGH

I enter the game room. The kids are huddled together in a circle, their eyes on a cell phone.

"Come on, Aunt Cookie, that's right, step on the gas," chuckles Scottie. "Get her up to forty-five!"

"Lee," says Polly. "Please take Flame and go get her. Cookie is obviously scared to death."

"What the hell is going on?" I ask Scottie.

"Aunt Cookie is driving on I-90. The cars are whizzing by her as if she's standing still."

"She almost is," laughs Jonas. "Aunt Cookie's been driving for almost three hours. She was going thirty-five. She just took it up to forty-five." He glances at the phone. "And she's back down to thirty-five."

"Jesus Christ," I bark, stalking to the door.

"Leave her be," orders Lee. "Cookie's safe and learning how to drive at night on the highway. She only has a few more miles to go, and then she's in Pony."

"Lee!"

51

"Polly, the woman is doing fine. It isn't snowing, and the roads aren't slippery. Christ, she's only going a bit slower than you drive."

"That's true, Mom. You drive like a granny," affirms Conan.

"I drive just under the speed limit, unlike your father," huffs out Polly.

I chuckle and drop down on the couch next to General. Then, I pull out my new iPhone.

"Got yourself a new cell," says General, glancing at my apps. "With all the bells and whistles."

"Hmm," I hum, downloading the tracker app.

I didn't realize it was after nine. It took me hours to cancel all the utilities and close out the leases on Elizabeth's apartment and SUV. Verizon was a zoo. I had to buy a new plan because I forgot Elizabeth and Jason were on the one I had. Then, I needed to add Cookie to the new one.

"Did you get all the utilities and leases sorted?" asks General.

"Yup," I confirm, getting a bead on Cookie's SUV. She has just entered Pony. I smile. Now she's driving twenty miles per hour.

"I got a call from Cam a bit ago," says General, taking a gulp of his Jameson. "He wanted to let me know he's hired a new songbird."

"Cam Forester of the Heartbreakers?"

"Aye. Seems someone fitting Cookie's description walked into Blue Heaven looking for a gig." General chuckles, "Cam needed to go out and park her SUV. The ass end was out in the middle of the street. People weren't too happy; they were blowing their horns at her and shite."

"Fuck," I growl.

"Aye, we need to work on parallel parking. The Heartbreakers are going to finish out the week at Blue Heaven and do a regular gig at Callaghan's Bar." General chuckles, "It'll be safer for Little Bit, and it's closer to Cam's ranch."

"Little Bit?"

"That's what Cam calls Cookie. He said he'd be afraid to fuck her for fear he'd break her. Though he was amazed; her tits were God-given."

I whip my head around, glaring at General.

"Relax, Cam has a wife and kid. He lifted Cookie off the stage so she wouldn't break her neck."

"He shouldn't be looking at my Aunt Cookie's pillows," growls Conor.

"I agree," I chuckle, growling back.

Cookie comes in the door with her guitar cradled in her arms and her hobo bag weighted down at her side. Her face is tear-streaked, and she looks worn out. She slides down the door, and her ass hits the floor with a bounce.

What...the...fuck?!

"Aunt Cookie!" shouts Scottie, running over to her.

She looks up at him, bursting into tears. "They were beeping and honking and giving me the bird and cursing at me, and I can't parallel park, and I had to do a roundabout."

"Christ, I think those are the most words I've ever heard her say," chuckles Flame.

Scottie hugs her. "I monitored you all the way using Uncle Flame's tracker app. You did it. So it's a win, Aunt Cookie."

"Lee, I told you to go get her," scolds Polly.

Lee chuckles, "When you first learned to drive, you came home blatting, too. Now you can drive anywhere, baby."

I leap over the couch and strut over to Cookie. I bend down and lift her into my arms. "Tough day?" I murmur onto her lips.

She nods, relaxing into me. "I went to Butte," she confesses. "I got a gig at Blue Heaven. Off the books."

"Next time you're upset and feel like going for a joyride, you need to let someone know," says General, shrugging on his coat. "Jonas, Scottie, grab your shite, it's time to make tracks." He kisses Cookie on the temple. "We love you, lass."

"Lee, we need to leave, too. Conan, Con, grab your things," orders Polly, coming over to us. "Cookie, I'm sorry we left you at Urgent Care. None of us knew you stayed. Please forgive us and come back."

"Thanks, Polly, but I can't. I..." stutters Cookie, starting to cry all over again.

"Shh, Polly doesn't need an explanation. You resigned, that's enough," I assure her and kiss her lips.

"No, I don't need an explanation," smiles Polly, kissing her temple. "Sisters forever, girlfriend."

"Hurry up, Aunt Polly's becoming a mushmelon. Later, Aunt Cookie," yells Jonas, zooming out the door.

"Come here, Jonas Kincaid, let me smooch those cheeks," teases Polly, following him.

Cookie giggles. I look down at my woman, grinning.

"See ya, Aunt Cookie," bellows Conor, making *vrrrmmm, vrrrmmm* and then squealing tire noises, peeling out the door.

I chuckle—the little ballbuster.

Scottie shakes his head and kisses Cookie on the cheek. "Glad you're home, Aunt Cookie. Next time, try to go fifty on the highway. We'll work on parallel parking in Uncle High's truck. He has good insurance for when you take his bumper off."

Cookie giggles again.

I shake my head, laughing. "Thanks a lot, nephew."

"You did great, Aunt Cookie," says Conan. Then he does an animated slow-motion moonwalk out the door.

Flame struts over to us. "I need to beat feet and put my wife to bed. Pick and Corrie are working on your case tomorrow, High." He kisses Cookie on the forehead. "Next time, give someone the heads up you're tweaked the hell out. We all have ears and shoulders, Cookie." He grins at her. "Though, you're aware I don't do emotional crying bitches, so save that for your man."

Cookie smiles up at me. "Who's my man?"

"Me," I whisper onto her lips. "If you'll have me."

Cookie looks into my eyes. "It isn't a question of me having you. These past two days, I learned you're a part of me. Whether we're together or apart, you'll always be a part of me. You're the one I want when I'm scared or happy or sad. I don't know if I can share you…"

I furrow my brow. "Share me? You're not going to share me with anyone, baby."

"Elizabeth…"

"Elizabeth is gone. You were never in competition with that bitch."
I grin. "I got you a present today."

"A gift? Thanks, but I don't need anything."

"Baby, you need this," I say, walking through the game room and
up the stairs. "Put your eye to the scanner, babe, and push open the
door."

The door swings open, and Cookie's eyes become round as
saucers. "Are those your clothes all over the bed?" Her head swings to
the left. "Is that your dresser?" She moves her eyes up. "And gun rack
on my wall?"

"Yup," I chuckle. "We're taking the next step, baby. We're living
together."

Cookie inhales and blows out a long breath. "Amour, you're
moving at warp speed. We slept together one night, and *boom!* You
moved in," she giggles. "Put me down so I can clean *our* room."

"First, I need a selfie of us together." I drop her onto the bed and
plunk down beside her. "Kiss me," I order, holding up my phone.

She furrows her brow. "Did you get a new cell?"

"Kiss me, so I can snap the goddamn picture."

Cookie puts her lips to mine, giggling.

"Christ," I laugh, snapping the picture. Then I look at the photo
and show my woman.

"That's a good one."

"One more." I jump up and open my top drawer. I take out Cookie's iPhone. "This one is for you."

She stares at it, her eyes widen. "You got me an iPhone. How much
is the monthly bill? I have a TracFone..."

I hand her the cell. "Baby, I'm taking care of the bill."

"*Non*, it doesn't work like that, Amour. We share all monthly
expenses." She leaps up and pulls open her nightstand drawer. Then,
she takes out a spiral notebook. "My ins and outs." She thumbs
through it, biting her bottom lip. "If I reduce my monthly mad
money..."

I take the notebook from her and toss it back into the drawer.
"You're not giving up shit." I tip her chin up to look at me. "We're part-

ners. You do shit for me, and I do shit for you. You tell me what's in that head of yours, and I'll let you know what's in mine. I never had that, Cookie, and I want it with you. The brothers and their wives taught me a lot about relationships. I knew, because my mom and dad have as close to a perfect marriage as any couple can. But, somehow, I got screwed up along the way. Now, I have my head on straight, and I want it all with you."

Cookie's talking in rapid French and crying at the same time. I catch about every third word—something about dreams, wishes, houses, and stars.

"Baby," I chuckle, wiping her tears away with my thumbs. "Use English. I haven't spoken French in twenty-three years."

"No worries, it will come back," laughs Cookie. "Thank you for my iPhone. Will you show me how it works?"

"Yeah, baby," I murmur against her lips. I hold up Cookie's cell and snap a picture of us passionately kissing.

CHAPTER 10

ZERO EXPERIENCE WITH COUPLES — COOKIE

High is lying stretched out on *our bed*. It still seems too surreal. Girls like me, we don't dream of handsome husbands, big houses with white picket fences, or babies. We survive.

Oui, I'm worried. The one time I took a chance and dared to dream, it turned out to be the biggest mistake of my life. I guess, if I use that as a comparison, High couldn't top it, other than dying. High not breathing would be worse than anything I can imagine. *Non, you wouldn't come back from that.*

I hang the last pair of High's jeans and stand back. Our clothes look right together. I bury my face in one of High's Henley thermals and inhale deeply.

"Baby, you've been in the closet, staring at our clothes, for ten minutes. Now you're sniffing my shirt," chuckles High. "Come and smell me."

Talking, sharing feelings, telling people what is on my mind isn't something I'm used to. Growing up the way I did, I didn't talk to anyone other than myself. I didn't have a childhood: playmates were something foreign to me. Toys were nonexistent. I expressed myself through music. I put my feelings into song lyrics and sang in coffee-houses and bars. When I did speak to people, it was about music.

Jewel was my first friend, the first person I opened up to. She doesn't judge or look down on me. Now, I have High, and I want an honest relationship.

"Baby," calls High.

I pull my face away from his shirt. Good lord, he's leaning against the doorjamb, watching me.

"I was just checking to make sure I washed this one," I lie.

He grins. "Yeah, you washed that one." He walks over and lifts me into his arms. "Baby, lie with me and tell me about your day."

"First, I need to get ready for bed."

He kisses my lips, setting me on my feet. "Go get ready."

I walk over to my dresser. "High, did anyone feed Puddin'?"

"Puddin', the thirty-five-pound bobcat you keep in the barn?" he chuckles. "Yeah, baby, Merrill fed him. I told him to up his rations. I don't want Puddin' eating you."

"He won't. Puddin' loves his mama," I giggle, grabbing a pair of clean panties. Then, I choose my silky pink pajamas—they're girly, sexy, with a scooped neck and low-rise waistband. They're cute.

I head into the bathroom. High and I have slept together lots of times, but not as a couple. I have zero experience with couples. I didn't grow up with a father, and I was more of a parent to my mother than she was to me.

I strip, tossing my clothes into the hamper. Then, I examine myself in the full-length mirror attached to the door. Thank god I kept up my waxing. I considered stopping because the body wax is expensive, but High always seemed to like my pussy clean. I was lucky enough to find the wax at the flea market for half the cost.

I run my hands over my hip bones—they're more pronounced than usual. It's not surprising. I lose, on average, two-to-three pounds when I'm performing. No eating in combination with running around on stage under the hot lights, it's inevitable. I cover my size C boobs with both hands. High loves my breasts. I know this because he smothers his face into them, growling his low, sexy-as-heck growl.

My breasts are the only thing Sylvie gave me. I suppose my father gave me my five-foot-three, fine-boned frame, my blue eyes, and my wavy blonde hair. He also gave me my voice—Sylvie can't sing a lick.

My mother is a tall, large-framed brunette with dark brown eyes. Unlike most drug addicts, Sylvie is not a string bean. Heroin has the opposite effect on her; it gives her a humongous appetite. Any food I brought home was gobbled up before it hit the fridge or shelves.

Sylvie has three talents: spreading her legs, shooting up, and using me as her cash cow. When my mother found out I could sing, she was all over it. I was five when she procured a secondhand acoustic guitar from god knows where—it was probably stolen from one of her johns. She handed it to me with a used guitar primer and told me to learn how to play. Unbeknownst to my mother, the guitar saved my life. I've never put the instrument down. The piano came two years later. I was seven, busking on the streets and playing in coffeehouses. I'd earned enough money to move us out of the homeless shelter into a rundown one-bedroom studio. I slept in the walk-in closet. The basement had an old piano. By then, I'd taught myself how to read music. I knew from busking that people love to hear covers of the rock legends. I made it my mission to learn them all.

Living in various homeless shelters for the first seven years of my life, formal education wasn't available to me. I was educated by the Catholic nuns who volunteered. For two hours a day, from 9:00 to 11:00 a.m., seven days a week, the nuns taught me math and to read and write in English and French. It stopped when I turned fourteen. "Chéri, you've gained all the knowledge we have to offer. God has given you the gift of music. You are a prodigy, Chéri, don't waste it," said Sister Bernadette. "Go with God, child."

I don't have a high school diploma, and I don't know anything about science or history.

I snort. How do you tell a man like High all that? He had the perfect upbringing: two parents who loved him, a real home, friends, and school. How do you tell him about Brian Stratton and what he did to you in the freakin' motel room? How do you tell him you begged Pick to let you die on an alley grate?

I grab the cold cream and angrily smear it all over my face. I've watched how General and Raven, Horse and White Dove, Pick and Hialeah, Mafia Man and Maggie, Tank and Jillian, Flame and Princess, Raine and Buck are with each other. The Sinners' couples are open and honest. They give and take; above everyone, their partner comes first. I want that for High and me. But I need to find the words to tell him about my past and hope he doesn't cut and run.

I yank a few tissues out of the box and wipe the cream off my face. I stare at the image in the mirror: the confident rocker girl has been wiped away. Left in her wake is Chéri Fayette, aka Cookie—High's woman and aunt to the Sinners' kids.

The bathroom door opens. "Baby..." High stops. His eyes become as dark as the midnight sea at the sight of my naked body. His boxers tent with his engorged, ginormous cock. My pussy drips wet. I should be embarrassed, but I'm not. He's High, my man, and I love him. After three long months, I want to pleasure him, smell his musk, and taste him.

I lick my lips, my eyes pinned on his cock. "Amour..." I tell him in French how much I need his cock, his balls, and his ass.

High stalks over to me, lifting me into his arms. "You need me," he growls into my ear. Then he chuckles low. "Baby, what exactly are you going to do to my ass?"

I grin. I'm not telling High Jewel has educated me on a man's sacred hole, or about the virtues of full-body orgasms. *Oui*, my best friend and I share.

CHAPTER 11

FULL DISCLOSURE — HIGH

"Goddamnit, baby," I growl, loving her warm, wet mouth. "Cook, Jesus, fuck," I snap. My head comes off the pillow to watch my woman taking me.

I'm fucking enormous and so goddamn hard. Cookie relaxes her throat, taking me to the root. She buries her nose in my hair, snuffling and rooting. Her tongue is magical, massaging my length. Christ, her little fingers circle, prodding my asshole. My balls quiver; my hips come off the bed when she pushes past my sphincter. I grunt, baring my teeth at the burn and the incredible feeling of getting my ass fucked.

I moan, fisting her hair. My woman grips the base of my cock, jacking me off as her beautiful mouth and fingers fuck me.

"Christ, babe," I groan, running my finger between her swollen pussy lips. *Goddamn, drenched, and wide open for me!*

Knock knock knock! "Cookie, it's me, Celia. I need to talk to you. It's an emergency."

Cookie stops, drops my cock, and pulls her fingers from my ass, her eyes pinned to the door. "Jewel or one of the guys might be hurt," she whispers, leaping off the bed, dashing for the bathroom.

"I am going to fucking kill you, Marshmallow!" I roar, swinging my legs off the bed.

Cookie and I are making it official, and the bitch ruins it! Someone had better be goddamn dying or dead.

"High? What are you doing in Cookie's room?"

"I goddamn live here," I bark, grabbing a pair of sweats.

The door handle jiggles. "Is Cookie in there? I need to speak to her immediately."

I yank open the door, my hands going for her goddamn neck. Marshmallow squeaks, skirting under my arm.

She sniffs. "It smells like sex in here." The bitch looks around the room, clocking my dresser and gun rack. "Are you two...like, together?"

Cookie comes out of the bathroom in a black silk short robe. Her hair is pulled back into a ponytail, her lips red and swollen from my cock. *Pure beauty.*

Yeah, I'm going to strangle the bitch, and then Cookie and I will continue to make it official.

"Cookie." Marshmallow races over to my woman. "General told me I'm being replaced because the audience is dissatisfied. *HE'S FIRING ME, COOKIE!*" She tosses her hands up in the air, pacing. "It's not me. My voice is pitch-perfect. You know it's the songs, Cookie. They're old...outdated. I need your songbook. I heard you playing them. The melodies are fresh, haunting, and they'll fit beautifully with my tone. Together, your songs and my voice will bring in the crowd."

Cookie backs up, shaking her head, tears brimming her eyes. *"Non,"* she whispers. "I...I can't."

"Go to hell, Marshmallow," I snarl, my nostrils flaring. "Cookie is not giving you her goddamn songbook. *GET THE FUCK OUT, NOW!*"

Jewel comes running into our room, taking in the scene. "Are you crazy?" she asks Marshmallow. "High is going to kill you!"

"Jewel, I need—"

Jewel grabs the bitch's arm, yanking her toward the door. "What you need to do is leave High and Cookie alone!" She gives Marsh-mallow a hard shove, pushing her out of the room. "You won't live to see the sunrise if you continue to poke High." Jewel closes the door behind them.

I strut over to Cookie, wrapping her into my arms. She hugs my middle, burrowing her face into my chest.

Cookie sniffs, hugging me tighter. "I think Marshmallow inter-rupting us was a sign."

"Nope." I kiss the crown of her head. "Marshmallow is a dumb, selfish bitch who needs to go."

Cookie pulls out of my arms and sits down on the edge of the bed. She folds her hands in her lap and then looks up at me. She nods, exhaling. "The Sinners' couples have full disclosure in their rela-tionships."

I drop down beside her and take her hand. "Yeah, baby, they do."

Cookie glances at me. "You've told me about your life. I need to tell you about mine." She looks back to her hands. "It's only fair. You might not want to be with me…"

I scoot to the middle of the bed, taking my woman with me. "Cook, there is nothing you're going to tell me that would make me leave you." I bring her into my body, cocooning her. Then, I do it…I tell her how I feel. "Cookie, I love you."

My woman's body goes solid. "You…love…me?" she stutters into my chest.

"Yeah, babe," I murmur onto her crown.

"I love you, too, High," she confesses, relaxing. "More than the sun, moon, and stars…more than Puddin' and Jewel and music."

I chuckle, "That much, huh?"

Then Cookie tells me about her life in Quebec. Christ, she lived in homeless shelters until she was seven. My woman had a drugged-out prostitute for a mother. At seven years old, she sang in coffee shops and on the streets; at fourteen, she worked in goddamn dive bars. It was as if she lived in a goddamn third world country—no school, no friends, no one to depend on but herself. Then Cookie tells me what freaked her out about the clinic—her mother's STDs and HIV.

"Jesus, baby. I'm so sorry you went through that," I murmur, holding her.

Cookie tips her head up, looking at me. "High, can I tell you about Stratton Records?"

The way my woman asks, a tremble in her voice, lets me know this will be worse than anything she's already told me.

I tighten my arms around her. "Yeah, baby."

"I was gigging at Rouge. Brian Stratton walked up to me and handed me his card. He said my voice was money in the bank; he wanted to sign me to his label. I didn't believe him at first. Geoff—he played the keys in the band—told me Stratton was legit. It was my chance to break into the American music business."

"Baby, you signed the contract without a lawyer?"

Cookie nods against my chest. "*Oui*, Stratton told me it was the standard contract. He promised me recording time in a real studio and worldwide tours, opening for the top rock bands in the industry. I was scared out of my mind, but I agreed. It was America—Celine Dion, Justin Bieber, Shania Twain, Alanis Morissette, and a bunch of other people had done it. So, I took my shot."

My nerves fire, burning with anger. Stratton knew Cookie was on her own. The fucker took advantage of her. All the artists she named had good people looking out for them. My woman had no one.

"The next morning, we took off from Jean Lesage in Stratton's private jet. I was so scared; I'd never been out of Quebec. Stratton told me we needed to stop in Helena, Montana. He had another artist to check out." Her entire body is quaking in my arms.

"Hey, I'm right here, baby," I murmur onto her crown. "No one can hurt you. I'll put them to ground before they come close."

Cookie hugs my arms, blowing out a long breath. "We took a cab to a seedy motel. It didn't seem right. I mean, we just got off a private jet. Stratton checked us in. I had my own room, so I thought I'd be all right." She digs her tiny nails into my arm, shaking.

God no! I force my body to stay relaxed. I don't want to ask, but I do, for her.

"Baby, did Stratton violate you in the goddamn motel? Did the fucker take your virginity by force?"

She nods, crying. "He tied my wrists above my head. I was fighting and screaming. He hit me over and over again, yelling at me to shut up and take him."

Rage burns inside me, threatening to ignite into a fucking inferno. I use everything I have to lock it down for my woman.

"Okay…I've got you. I have you, Cookie."

"I didn't feel his slaps or punches. My privates hurt so freakin' bad. I don't know why; he had a tiny nub of a dick." She tilts her head up to look at me. "I don't know why that sticks in my mind. It shouldn't have hurt that much."

"Christ, baby, you were dry and a virgin; your body was tense. You were fighting for your life," I explain onto her temple.

"*Oui*, that was it. High?"

"Yeah, baby."

"I don't know what happened. Stratton made a grunt and died on top of me. I couldn't think; all I wanted to do was escape. I got my wrists loose, grabbed my bag and guitar, and bolted. I didn't have any money or a visa. I just ran until I couldn't run anymore."

"Baby, Jesus," I murmur. A tear runs down my cheek.

"I was so cold. I had left my coat at the motel. I didn't know where I was, and I had no one I could call. I stumbled into an alley and lay on a grate."

"Baby, fuck," I murmur, tightening my hold on her. *Christ, she's killing me.*

"I remember looking up into the stars. It was snowing lightly and the flakes were melting on my face. It was angelic, as if God had chosen the perfect place for me to die. So, I gave myself over to him."

"Baby, Christ, no."

"In the morning, this huge, tatted, muscled older man with the most beautiful golden eyes was hovering over me. At first, I thought he was God."

"Pick?"

"*Oui*. Pick lifted me into his arms and told me he was bringing me to the hospital. I told him, *non*, to leave me alone; I was waiting for God." Cookie tilts her head up, smiling. "He growled at me, said God didn't want me until I was old and gray. I woke up a few days later in Sinners' clubhouse. The rest you already know."

"Yeah, we took a young girl and made her a goddamn sweet butt," I sneer. "That's real fucking godly."

"No one knows what happened to me except for Jewel. Pick and General probably figured I was a prostitute." She snorts. "I was a terrible sweet butt, High. I only had sex with Brainiac and you. Oh, and Guard Dog, once, because I was afraid General would toss my butt out. Brainiac and I ended it when he realized I loved you."

"Brainiac knew you loved me? Did you tell him?"

"*Non*, he guessed it when things didn't...you know."

"Yeah," I growl. "I don't need to know the details."

Shit, I don't want to tell her Stratton isn't dead, but I have no choice. I need to make a trip to LA and put his ass to ground.

I hug her close. "Baby, Brian Stratton isn't dead."

"*Non*," she shakes her head. "The devil is in hell, where he belongs."

"Baby, Brian Stratton signed the letter he sent you. I need to take off for a few days. I'm going to end the fucking bastard."

Cookie looks up at me. "I didn't look at who signed the letter. How can Stratton be alive? He wasn't moving. Oh, god." She starts shaking.

"Babe, stop. The bastard will be dead by the end of the week," I assure.

"You're going to kill him? For me?" She thinks for a few beats. "I'm your woman." Narrowing her eyes, she says in French, "End the bastard."

I smirk. Nothing says love like a little murder.

"Amour, don't get caught. Now that I have you, I can't live without you. Ever!"

"You won't lose me, Cookie." I inhale, then blow out a breath. "Baby, Elizabeth is making waves. She's claiming we're married by common law. But I don't want you to worry. Princess and Pick have the case covered."

A volley of French comes out of my woman's mouth. Again, I catch just a few words: lazy, moneygrubbing, lying witch. Fawn was mentioned somewhere in there.

"Users! They took advantage of your kindness, your generosity, and your love!" she bellows irately. "And Megan. I'm going to have a talk with her, Amour. She needs to know how much you love her. *You* put a roof over her head, paid for her food, clothes, college, and...and everything. I know she's your daughter, but I will not stand for her disrespecting you. *IT ISN'T RIGHT!*"

I chuckle. "Calm down. I already laid down the law with Megan. I also cut off my support to Fawn and Elizabeth today."

"Good, that's excellent, Amour." Cookie snuggles into me. "Now, if it doesn't hurt too much, tell me about your cabin."

"My cabin? Do you mean the shack up the road?"

"*Oui.*" She nods. "I want you to describe it to me."

"Cookie, it's a shithole," I chuckle. "It's cold as ice in the winter and hot as hell in the summer."

"Does it have a kitchen?"

"Yeah, baby, it has a kitchen, a living room with a fireplace, three bedrooms, and a bathroom. The fifty acres are beautiful—all wooded. It has a view of the Rockies, and there is a small, spring-fed lake. Cook," I say onto her crown, "do you want to move to the cabin?"

"*Oui*, it sounds cute and cozy. Like that show, *Little House on the Prairie*, Mama Cass used to watch." She looks up at me. "Would it be too painful? You lived there with Fawn and Megan."

"Nope, we'll ditch all the shit and start fresh. I need to plow the road. We'll start on it next Sunday."

"Oh, my god," she shrieks, kissing me all over my face. Then my woman rips her body from my arms and does a happy dance, running around the bed. Then she yanks open her nightstand drawer and pulls out her spiral notebook. She starts flipping wildly through the pages.

I turn over, laughing at her. "Babe, what in the hell are you doing?"

"Checking my ins and outs, Amour. I need to hit the flea market." She beams the brightest smile at me. "I'm going to make your cabin our home with colorful pots and throw pillows, and, oh, I saw the best dishes. They were Lenox...new, still in the boxes. So cute. They had fireflies on them. Lord, please let them still be there."

I grab her around the waist, pulling her into bed with me. Then I take her notebook and toss it onto the floor. "I'll pay for the shit you want," I murmur against her lips. I give her a deep, tongue-tangling kiss. She moans; I answer with a groan.

Cookie breaks our kiss, scurrying down the bed. She takes off her robe, letting it flutter to the floor.

I shed my sweats, my eyes on her amazing tits. My woman throws her leg over me, positioning my hard cock to her hole.

Slowly, she slides down a few inches. "Ooo," she hisses, stretching around me. "*Énorment*, Amour." She whimpers, "I want to come."

I put my soles flat on the bed, lifting my hips. I grab my woman's ass, helping her ride me. I grunt, lubing my finger with her slick lady juice. I reach around to her ass and push past her sphincter. "Not yet. Ride my cock and finger, baby."

"Amour, please," she cries out. "I want to come."

Her scent surrounds me, enticing me. My cock grows longer and thicker. I snarl, needing to fuck like a bull in heat. Spreading her wide, I fuck wildly up into her slick, warm wetness.

My woman tosses her head back, keening in French. I do a sit-up, burying my face into her tits, grinding her down onto me. Her pussy walls flutter.

"Goddamnit, baby, wait for me," I snap, flipping us so that she's on the bottom. I put her legs up, her toes touch the headboard. Thank god, my woman is Gumby.

I fuck fast in long, powerful strokes with a couple of humps at the end. I grunt, my eyes on our connection. My woman's pussy is beautiful, open to me, sheathing me. Her rosette is winking with every thrust. I have the sudden urge to be there, too. Cookie is too small to take me without lube. I pull out, put my head to her hole, pushing in an inch.

"Christ, ah, fuck," I bellow, sweat running down my temples.

Cookie mewls, tossing her head on the pillow. "*Plus, Amour! Plus...! Plus...! Plus, profonde!*"

I almost laugh at my woman, trying to make me understand what she wants.

"Shh," I soothe against her lips. "I can't give you more or go deeper. You'll tear, baby."

I pull out and slam back into her pussy. My woman's entire body trembles, her toes curl, every muscle in her body becomes rigid. There is a gush of warm liquid bathing my cock. Her pussy spasms around me, milking me.

"Fuck," I groan, sending my hips flying. The tingling hits my lower spine, shooting to my balls. My cock jerks, letting loose my jizz. I stay deep, covering my woman as I hump and grind. Cookie's pussy doesn't let up its intense spasms. I look down at her; she's in a euphoric haze.

"Christ, baby," I growl between harsh breaths.

I try to clear my mind, aware I need to take care of my woman. I read about full-body orgasms and squirting. The brothers talk about how amazing it is to witness, but I never had a woman I wanted to give one to until Cookie.

I lower her legs and cocoon her with my body, keeping my cock deep within her pussy. I pull the comforter over us, knowing we're going to be sleeping in a wet spot.

I touch our connection. "Cook, relax your pussy for me, baby." Then, I run through all her body parts, telling her to relax them for me. "Love you, baby."

After a good five minutes, Cookie stirs in my arms. She puts her nose to my pit, mumbling, "Pheromones," snuggling into my body.

I chuckle. "I just thought you loved my stink."

"*Oui*, I do," she murmurs against my skin. "I need to change the sheets, Amour," she slurs. "You hate the wet spot."

"Nope, I'll deal for tonight. It's late, baby. Sleep."

"High?"

"Hmm, baby."

"I love all of you."

I kiss her head. "I love all of you, too, baby."

"High, have you ever done that before?"

I chuckle; I guess we're not sleeping. "What? Getting my ass fucked and making a woman squirt?"

"*Oui.*"

I laugh low. "Nope, it was a first."

"I liked it," confesses Cookie. "Jewel was right. Full-body orgasms are sublime…and the other thing you did to my butt…and touching your sacred hole."

I guffaw, shaking us both. "Good to know, baby. Let's not share with Jewel."

"We're best friends; we share, Amour. I'll just her tell a little bit," she giggles.

I chuckle. After everything my woman's been through, I'm happy she has Jewel.

"Love you. Sleep, baby."

"Love you back. I'm going to dream about our cabin in the woods," she yawns, reaching over and setting the alarm on her new iPhone. My woman sets it down gently, as if it's the most precious thing she owns.

No doubt: I'm bulldozing the cabin and building her a house with a white picket fence this spring.

CHAPTER 12

JEWEL'S TRUE IDENTITY - HIGH

Cookie and I were up before the crack of dawn. She insisted on driving herself to Butte. Before she left, we went out to the barn to feed Puddin'. He was glassy eyed, stiff as a board—dead. Judging from the froth coming from his mouth, someone had poisoned him. I'd bet all my money Marshmallow did it. My woman cried for an hour in my arms. I was ready to put Marshmallow's ass to ground, but Cookie said we didn't have any proof. I swear to god, if the bitch comes within fifty feet of us, she won't be breathing.

Then, I tracked Cookie and knew she was going to be late. She was driving thirty-five on the goddamn highway. I called Cam so he wouldn't worry. He busted a gut over her driving that slow. "Don't fucking fret, High. I'll park her when she gets here." He was still laughing as I disconnected.

Now I'm taking shit from General. I bang my fist down, rattling the war room table. "All I'm asking is for Beau, or Mafia Man, to fly me to LA tomorrow. No one needs to know why or be involved," I shout, glaring at him.

Mafia Man runs a hand behind his neck, something he does when he's stressed. "Jesus, High, it's fucking obvious something happened, and you're out for blood. Beau, General, and I are the only ones in this room. Tell us what the hell happened."

I run a hand over my face. *"Rrrrah!"* I growl. "Goddamn, fucking shit!"

Beau sets a tumbler of Jameson in front of me. Then, he clears his throat. "Jewel told me you and Cookie moved in together."

I take a gulp of Jameson. "Yeah, we're cleaning out the cabin on Sunday. It's a shithole, but she wants to live there."

Beau nods. "Makes sense. She's a woman, she wants her own place. I'm assuming the two of you talked, and you're going after Stratton Records."

I narrow my eyes on him. "What the hell do you know about Brian Stratton?"

"Not much, only he signed Cookie to a contract. Somehow she ended up in Helena half-dead on a grate. Given Cookie's reaction to the envelope, and Jewel being as jumpy as a cat on a hot tin roof, my guess is Brian Stratton beat the shit out of her."

I hang my head, exhaling. "The cunt violated her. She was a goddamn virgin."

"My fucking god," growls General.

"Yeah, she was eighteen. Her life before that was a horror story." I snort. "She thought Pick was God when he found her."

Mafia Man nods, understanding because his four sons—five, if I count Patriot—were abused by their biological mothers. "So, we're going to LA to take out Brian Stratton. Torture or clean?"

I smirk at him.

He smiles. "Torture it is. We need intel on him, where he lives, his daily routine, and where we're going to do the deed without being seen or heard."

"Beau," calls Jewel from the stairs. "Use the beach house's garage. Toss the bastard into the ocean for fish bait."

"Jewel, Jesus Christ," barks Beau.

"Mafia Man and General know who I am. High is Cookie's man;

72

he's not going to tell anyone." Jewel looks at me. "I am Reagan Sawyer."

"Reagan Sawyer? The movie producer was your father? Jenna Sawyer, the author, founder of Pony Library, was your mother?" I moan. "You're the goddamn urban fashion designer. That's why Maggie and Mafia Man recognized you. Jesus, what the hell were you doing as a sweet butt?"

Jewel smiles at me. "It's a long, ugly story, High. I would appreciate you keeping my identity a secret, even from Joker. Thank you for doing this for Cookie. If you need money, Beau will access my account. I'd say to enjoy the beach house, but I think that will be a bit challenging, given what you need to do." She turns, walking back down the stairs. "High, make sure you access Stratton's computer and erase all evidence of Cookie's contract," she orders from the bottom landing.

"What...the...fuck, Beau? Reagan Sawyer! You're living in her country house ten miles up the goddamn mountain. You were her father's friend!"

He looks down at his folded hands, saying nothing.

"High, Jewel's situation is more screwed up than Cookie's," says General. "Just be thankful the girls are alive, and they have us."

"Yeah," I bark, running my fingers through my hair. *This shit is unbelievable!* "Who else knows about Jewel?"

"The adults in my family, Beau, General, Maria, Cookie, and now you," says Mafia Man.

"Maria? Who the hell is Maria?!"

"Jewel's housekeeper in Malibu. Actually, she's more of a family friend," says Beau. "I understand if you're unwilling to keep Jewel's identity a secret. It goes against the brotherhood. I'll move her if—"

"No." I shake my head. "Jewel is Cookie's best friend. I'll keep my mouth shut."

"Thanks," he says. Genuine relief crosses his face. I get the inkling Beau loves Jewel. I'm not sure in what capacity.

"I need to do some research," says Mafia Man. "We'll meet here tomorrow morning and plan the hit." Mafia Man is a badass ex-Irish Mafia boss and a computer whiz. If it's on the web, he'll find it.

I nod, down my Jameson, and stand. "I can't do it Friday. Cookie's gigging at Blue Heaven in Butte; I need to be there to support her."

Beau chuckles, "Yeah, we're aware. Jewel is sending me in her place."

I snort, bound down the stairs, and come eye-to-eye with my daughter.

"Megan," I say, rounding her.

"High, are you moving your girlfriend into the cabin?" she asks snottily.

I turn slowly, giving her the fatherly death glare.

"I, um, overheard Jewel talking on the phone to Cookie. I didn't know you were seeing anyone. The dancer..."

"Trudy played me. It's none of your goddamn business, but I never slept with the bitch, Megan."

She nods and then furrows her brow. "Cookie is young...two years older than I am. She's very tiny and beautiful. Jewel said she's a musical genius."

I stare at my kid, waiting for her to get to the point.

"I don't want Cookie to get hurt by Elizabeth, High," she blurts out.

"Elizabeth is fucking gone, Meg. I haven't had anything to do with her physically in years. I ended all ties with her yesterday." I pull out my iPhone. "Smile for your old man," I order, holding it up.

Megan laughs and strikes a pose the way she did when she was ten. She used to love it when I took her picture.

She shuffles her feet, appearing nervous. "High, can I meet Cookie? And go to the cabin with you? I'd like to see my old room."

I blow out a breath, running my hand down my face.

"I won't make trouble. I've talked with Aunt Faith and realize the divorce wasn't all your fault. Mom and Ed..."

"Megan, your mother and I both made mistakes. Fawn loved Ed and took you from me. You didn't want anything to do with me. I provided for you the best I could. That's it; end of the story. It happened ten years ago. I've moved on and built a life in Pony with the Sinners. Now I'm with Cookie, and I don't want her reliving my past."

She nods, tears brim her blues. "It's too late for me to be included in your life with Cookie? She's young, and you'll have more kids with her—out with the old, in with the new."

"I didn't say that, Meg. Cookie knows all about you. And, provided you keep your attitude in check, she'll love you." I chuckle, "If you don't, you're going to meet up with Chéri, the badass Frenchwoman."

Megan grins. "She's French Canadian, like your father."

"Yeah, Meg, from Quebec. She loves me; she won't tolerate disrespect. Be here at nine tonight; you can meet her then. On Sunday, we're cleaning out the cabin."

"I'll be here," says Megan, all smiles. "I need to get to the Reservation. I'm teaching advanced algebra." She giggles. "Aunt Raven sucks at it, and Uncle Sean is tired of trying to work out the problems."

A low chuckle comes from behind us. "Your aunt gets her panties in a knot over math. Thank god Aaron is teaching calc," laughs General. "Those problems are a bitch."

Megan giggles again, running for the door.

I blow out a breath. No "bye, Dad, love you, Dad," or "see ya, Dad," but it's a start.

CHAPTER 13

COOKIE HAS TURNED MY LIFE AROUND – HIGH

Princess is in the war room; Joey is at her tit. Flame is behind her, supporting their baby. It's become the norm, witnessing the two of them breastfeeding their triplets. Fawn didn't breastfeed Megan. Something about inverted nipples and not getting Meg to latch on. A screwed up thought comes into my mind: I want to help Cookie breastfeed our kid.

"High, are you with us?" asks Princess.

"Yeah," I nod, refocusing on my problem.

"It's going to be a challenging case to win if Elizabeth goes through with her claim of marriage," says Princess, changing boobs with Flame's help. "She has the statements to prove you've been providing for her. The law is on her side."

I run a hand down my face. Christ. Do a good deed, and it comes back to bite you in the ass.

"Daddy and I received a call from Margo Cooper today," announces Princess.

I furrow my brow. "Margo Cooper? Elizabeth's mother-in-law?"

"The one and only," confirms Pick. "Roger Smith referred her to us. Apparently, Elizabeth is suing Margo for the property Jason Sr.'s grandfather left him. In Jason Sr.'s will, he bequeathed it to his mother, Margo. Margo is claiming Jason Jr. was not her son's child. He was duped into the marriage. We don't want any blowback on you, so Doc is going to take a sample of your DNA."

I pound the table with my fist. "I am not Jason Jr.'s fucking father!"

"We know that, High," says Doc. "It's just a precautionary measure. So spit in the goddamn tube."

"Christ," I breathe out, then spit in the tube. I sign on the line, validating it's my spit.

"Mrs. Cooper has enough money to keep Elizabeth's case tied up in court for years. We think Elizabeth will come at you hard and heavy for cash, given you cut all your support. Jamie and I talked…"

Flame is Sinners' Sergeant of Arms. A badass to the max. Being Princess's husband, he is Jamie or Schnooks to her.

Flame grins, releasing Joey's lips from Princess's nipple. He tucks Princess's tit back into her bra and then tilts Joey up, rubbing his back while talking to me. "Brother, the choices are simple. You pay the bitch off, or we dig up dirt on her. If Jason Jr. was not Jason Sr.'s son, she has skeletons rattling around in her closet. We need to find them."

I grin, hearing Joey give his father a belch. "What do you have in mind?"

"I'll tap into the security system in the apartment building and the street cam. If the bitch is seeing someone, we'll have proof. Then, we'll do some surveillance and catch her red-handed."

"High, Margo asked about you," says Pick. "We gave her the gist of your situation. She wants you to be at our meeting; she's looking for insight into Elizabeth and the Wheelers."

I nod. "When and where?"

"This Friday, at Callaghan's Bar. Butte is a large city, but people talk."

I push back my chair and stand. General tosses an arm around my shoulder. "You have a lot on your plate. How are you holding up?"

"I'll be okay when Stratton is taken care of. Elizabeth is just a goddamn thorn in my side."

General drops his arm. "Do you need any help with the cabin on Sunday?"

I chuckle, making my way down the stairs. "Nope, Megan and Cookie will be there."

I walk over to the bar, grab a beer, and then make my way over to the couches and drop down next to Megan.

JJ leaps onto my lap, holding up a phone. He's tracking Cookie. "Look, Aunt Cookie is almost home."

I chuckle, seeing my woman do her usual twenty mph up Diva Mountain Road.

"Why is Cookie going so slow? Is she having car trouble or something?" asks Meg, her eyes pinned to the cell.

JJ shakes his head no. "Aunt Cookie is scared to drive fast."

Megan giggles. "I think I can run faster than your aunt is driving."

The door opens, and Cookie walks in, loaded down by her hobo bag, several other bags, and her guitar.

Meg's eyes go wide. Yup, my woman is decked out in her rocker clothes—skin-tight leather pants, a sexy-as-hell off the shoulder red sweater, and kick-ass high-heeled biker boots.

I stand with JJ on my hip and walk over to her. Leaning down, I give her a kiss. "Was the drive better tonight, baby?"

She grimaces, setting down her bags. "*Non*, people are so rude! On my way home, I needed to stop at a garage sale. It was six o'clock—the lady was packing up her things, so I needed to pounce."

Megan and Jewel giggle beside me.

"You'll learn quickly Cookie is the number one bargain shopper," whispers Jewel to Megan. "I can't believe the amazing things she gets for little to no money."

Cookie smiles, pointing to her packages. "All new Cannon towels, including washcloths and hand towels, still in the packaging, with the tags attached, for—get this—five dollars! A full set of ten in the perfect color: burnt orange. The lady said she bought them for her friend's wedding shower and it fell through. I also got a full set of multicolored ceramic mixing bowls for two dollars, and a KitchenAid stand mixer for ten. It was a little more than I wanted to spend, but I couldn't pass it up." My woman looks up at me. "Amour, remind me to put them in my outs column." Then she steps forward, grinning at Megan. "I'm Cookie." She slides her arm into the crook of Megan's arm, leading her over to the couch. "Tell me about yourself, Megan. I want to know you."

"Christ," laughs Flame, kissing Cookie on the temple. "High made you chatty. Do you want a glass of wine, Cook?"

"*Oui*, thank you," she laughs.

Jewel smiles up at me, mouthing, "Thank you."

I grin and mouth back, "No thanks needed." Then, I follow Jewel over to the couch.

JJ's staring at his aunt. "Aunt Cookie is glitzier than Aunt Maggie. And she has big—"

I cover his mouth, shaking my head no. When I lift my hand, JJ cracks up, whispering in my ear, "Boobies."

I chuckle at my four-year-old nephew.

For the next hour, we listen to everything about Megan: her life in Denver, her experience at Stanford, and her internship at the Reservation. Whenever Megan asks a question about Cookie, one of the Sinners jumps in, deflecting it.

Flame was wrong; my woman isn't chatty. She's a good listener—attentive, making everything about Megan.

Meg smiles at Cookie. "You're an artist."

JJ gets there before anyone else. "My Aunt Cookie is the lead singer in a band—the Heartbreakers. And she's part of the cooking club. She makes me tarts, quiche, crepes..." He keeps going, listing every food Cookie has ever made for him. He nods, grinning proudly at Cookie. "She speaks French and likes lots of wine and chocolate. She doesn't like chips, soda, Cheetos, or bugs. She thinks the coffee at the club is piss water. And she's thrifty."

I chuckle, looking over to my woman. Her face is beet red.

Jewel giggles, "I guess that pretty much sums up Aunt Cookie."

"Yeah," laughs Flame. "He didn't leave anything out."

Megan turns to Cookie. "I'd love to go to the flea market with you."

Princess chortles, "No, you wouldn't. First, you need to dress as if you're indigent, so the vendors think you're poor. Then there are her six rules. Number one: make a list of items you want, and don't be an impulse buyer. Number two: don't act excited over something you like. Number three: set the price you're willing to pay, and don't back down. Number four: walk away if the seller refuses to deal. Number five: don't buy anything from the food vendors; they are gougers. Number six: don't shop with anyone; the sellers push the prices up when they see two people looking at the same item."

Cookie laughs. "I'm not that bad. You're welcome to come with me on Saturday morning. We need to be there at seven o'clock sharp. I usually try to go at the end of the day, because the vendors don't like to cart their wares back home, but there's no help for it. I want to be fresh for Sunday."

Princess nods slowly. "See? Told you. Cookie's going to make you park *far, far* away from the building, so no one sees what type of vehicle you're driving."

"High?" says Megan.

"He's Dad or Daddy to you, Megan," scolds Cookie. "You're lucky enough to have a father who loves and supports you. High deserves the title."

Flame, General, and I just about choke on our drinks.

Joker chuckles, "Chéri Fayette is coming out to play, Megan. Take cover. You disrespected her man."

"*Dad,*" emphasizes Megan. "Are you going to the flea market with Cookie?"

I bite my lip to keep from laughing. "Yeah, Meg."

"Do I get to keep my room in the cabin? Or..."

"Of course you get to keep your room, Megan. Your father wants you with us," assures Cookie.

But Cookie and I are loud when we get our groove on, and thin walls don't make for a hell of a lot of privacy.

"Bring headphones with you, Meg. Cookie and I get busy at night and in the morning."

"Ew, Dad," giggles Megan. "I don't need to know that."

I throw back my head, laughing. "You don't need to hear it, either."

Cookie has turned my life around; she's given me back my daughter.

CHAPTER 14

I look at Patriot. For some reason, Mafia Man gave him the intel about Cookie. It's Wednesday; time is ticking. I need to put Brian Stratton to ground before Friday—Cam called me and asked if the Sinners could provide security at Blue Heaven that day. Apparently, word spread that my woman can sing. Cam is worried about the crowd size, given the university and the community college.

Patriot lowers the large white screen and plugs in his computer. "Dev told me what was going down with Stratton and wanted my expertise on his health." He clicks on a picture.

I scrunch up my face. "Christ, is that the fucker's cock and balls?"

"Yeah," nods Patriot. "Stratton has seen multiple doctors for his diagnosis of micropenis; it's a rare but real condition. As you can see, the guy has a two-inch penis...three with an erection. To make matters more interesting, the asshole has a severe case of Peyronie's."

"Peyronie?" I repeat, grimacing. "What the hell is that?"

"A curved penis," defines Patriot. "It makes sex unpleasant for the woman."

"Christ," I bark.

"Yeah," nods Patriot. "And the topper: Stratton has cardiovascular syncope, a condition that causes him to faint and spontaneously recover. My guess is the asshole's pacemaker malfunctioned, seeing's how he had it replaced the day after he violated Cookie." He clicks to another picture. "This is Stratton. He's fifty-five, decent-looking, with a believable face. The asshole is of average height—five-foot-ten—and weighs in at a buck-eighty. Stratton lives alone in an upscale neighborhood. He's never had a girlfriend or wife; more than likely, it was related to his messed-up self-image. He has been seeing the same psychiatrist for the last forty years. He has no social life that we're aware of; he eats, sleeps, and works."

I sneer at the fucker's picture. "Arrest record?"

"Five," answers Mafia Man. "Five women came forward over the last ten years, claiming they were assaulted by Brian Stratton—beaten and attempted rape. Cookie was the smallest, easiest to subdue."

"Convictions?" I bark, my rage rising.

"None, brother. They all took back their statements before he was tried. High, the women are put through hell on the stand. Their lives are torn apart and exposed," says Mafia Man.

"There is a lot of psychological bullshit attached to rape. Often, women and men don't come forward," explains Patriot.

Patriot was sexually abused as a kid. He understands the trauma better than anyone.

"Are you okay with all this shit, brother?" Jesus, I don't want this to cause him to have flashbacks.

"Yeah, High. No worries. I worked out my shit a long time ago."

"I broke into his computers and wiped them clean of Chéri Fayette, brother," says Mafia Man. "It's LA; there are cameras on every street corner. He lives in a gated community. The office building is high-tech. Stratton uses Uber to and from work. We need to be the cunt's chauffeur. I looked at his calendar. Tomorrow night, he has a two-hour meeting from six to eight. We'll take him after the meeting; it'll be dark. Patriot is going to give us diazepam to knock his ass out. We'll take this route"—He runs his finger over the highway and streets

—"to get to Jewel's beach house. Beau and Patriot will be waiting for us," says Mafia Man.

"We'll Narcan his ass to wake the bastard, and then he's all yours," says Patriot.

"After, we'll take my boat out into the ocean, and he's fish food," says Beau. "We're back home by early afternoon."

Liam, Guard Dog, and Rocky step out of the shadows.

I moan. Goddamnit, Mafia Man told his brothers.

"We're in," announces Liam. "Tommy stays in Pony."

"Uncle Liam," growls Patriot. "I'm not staying in Pony!"

"Your ass stays here, and that's the end of it," yells Liam.

I need to bite my tongue to keep from laughing. Uncle Liam has spoken.

"We leave at nine tomorrow morning. That puts us in LA at noon. We'll scope out the area; there might be a better route," says Liam.

"Liam, goddamnit, it's planned," whines Mafia Man.

"Dev, it never hurts to look at alternative routes," barks Liam. "You did less than twenty-four hours' worth of surveillance on the asshole. This needs to be foolproof. No one wants to be locked up for twenty-to-life."

Beau and I look at each other, chuckling. Badass big brother Liam is overriding badass little brother Mafia Man. It will be an interesting trip with the four Kincaid brothers.

CHAPTER 15

THE TORTURE — HIGH

It's one p.m., and it's stop-and-go, bumper-to-bumper traffic out of LAX. Adam, the manager of LA Top Gun Security, picked us up, and now we're headed back to the office to drop him off.

Adam is an ex-enforcer for the Irish Mafia. A badass at age thirty, he was hand-picked and trained by Liam. Given how he greeted Liam with hugs and kisses, he loves the ex-mafia boss like a son loves his father.

Adam looks at me and then to Guard Dog, settling his eyes on Liam. "Any particular reason the six of you decided to show up in Los Angeles on a Thursday afternoon, without notice, loaded for bear, boss?"

Liam ignores his question and mumbles something, running his finger along the highway to Malibu. "Adam, we need to check out West Hollywood…Santa Monica Boulevard."

"Boss," smirks Adam, "the boulevard is fourteen-and-a-half miles long. Got an address?"

"Hmm," hums Liam. "1222."

I look over at Mafia Man. He's pouting like a petulant child, clearly not happy about big brother taking over *his* operation.

I pull out my cell to text Cookie like I promised.

> Me: Hey, baby, we made it to LA.

> Cookie: Be careful; love you, Amour!

She sends me a man-and-woman-kissing emoji.

Nope, I don't do emojis. That's Mafia Man and Maggie's thing.

> Me: Back at you, baby. I'll text later.

Rocky looks over at me. "Is Cookie all right?"

I nod, tucking away my phone. "Cookie's in Butte, practicing with Cam for the gig on Friday. Are you going to be available to do security with me?"

"Yeah, brother, we'll all be at the Blue Heaven. Pick, Hialeah, and Running Bear are babysitting all the kids. Flame and Corinne are trying to work it out," says Rocky.

"The triplets are still on their mother's tit," announces Guard Dog, as if we all don't know that piece of info. He laughs, "Corinne's a goddamn milking machine. It's kind of hot, in a weird sort of way. Not that I want Corinne; she's like a sister."

"AJ, Jesus," barks Rocky, his voice full of disgust.

Adam chuckles, "Aaron still has his titty fetish."

Beau and I look at each other, laughing. Guard Dog is the third brother in the Kincaid clan. He's AJ to his blood brothers, Aaron to the ex-enforcers, and Guard Dog to the Sinners' brothers. Most of the time, he's the peacekeeper of his family—and fucking hilarious. And yeah, he has a serious titty fetish. I just about pissed myself when Rocky blamed it on their father for not making their mother wean him soon enough.

Liam points to a glass-fronted two-story building. "Adam, pull over. The building is right there."

Adam pulls over to the side of the street. "Stratton Records." He furrows his brow. "We updated their security system a month ago." He looks at Guard Dog. "I sent the invoice to Mac. We're still waiting for payment."

Liam grins. "Their service has just been cut off. Drive around to the back. I want to check out the parking lot."

Adam sighs, driving around to the back. "Boss, I know the building. Whatever is going down, I'm in."

I stare at the back door, deciding to give Adam the intel. He's trustworthy. "Brian Stratton hurt six women, including mine. We're putting him to ground, tonight."

Mafia Man gives Adam his version of the plan.

"Shit," breathes out Adam. Then he shakes his head. "The Malibu beach house is too goddamn close to other homes to torture the asshole in the garage."

Liam nods. "Agreed."

"But Stratton Records clears out by eight p.m. and doesn't start up again until nine in the morning." Adam points to the foundation. "The building has a windowless basement; we can take the cunt down there. We'll cut the feed to the security system; High will do his thing. If we use the Top Gun Security van, no one will question it."

"Disposal?" I ask Adam.

He thinks for a few beats. "We can feed Stratton to the fish, but we'd need to drive forty-five minutes with a goddamn corpse in the back of the van. Plus, it's a wealthy neighborhood; folks are nosier and more suspicious. Dropping the body off in an alley of the gang-infested part of Hollywood would be safer. Dead bodies turn up there every goddamn night. It's a ten-minute drive from here. The gangs have shot out ninety-five percent of the cameras—easy in, easy out. It's done."

Liam looks at me. "High, it's your call."

I glance at Beau. "Are you comfortable with the alley, brother?"

"Yeah, we'll cover the body with lye. It'll erase all traces of us."

"Guard Dog?"

"Yeah, High. It's a good plan."

I look over at Mafia Man. "You, brother?"

He grins at Liam. "You planned to get Adam on board. When, big brother, did you call him?"

Liam smirks at his little brother. "Five minutes after you told me about the asshole violating Cookie."

Mafia Man snickers. "Yeah, High. It's the basement and the alley."

At 8:00, my nerves buzz from the adrenaline flowing through my veins. I clench my fists, listening to the pimply faced young girl trying to belt out Miranda Lambert, "The House That Built Me." It's her fourth song; this one is more painful than the others. But the kid's mother insists she has what it takes to be a big star.

"Christ, just cut her loose."

"Settle your ass down," growls Beau into my ear. He's plastered to my back in the small janitor's closet that shares a wall with Stratton's office.

"If I need to listen to one more goddamn song, I'm going to kill the mother, too," I growl back.

The brothers' snickers come through my earpiece.

Stratton sighs. "Mrs. Burdick, my head is pounding. Your daughter will never make it in the music industry. She doesn't have the looks or the moves. Her voice is like listening to nails on a chalkboard—off-key screeching. The door is behind you; please use it."

The little girl breaks out in loud sobs.

"It's okay, darling. Mr. Stratton wouldn't know talent if it hit him in the nose. Come, Sweet Pea, we'll find a real agent to back you."

A door bangs closed, shaking the walls of the closet.

"The building is clear," says Liam through our earpieces. "Take the asshole now."

Beau and I slip out of the closet and walk the ten feet to Stratton's door. I open it and strut in. Stratton's at his desk, shuffling through papers. He looks up at me, startled.

"Look, if you're the girl's father—"

"I'm not. I'm Chéri Fayette's man," I say, keeping my voice even.

Stratton tries to see around me, smiling. I know his little crooked cock is hard, just by the way his hand slips to his crotch. *The goddamn pervert.*

"Is Chéri with you—"

"Nope." I yank my Glock from my waistband and stride around the desk. I tap him on the head with the barrel. "Fucking move!"

Stratton's eyes widen, his pupils dilate, his breathing accelerates. Beads of sweat pop out on his brow. "Look, I don't know what Chéri told you—"

"We both know what you did to my woman," I bark, yanking him out of the chair. "Now you and I have a date in the basement."

Stratton starts blatting and blubbering about how he's going to make Chéri a star...bigger than Mariah Carey, Beyoncé, Whitney Houston, and Adele.

"She has the 'it' factor: the voice, the moves, and the looks," he cries, stumbling down the stairs.

We hit the basement, and he's still blubbering. "Just let me talk to her. I have a heart condition; it made me crazy." He screams, "Lack of oxygen! That's why it happened, lack of oxygen to my brain! My pacemaker battery died!"

Guard Dog looks at him with disgust. "Asshole, I know you don't have a set of balls, but Jesus, you're crying like a newborn babe. For Christ's sake, die with dignity."

I shrug off my cut and hand it to Beau. "Take off your fucking jacket," I growl. "I'd cut off your cock and feed it to you, but it doesn't mean that much to you."

Stratton starts groveling, "Please, wait, just wait. I have money—"

"Too late!" Quick as lightning, my fist flies, *jab...jab...jab*. I connect with the asshole's face and then throw an uppercut to his left jaw. He falls onto the cement floor. A river of blood pours from his nose and split lips—Stratton's drooling, crying, and trying to crawl away on all fours.

"Where do you think you're going, Pumpkin?" laughs Adam, lifting him up by his shirt. "High is just getting warmed up." He shoves him back toward me—Stratton staggers. The smell of piss and shit infuses the air.

"Christ," barks Mafia Man. "Did you need to shit yourself?!"

Jab...jab...jab! His head whips back and forth like a goddamn speed bag. *Crunch*...his nose flattens. Stratton screams, putting his hands to his face. I do a roundhouse kick. *Crack*...his jaw separates. Stratton's eyes roll back into their sockets; he face-plants into the floor.

"Are you kidding me?" barks Rocky, staring down at the asshole's body. "What a fucking pansy-ass pussy!" He looks at me. "You didn't even break a goddamn sweat."

Liam chuckles, "Finish the fucker off, High."

I drop down onto one knee, put him into a headlock. "This is for my woman, asshole." In one smooth jerk, I snap the fucker's neck.

Beau nods, bumping temples with me. "Let's roll the fucker up in plastic, get him out to the van, and bleach the room."

Disposing of Stratton's body was as easy as snapping two fingers. We tossed him in an alley, covered him with lye, and got the hell out. Then, Adam gave us a ride to the airport.

I give Adam a fist bump. "Thanks for your help, brother. You have my marker."

"No problem, High. We'll call it even; you took our backs with the Italian Mafia."

Adam hugs Liam as a son would his father. "Don't be a stranger," he says into Liam's neck.

Liam kisses his temple. "You know where I live. You're welcome anytime."

Mafia Man, Beau, Guard Dog, and Rocky give Adam bro-hugs.

"Hug Maggie, Polly, and the kids for me," says Adam. "Tell everyone I miss them."

"Will do," says Mafia Man. "We'll wait for Stratton's body to be identified, and then we'll sue his estate for the money the asshole owes Top Gun."

Adam chuckles, "Always the accountant. Love you, brother. Fly safe."

I pull up the steps to the jet and close the door. Mafia Man is our pilot, and Rocky takes the copilot seat. I raise an eyebrow, looking at Beau.

He chuckles, "I'm taking the ride."

I nod and text Cookie—

Me: Baby, it's over. We're on our way home.

I get a paragraph in French back. Beau looks over my shoulder, reading it. *"Je t'aime* means love you. Cookie asked if you're all right. She also said she is having a sleepover with Megan and Jewel. They're watching *Last Comic Standing.* Megan picked it. Jewel and Megan are laughing their butts off." He chuckles, "Cookie's complaining she doesn't understand the jokes; she needs you to explain them."

I smirk. My woman doesn't watch television. She likes to read, write songs, and listen to music.

Beau grins. "She also said your daughter loves jalapeño chips, just like you." He laughs. "She'll scooch over so you can fit in bed with them when you get home. She needs her snuggle and to...*smell*...you." Beau glances at me. "I'm not sure Cookie had the right word, 'smell.' She probably confused the words."

I chuckle. Nope, my woman meant "smell."

"I don't know how in the hell Cookie thinks the four of you will fit in a queen-sized bed." Beau points to the French words, explaining: *"Amour,* love. *Tu,* you. *Plus,* more. *Que,* than. *La vie,* life. That's all she wrote."

I need to brush up on my French. Christ, if I don't, Beau will know all our business.

CHAPTER 16

THE FONTAINES — COOKIE

I rush up to the Happy Hot Dog food truck. "Sorry I'm late, Al. The practice session ran a little long because of the gig tomorrow night," I explain, pulling my guitar out of its plastic bag. "You're coming to Blue Heaven, right?"

"Yup, lookin' forward to it."

"Make sure you let the guy at the door know you're my special guest. He'll bring you to the VIP section."

Al chuckles and serves the next person in line.

Good lord, it's like the Arctic out here—freezing. I wiggle my fingers to warm them up. I need a tune I can move to.

"What will it be today, Al?"

"Hmm," he hums. "How about a little Celine Dion?"

I laugh. "'I'm Alive' it is." I start strumming and humming, letting the music take me away. When I get to the hook, I close my eyes and bounce on my toes. "Come on, Al, sing with me!" I smile, hearing him bellow out the lyrics. At the end of the song, I notice a lot of people are surrounding me, pushing in.

"Hey, back up," shouts Al. He comes out of the truck. "I said, back the fuck up!"

A tall man pushes his way through the crowd, standing in front of me, protectively. I get a whiff of a very familiar scent. I furrow my brow; he smells like High.

"Put your money in the can, show's over," shouts the guy.

Inhaling deeply, I widen my eyes. He sounds like High!

"Thanks, Mr. Fontaine," says Al. "I was afraid they were going to hurt Cookie."

Mr. Fontaine? Non, it can't be a coincidence.

When the man turns to look at me, I sway on my feet—black spots dance in my eyes.

"Hey." He catches me. "You're all right. They're gone."

I open my mouth. All that comes out is a half-choked "Christian," in my French accent. I put my palm to my forehead, trying to remember my English.

"Do you know my son, Christian?" he asks back in French, staring down at me.

I nod, then speak in rapid French. "He's my man. We live in Pony, with the Sinners." I stupidly turn, pointing in the direction of Pony. Then I launch into how much High misses him and his mother, and he's sorry for everything he did. Tears brim my eyes. I say in French, "You need to forgive him, because he's a good man, and he takes care of Megan and me and the Sinners." I throw up my hands. *"Toutes les personnes!"*

"I think she may be havin' some kind of episode," says Al, pulling out his phone. "She's been workin' her little ass off. I need to get her checked out."

"No, Al. She is my son's woman," laughs Mr. Fontaine. "Cookie is speaking French. Very rapidly," he chuckles.

In combination with my nervousness, the cold wind is making me tremble, and my teeth chatter.

"Do you have a car, Cookie? I just dropped mine off at the shop."

I nod vigorously. "You'll come back with me to Pony to see High? I mean, Christian. I can bring you back here tomorrow. I have a gig at the Blue Heaven tomorrow night." I point a shaky finger in the direction of the bar.

"Al, I'm going to get Cookie into the car," says Mr. Fontaine.

Al's gaze flits to High's father and then back to me. "I think that's a good idea. I'll see you tomorrow, Cookie."

Mr. Fontaine wraps an arm around me and takes my guitar and coffee can. "Where is your car, Cookie?"

"In the parking lot. It's the Cayenne." I look up at him. "So, you'll come?"

He smiles down at me. "*Non*, my wife is at home. Maybe you would consider coming to my house and telling her about Christian? Dana would love to meet you."

I nod and dig out my keys from my hobo bag. I hit the fob to unlock the doors. Then, I blow out a breath; it's 5:00, rush hour traffic time. I swallow, slide into the driver's seat, and put on my seat belt.

"May I have your address, please? I need to put it into my GPS."

Mr. Fontaine chuckles, "I'll direct you."

I think about that for a second; I get nervous when people give me directions. *Oh, god, I want High.*

I blow out a quick breath and put the SUV into gear. I crawl out of the parking lot and make a right into traffic, white-knuckling the steering wheel. We're going fifteen mph. People are beeping their horns, but I've learned to ignore them.

Mr. Fontaine gives me directions to his home. Twenty minutes later, I'm pulling into his driveway. I smile; the house is just as High described it—a big white house with black shutters and a huge front yard. Tears prick my eyes; it has a white picket fence.

Mr. Fontaine furrows his brow. "Are you okay, Cookie?"

I nod, smiling. "High described your home to me. I thought it sounded like the most beautiful house I could imagine." I breathe out, "It is."

"Where are you from?"

"Quebec."

"What part of Quebec?"

I shrug, smiling. "Just Quebec," I answer, not wanting him to know I'm from the poverty district.

He smiles. "Okay, Cookie from just Quebec, let's go in and say hello to Dana."

I follow him up the cobblestone walk. He opens the door, shouting, "Baby, I brought home a guest."

My eyes go everywhere, taking in everything. Maggie and Mafia Man's home is gorgeous, but High's parents' house is magnificent. The hallway is as big as our whole apartment was in Quebec. I drop down on my butt and untie my boots.

Mr. Fontaine looks down at me and shakes his head, chuckling. "Rene?"

I look up...up...and up. A beautiful, thin older woman is staring down at me. She has silver hair pulled back into a ponytail and piercing sky-blue eyes. And she's tall—maybe five-ten, like Maggie and Princess. I furrow my brow; she's wearing a knit cream sweater dress that ends just above her ankles. She looks like one of the ladies who would shoo me away when I busked too close to their storefront doors.

"Child, what are you doing on the floor?"

Mr. Fontaine chuckles again; High has his deep, rumbling laugh.

"Baby, this young lady is Cookie. She is Christian's woman."

Mrs. Fontaine's eyes widen. She takes a sharp inhale, covering her mouth. "Rene," she drawls, her eyes fill with tears. She looks up at her husband. "Where did you find her?"

He laughs, bending down, and lifts me up. "Now that is a story, baby."

I stand statue-still, not knowing what to say or what to do. I shouldn't have come; I should have just gone home and not bothered these people. I need to get out of here.

"I..." I stutter. "I'm...I'm sorry, I need to go. Christian will be worried about me." I drop back down on the floor, trying to pull on my boot with trembling hands.

"Rene, what is she doing? Cookie, what are you doing?! You can't leave. Rene, she can't leave!"

Mrs. Fontaine plops down on the floor in front of me. She reaches for my hand. I pull away like a scared rabbit. These people, this house, it's too much.

Mr. Fontaine crouches beside me. "You asked me to forgive my son." He's talking softly in French. "There is nothing to forgive. Christian left Dana and me. We did not leave him; we would never leave him." He switches to English. "We love Christian. Cookie, you asked me to go to Sinners with you. If the offer is still open, Dana and I would love to go."

Mrs. Fontaine leaps up, and I skitter back on my butt. "Oh, god, I scared her. I will never hurt you, Cookie. Rene, get her a cup of coffee —cappuccino, she's French. I'll pack…"

I look up at Mrs. Fontaine, my eyes swim with unshed tears.

She smiles the most beautiful smile down at me. "Rene makes the best cappuccino with whipped cream and cinnamon. And we have croissants filled with chocolate. Rene gets them from a French bakery in Alberta."

"Baby, go pack. I'll take care of Cookie." Mr. Fontaine looks at me. "Would you like a cappuccino and a croissant?"

I shake my head no. I want High; he knows this world—a civilian world of family and big homes with picket fences. Where people offer you coffee and pastries out of kindness.

As if someone has transformed Mr. Fontaine, he becomes a badass caretaker like High. He lifts me up and carries me through his living room, into the kitchen, where he sets me on a stool at the island. I look around; the Fontaines' kitchen is light gray with white glass-front cabinets and a dark gray tiled floor. He stalks over to the stainless steel fridge and pulls out a bowl of fruit and a Tupperware bowl of whipped cream. I watch him scoop the fruit onto a plate and add a spoonful of cream. He slides the plate in front of me, then takes a strawberry and dips it into the whipped cream. He holds it up to my mouth. "Bite and chew," he orders.

"*Merci*," I murmur, taking the piece of fruit. I set it back onto the plate. If I eat, I'll puke.

Mr. Fontaine nods. "I'll make our coffees. Do you want to hear about Christian?" he asks, fiddling with an expresso machine.

"*Oui*," I respond, watching him.

Mr. Fontaine tells me everything I already know—High was into MMA, hunting, and fishing. He still goes hunting and fishing with Joker. High used to love football and baseball. I knew that, too; he watches the games on television. High was a junk food junkie.

I giggle, "Jalapeño chips are his favorite."

"*Oui*," laughs Mr. Fontaine. "Christian got his like for spicy foods from me." He slides a cup of cappuccino in front of me. "I have a confession to make, Cookie."

Mr. Fontaine sits on the stool next to me, taking my hand. "I have been spying on my son for twenty-one years. I know Christian has a daughter, Megan, and he's divorced." He smiles. "I also know he's cut ties with Elizabeth Wheeler-Cooper. Margo Cooper is a friend of mine. Elizabeth is about to make a lot of trouble for him. I want to help my son."

I explode with a volley of French: "She is a moneygrubbing leech and took advantage of my man's kindness for her own gain." I look up at Mr. Fontaine, anger burns in my eyes. "Christian takes care of those he loves. Though he hasn't loved Elizabeth for a long...long...long time. He honored their friendship and paid her bills. The witch paid him back by claiming they are married by common law. *Non*, they are not! High has not been with her in ten years! The witch wants half his money, and she didn't work for a penny of it!"

Mr. Fontaine smiles down at me. "You do have fire in you, *mon chéri*. No worries, we'll cut Christian loose from the"—he laughs—"witch." He tilts his head, looking at me. "What is your given name?"

I take a sip of the cappuccino. It's delicious; I savor the dark roast and rich cream rolling across my tongue. "Chéri Fayette," I say, taking another sip.

Mrs. Fontaine drops a suitcase on the floor next to me. She smiles. "I told you my husband makes the best cappuccino."

I nod, "*Oui*, Mrs. Fontaine."

"We are Dana and Rene to you," says Rene, smiling.

I slide off the stool, taking my cup and dish to the sink. "We need to get going. Christian will be anxious if I'm later than nine o'clock."

"Chéri, it's only six," says Dana, taking the fruit and putting it in the fridge. "Pony is only an hour away."

I giggle. It's a three-hour ride for me, but I refrain from telling them that. I wash and dry my cup, putting it back into the cupboard.

Rene grabs the suitcase, and we're out the door. My nerves are buzzing with excitement. High is going to be overjoyed to see his parents.

"Seat belts," I order and put the Cayenne into gear. I do my usual twenty mph until I hit the highway. Then, I take the Cayenne up to thirty-five. The other drivers are honking and flipping me the bird. I ignore them. It's starting to snow; I hate driving on snow-covered roads. I white-knuckle the steering wheel, my hands at three and nine, just like Brainiac taught me, and slow to thirty.

"Pull over," orders Rene. Dana giggles in the back seat.

I chance a glance at him. I decide he must need to pee; he appears uncomfortable. I slow down to five mph and pull to the side of the highway.

He leaps out, comes around to the driver's side door, and opens it. "Climb over the console," he says, laughing.

I look at him, confused.

Dana titters, "Rene wants to drive, Chéri."

I furrow my brow, looking at Rene. "Am I driving too slow?"

"If you drove any slower, we wouldn't make Pony 'til morning," he laughs, giving my butt a nudge.

I climb over the console. Rene leaps into the driver's seat, and we're flying down the road.

Good lord, Rene drives like High—pedal to the metal.

Dana is chatty, asking me about Quebec and my music career. I've learned how to answer questions without revealing too much of myself.

Rene gives me a sideways glance, changing the subject to Dana. She's a retired teacher and does all sorts of charity work for under-privileged children. We're in Pony within forty minutes.

I smile. "Would you like me to drive the rest of the way?"

Rene chuckles, "*Non*, just tell me where to turn."

When we get to the gate, Cue Ball and Rascal come over to my SUV. Rene lets down the window.

Rascal furrows his brow, looking at me. "Cookie, are you okay? Who are these people, and why is this guy driving your Cayenne?" He glares at Rene. "You better not have fucked with her."

I know he's ready to make Rene get out, so I quickly introduce High's parents to the two Sinners' brothers.

"Sorry," apologizes Rascal, holding out his hand. "Cookie is tiny and timid. We worry someone will screw with her."

Rene takes his hand for a brief shake. "No apologies needed. Dana and I got that."

Dana pops her body between Rene and me. She leans over Rene, smiling at Rascal. "I'm Dana. You have nothing to worry about; Rene took good care of her. He saved Chéri from the people threatening to crush her on Lexington Avenue."

"Dana, Jesus Christ," growls Rene.

Rascal's eyes dart to me. "Cookie, explain!"

"It was nothing, Rascal. The people liked my singing and wanted to get close. We need to get to the club. High will be worried." I wave my hand. "Go, Rene."

"Yeah." Rascal eyes me skeptically, not taking his hand off the SUV. "That was the last trip you make to Butte alone. Do you understand me, Cookie?"

I nod, keeping my eyes straight ahead. Badass bikers are protective and bossy.

"Nice to meet you both. Go, Rene," orders Rascal.

Rene glances over to me, driving down the road. "How much trouble are you in?"

"None," I answer. "The Heartbreakers and I will gig at Callaghan's Bar after Friday." I frown. "I'll need to give up busking with Al."

Rene pulls up to the Sinners' clubhouse. "Chéri, does Christian know you were singing on the streets of Butte?"

"*Non*," I say, opening my door. "High would be a thousand times worse than Rascal. But we're moving to the cabin. I want to make extra money for the flea market. I'm not a leech—we're going halves on everything."

I leap out, grabbing my guitar and coffee can. Dana hooks her arm into mine, smiling down at me.

"I'm a little nervous," she confesses.

I nod, tightening my arm. "The Sinners are badass bikers with their own set of rules—family, club, God, and then comes country. You have nothing to worry about. You're with me."

Rene chuckles, grabbing the suitcase. He follows Dana and me up the steps. Pink Floyd, "Comfortably Numb," filters out onto the porch.

I open the door, and JJ comes flying at me. "Aunt Cookie, you got her up to ninety!" Then he notices Dana and Rene and growls in his four-year-old-badass way, "Who are these people, Aunt Cookie?" He points up at Rene. "Did you drive my aunt's car? Uncle Lee wants Aunt Cookie to drive, so she learns how."

"Baby!" shouts High, coming through the kitchen's swinging doors. He stops short, staring at the two people with me. "What the fuck?! Dad...Mom..."

"It's us," cries Dana.

Rene clears his throat. "I hope it's okay that Chéri invited us. It's been a long time, son."

High stalks over. "Yeah, Dad, it's been a fuck of a long time. I'm sorry..."

"*Non*, we're not goddamn going there," says Rene, grabbing High. He holds him, kissing his temple. "Love you, son."

High grips his father's coat, holding on tight. "Love you, too, Dad." Then he lets go, bending down, wiping his mom's tears away. High hugs her tightly. "Love you, Mom."

I take JJ and move him away. High needs alone time with his parents. That makes me happy and sad at the same time. I don't know where I'll fit, or even if I can fit in with Megan, Dana, Rene, and High.

"Let's go to my room. You can help me with my set for tomorrow."

JJ smiles up at me. "I'll be your costar."

I giggle, "*Oui*." I open the door and toss my things onto the bed.

Then I stroll over to my keyboard. "Let's warm up with a few scales. I don't need to do them; I sang all day. But I'll do them anyway, to give High time.

"Okay." I smile at JJ. "How about 'Everybody Hurts?'"

"R.E.M., awesome." JJ grabs my hairbrush, standing by me at the keys. "You start; I'll come in on the hook."

I laugh and start the intro. When I get to the hook, I point to JJ.

He tips his little head up and belts it out in his tenor voice. Our heads bob to the beat. He has his little eyes closed; he's singing his heart out. I smile, returning my eyes to the keys. I join in and let loose on the last verse. We end the song in perfect harmony.

Loud clapping comes from inside the room. I turn; High is smiling at me. He's holding JJ in one arm, a glass of wine in his other hand. Rene, Dana, Joker, Jewel, Raven, General, Princess, and Flame are all holding drinks, gathered in our room, and the hall.

"Cam was right; Little Bit has pipes," laughs General, holding up his bottle of beer.

"And good taste," says Dana, her eyes dart around my room. "This room is amazing."

JJ gives her a big, toothy grin, nodding. He points to the gun rack as if that's what Dana is referring to. "Uncle High's."

Dana giggles. "The weapons do give it a unique ambiance."

JJ announces, "Aunt Cookie and I are jamming. We're doing a set at the Blue Heaven tomorrow night. You're all invited."

"Nope," says his father, taking him from High. "You're coming here. Aunt Jewel, Papa Pick, and Grandma Hialeah are watching you, your brothers, and your sister."

"No, Daddy, I'm Aunt Cookie's costar. She needs me."

"You'll need to wait until Aunt Cookie sings at Callaghan's," smirks High. He struts over and gives me a deep, lingering kiss. Then he murmurs, "We'll be talking about you busking on the street in Butte."

I moan. "Your father narked me out?"

My man hands me the wineglass. "Narked you out. Jesus, you've been hanging with the kids," he chuckles onto my lips. "Yeah, baby. Not much scares my father, but that rattled his cage."

"Are you good with your parents?" I ask, taking a gulp of my wine.

"Yeah, really good, baby. My biker babe has my back. Thank you, baby."

I smile. I'm officially High's biker babe: I've been given my place. My man put Brian Stratton to ground for me, and I brought his parents to him—partners for life.

CHAPTER 17

THE COOPERS — HIGH

Rex struts over with beers for General, Pick, Joker, Flame, Beau, Dad, and me. He passes them around the table. "Heard we're gettin' a new songbird. One that doesn't squawk and chase the customers away. Happy for it. I'll keep an eye on her for ya, High."

I take a swig of my Fat Tire. "Thanks, Rex."

He sets down a club soda in front of Princess. "I think your clients just drove into the parking lot."

Princess shuffles the papers in front of her. "Thanks, Rex. We'll let them get settled, and then we'll order."

I look over to the door. Margo Cooper walks in with her mother, Willamena, Willy to her friends. My parents have been the Coopers' friends for years, so I asked dad to join us. Beau, Joker, and Flame are here for support. I was hit with the divorce papers to our non-marriage this morning. The bitch wants half of everything, including my Diva Mountain property. Cookie went stratospheric, ranting about using, lying, moneygrubbing, lazy women. If Elizabeth was anywhere in the vicinity, my woman would have killed her. Mom and

Jewel are with her at the club, trying to keep her ass calm. I wanted her to rest before the gig tonight.

We all stand. My father hugs Margo and Willamena, and then he introduces them to all of us.

I begin: "Mrs. Cooper, if you're uncomfortable with—"

"Please, call me Margo. And no. Mom and I are glad everyone is here."

"That little lying tart needs to be taken down a peg, boy," Willy says to me as I help her down into the chair. "I'll have a gin and tonic with a twist of lime. And a Cobb salad, double the bacon. I don't know why these restaurants skimp on the bacon."

"Mother..." drawls Margo, giving her mom big eyes.

"What, Margo? You said we were having a lunch meeting. I'm hungry."

Willy is in her late seventies with tan, wrinkly skin. Her long gray hair is in a top knot. Dad had told us Willy and her husband, Oliver, emigrated from Devon, England, to America. Willy was sixteen; Oliver was twenty. They bought their thousand-acre ranch just outside of Butte and raised cattle until Oliver died twenty-two years ago. Now, Willy lives with her only daughter, Margo, in Butte. Oliver left the ranch to his grandson, Jason, with the stipulation he could not sell without Willy and Margo's approval.

General chuckles, "I'll get your drink and grab menus. Margo, what would you like to drink?"

Margo was born and raised on the ranch. She's a tall, slender woman with big blue eyes. Dad said Margo attended Butte University and majored in business management. She met her husband, Tobias Cooper, at the cattle market. Together, Margo and Toby ran the ranch and the meatpacking plant until Toby dropped dead from a heart attack the same day his son died in the car accident. Margo sold off the cattle, closed up the house, and moved Willy into her home. Now, Margo runs the meatpacking plant with her husband's best friend, Hugo.

She smiles. "I'll have a beer, thank you."

"Margo, beer makes you pee. We'll be stopping every mile if you drink that. Bring her a wine," orders Willy. "Margo likes dry red."

Joker snorts, trying to hold in his laughter. "Excuse me." He pushes back, laughing all the way to the bar.

"Mother, please," says Margo through gritted teeth.

"Margo, we're going to the Blue Heaven tonight. We won't have time for you to be stopping every ten minutes." Willy turns to us. "Cam Forester has a band, the Heartbreakers. They're a rock band. Cam has a new singer. All of Butte is talking about her. She goes by the name of Little Bit. Cam invited us, so we need to get this show on the road. Margo and I can't be late."

"Mom, the girl doesn't go by that name. That is what Cam calls her because she's tiny." Margo looks at me. "I'm sure you remember Cameron Forester. He and Jason graduated a year ahead of you."

I nod. "We're doing security at the Blue Heaven tonight. Beau will be at the door…"

I'm about to inform them that Cookie is my woman when General and Joker come back to the table. They set Willy and Margo's drinks in front of them. General sets down nachos loaded with chili and cheese. Then Rex comes with the menus, waters, and plates.

"I already put your order in, Miss Willamena." He chuckles, "Double the bacon."

Willy orders Beau to scoop some nachos onto a plate for her.

Margo explains, "Mom grew up among the cowhands. Dad taught her how to be a rancher. She speaks her mind because my father didn't have the time or the inclination to figure out what she wanted."

Beau chuckles, "No worries, she's fine." He puts the plate in front of Willy and spreads her napkin onto her lap.

"Thank you," says Willy, digging in. "My grandson was everything to us. He was going to be a doctor. The trollop conned him into thinking she was pregnant with his babe. We all knew it wasn't Jason's baby. The girl was running around Butte, spreading her legs for anyone with a nickel in the bank. Rene can tell you. As hard as it was for Rene and Dana, they too refused to give Christian money."

Dad reaches over, patting Willy's hand.

"The Wheelers were bad apples in Butte. Always looking for the easy way out," says Willy. "Jason wouldn't listen to Toby; he kept giving Harrison Wheeler his money. The toad lost over a million dollars on bad business deals. So Toby, Margo, and I talked. It killed Toby, but he cut Jason off." Willy takes a gulp of her gin and tonic. "When the money dried up, Elizabeth wanted a divorce—and half of everything." She looks at me. "Sound familiar, boy?"

"I'm sorry," I apologize. I need to put Elizabeth to ground, for the Coopers, Cookie, and me.

"I know you are. You got a second chance with your parents. Don't squander it. Mr. Michaels told Margo and me you have a new lady in your life. He said she's a good one, a keeper. Your track record isn't so hot; if I were you, I'd mind my p's and q's and save what's in your pants for her."

I flinch at her words. Christ, the old woman has no filter.

"Mother!"

"The boy needs to hear it from someone, Margo. His mates aren't willing to tell him," says Willy, taking another swallow of gin. "That trollop isn't going to get him, too."

"Jesus," chuckles Flame.

"The authorities came and told us Jason had died in a car accident. That's what the coppers called it—an accident. It wasn't a bloody accident, Jason killed himself. He left his father a suicide note. Toby, Margo, and I found it in his bedroom. Minutes later, Toby had a heart attack on the living room floor. God took him to be with Jason and Oliver."

"Fuck," I breathe out.

Tears brim the old woman's blue eyes. "Jason had killed himself because he hadn't listened to his father. Jason somehow found out Hinkle fathered Elizabeth's child. The tart won. She took Jason and Toby away from us. I'll be goddamned if she gets my ranch, too." She reaches over, patting Margo's hand. "My girl has been through a lot of heartaches."

"Hinkle..." I glance at Margo. "Lewis Hinkle, Elizabeth's lawyer?"

Margo nods. "Jason and Elizabeth went to college with him. Lewis

Hinkle didn't come from money; he got in with his grades and student loans."

My father looks at me. "Hinkle married money—Virginia Osterhout. Bram Osterhout owns a brokerage firm in Butte. Bram is a good guy. Keeps his cash close to the vest, and he doesn't have a good word to say about his son-in-law."

"You know him, Dad?"

"*Oui*, I've known Bram Osterhout for years. His office is in the same building as mine. Bram complains his son-in-law is lazy; Lewis Hinkle has been fired from just about every law firm in Butte. Hinkle lives off his wife's trust fund money."

Rex comes over. "Everyone ready to order, or..."

I'm getting ready to tell Rex we need a minute when Willy shakes her head at me. "Margo will have a burger, medium, with the fixings. Add some fries to it." Willy smiles, winking at me. "My daughter is stressed out; she doesn't eat enough to keep a bird alive. I see to it she eats."

I nod. "It's bullshit you have to go through this, Margo."

She gives me a weak smile. "It's bullshit both of us need to go through this, Christian. But, together, we'll beat Elizabeth Wheeler."

"We'll all have burgers and fries, Rex," says General. "And bring us another round of drinks."

"Corinne and I received the documents from Elizabeth's *attorney*." Pick's voice is full of loathing for the asshole. "Elizabeth claims the ranch is rightfully hers. She was married to Jason and had his heir. The problem is the court may side with her...Jason left her penniless."

"Corbin, my son was duped into marrying Elizabeth Wheeler. She wanted money, and she used her unborn child to get it. But in no way was Elizabeth's son left penniless. He has a trust fund that has been sending his mother monthly checks for three thousand dollars. It stopped when Jason turned twenty-one. On his twenty-fifth birthday, he will receive a check for two hundred and fifty thousand. Regardless of his mother's deviousness, or who his biological father is, we took care of Jason."

What...the...fuck?! I know my goddamn mouth is hanging open, but I can't get my muscles to work.

"Didn't know that, did you, boy?" says Willy. "You bought the trollop's sob story hook, line, and sinker. My Margo has a heart the size of Montana. She wouldn't let that boy go without. Like you, my daughter was thanked for her kindness with a lawsuit."

"Does Jason Jr. know about the trust fund?" asks Princess.

"I don't know. I have nothing to do with it. It was a real, real bad time in my life," admits Margo. "I asked Hugo to set it up for me."

Willy adds her two cents into the conversation: "Hugo used Butte National Bank. Hugo is the trustee. You can call him; he knows all about it."

"Right," says Pick, sympathy laced in his eyes. "We need to prove Elizabeth Wheeler conned Jason into thinking he was Jason Jr.'s father. Even with Jason's letter, that's going to be a challenge."

"Elizabeth Cooper is broke," blurts Princess. "It's difficult to believe with all the money you and High have given her, but she doesn't have a penny to her name. If she wins a divorce settlement from High, she'll be worth a lot of money. Enough to keep fighting us in court for years. We don't want that."

"I told you, Margo, you need to let me kill the tramp," says Willy, all serious.

"About that, Willamena. You can't shoot at Elizabeth anymore," grins Pick.

"The tart was snooping around on my land! My Oliver told me I have a right to protect it."

That's it for Joker; he lays his forehead on the table, guffawing.

Princess smiles at the old woman. "Willamena, let my men get down in the mud with Elizabeth. We need you to stay clean."

"Corinne," says Pick, "we need to talk to Hugo about the trust fund. We'll need statements and proof the money was dispersed."

Princess is typing at warp speed on her laptop. "Okay, Daddy."

Flame pulls out a picture and shows it to Margo and Willy. "We've accessed the street cams and Elizabeth's apartment building's security footage. We've seen this guy coming and going from her place. He knows the security code and has his own key to the apartment. I can't do facial recognition on the guy; he's always wearing a ball cap with his head down. Do either of you recognize him?"

Margo and Willy stare at the picture, shaking their heads.

"May I see it?"

"Sure, Rene," says Flame, handing my father the picture.

"Christian, google a picture of Lewis Hinkle. I'm reasonably sure this is him."

I pull out my phone and do as I'm told. The two men have the same build.

"Wait." I home in on the guy's left ring finger, where there's a massive, thick gold band embossed with the scales of justice. "That's Hinkle; look at the asshole's ring."

Princess leaps up, coming around the table. She nods, beaming as if she'd just won the mega-prize on a scratch-off. "Jamie, we need enough circumstantial evidence on Hinkle to get a court-ordered paternity test. We also need proof Elizabeth and Hinkle are having an affair. Lewis Hinkle isn't going to want his wife or father-in-law to find out he's cheating; that would end his cushy life and cash supply. You and High need to video them in a compromised position—holding hands, hugging, kissing, or…" She gives her husband big eyes.

"Having sex," cackles Willy. "That's what she needs, boys. A good old-fashioned porn video of them rolling in the hay."

"Christ," laughs General.

Margo sighs, "Good lord, Mom."

"Yeah, Willamena. That would be a lock," chuckles Pick. "If we have that, we'll never see the inside of a courtroom. Elizabeth's credibility would be shot to hell."

Rex comes over with our food, grinning at Willy. "Extra bacon for the lady. I had the cook add cheesy toast and extra blue cheese."

Willy digs into her Cobb salad, cackling. "You're going to roll around in the mud with the sows, boys. Don't get caught."

I chuckle at Willy, taking a bite of my burger. One way or another, I'll end Elizabeth. Not for Cookie and me—we will survive no matter what. I need to do it for Willy and Margo.

CHAPTER 18

BLUE HEAVEN – COOKIE

High circles the block a fourth time, looking for a parking spot. I have no idea why there is so much traffic at 7:00—rush hour is over in Butte. But I can't ask; I have a hot pack to my throat with a wool scarf keeping it in place, and I'm sipping on a steamy cup of tea—my ritual before a long gig. The heat keeps my vocal cords loose.

I'm in the back seat of the Cayenne, tucked between Dana and Rene. Joker's riding shotgun, his eyes peeled to the sides of the street.

Rene pats my hand. "No worries, we have time for you to stretch."

I giggle, lacing my fingers with his. He's my man's dad, an older version of High. In a day, I fell head over heels in love with High's parents. They're coming back to Pony with us to help out with the cabin.

"Baby, you took a vow of silence." High growls, "No giggling."

Another rule of mine: I don't talk much before a gig.

Dana rolls her eyes, smiling. "Father *and* son are bossy."

Joker points to the sidewalk. "There's Megan, General, Raven, and the boys."

High lets down his window, makes a shrilling whistle to get their attention. Tristen, Mika, Robbie, and Cole jog over to the Cayenne.

"Walk Cookie and my parents inside. Joke and I will park." High turns in his seat. "Kiss, baby. I'll meet you behind the stage."

I give him a chaste kiss, hand him my tea and remove the hot pack from my throat. I wrap the warm scarf around my neck three times.

Dana slides out, and then me. Rene jogs around the SUV, wrapping an arm around me and taking Dana's hand.

Raven, Megan, and General join us. I open my mouth to thank them for supporting me, but Rene growls, "No talking."

Raven giggles, her eyes on Rene. "The apple didn't fall far from the tree."

Dana laughs, looking up at Rene.

"Let's make tracks. The boys need to be in the bar before the turn of the century," barks General.

Dana's eyes go to him. "Seems we have something in common, Raven."

I swallow my giggle and follow the others into Blue Heaven. Inhaling, I fill my lungs with the bar's aroma: hops, alcohol, men's cologne, and women's perfume. The place is filled to the rafters with young adults talking, laughing, and drinking. The noise level is deafening. The vibe's an electrical current going straight to the rocker chick who lives inside me. The stage is my domain—the only place I've felt comfortable being me. It's the only home I've ever known.

Cam motions us to the back of the stage. General, Rene, and the boys part the crowd for Raven, Megan, Dana, and me.

Several of the college kids yell out to me. Many have been here every day, listening to us during our jam sessions. Patrons start to push in, wanting pictures with me for their social media pages. Now that there isn't a threat from Stratton Records, I'm happy to pose for the fans.

Cookie and the Heartbreakers went viral a few days ago: according to Cam, we had over half a million views on YouTube. Cam, the guys, and I discussed fame. I needed them to know I would never sign with a record label or go on tour. To my relief, they were okay with it. Cam, Max, Woody, and Lex have wives, kids, and homes they love. Cam said, "I need to sleep with my wife and raise my kids with her, Cookie. The boys and I just need enough money to live comfortably. Local fame is fucking awesome. Worldwide fame isn't for us."

Cam struts up to me, croaking out, "Little Bit, Christ, woman, you look hot! Are your boobs going to stay in that top?"

Rene grumble something about we should have brought another shirt.

I refrain from rolling my eyes. When High, Rene, and the Sinners aren't around, Cam appointed himself as my guardian and protector.

It's our debut; I need to look the part of a rocker chick. Jewel created the sleeveless tee for me. It's split down the middle and held together at the nipple line with one big silver button. My jeans are faded and ripped in the right places. The waistband hits just above my pubic bone, and my boots are kick-ass stiletto heels, lace-up Nubuck ankle boots. I knew I looked hot when my man's eyes grew dark as the sky, and his gorgeous cock went hard as steel.

Dana giggles, "We double-sided taped her breasts. Hopefully, she doesn't sweat the tape off."

"Dana, when Little Bit starts to sweat, the tee is going to become translucent. Her tits will be on display for the fucking world," says Cam hoarsely, then wincing.

My eyes widen at the sound of Cam's voice. I point to his throat.

"I know, my goddamn voice is useless," he rasps out. "My wife has a cold, and she gave it to me. I gave it to the boys."

I think for a beat. High knows both my sets; he's done the male parts of each song. "High will do it," I whisper. "My girlfriends will sing backup."

Rene looks at me like I have three heads. "My son? The kid who refused to join the chorus is going to sing on stage with you?"

I nod, smiling.

Tristen looks at General. "Can the girls sing?"

"Doesn't matter," says Cam. "If they sound like shit, we'll distort their mics." He turns to me. "Little Bit, we have everything set up.

Three songs, and then you can yak up the crowd. One of the guys will bring you a tumbler of Crown."

I learned a long time ago, a band's job isn't just to entertain; we need to make the bar profitable. That means we sell booze.

Cam looks around. "High needs to work out security before he hits the stage. This place is a fucking zoo."

"We have that covered, Cam," assures General. "Tristen and the boys will control the front of the stage. The brothers will disperse and mingle among the crowd."

"The intro will be the same. We'll play the first bars of "Born to Be Wild." You come out from the wings singing. The girls will be to your right with a teleprompter."

"They need drinks, Cam," I whisper. "The lights are hot."

"We'll take care of the girls," says Rene. "You concentrate on you."

An hour and a half later, High is still complaining. "Baby, I can't fucking do this," he growls, stretching out my hips. "I can't goddamn sing."

"Amour, you're talented; you sing beautifully. Concentrate on me." I bite my lip to keep from giggling.

"Yeah, baby, that will be really great. Me on stage with a goddamn hard-on."

My man has an excellent package. My eyes drop to his crotch; my panties dampen. *Non-non-non, don't think about High's big eleven-inch.*

I turn my attention to Maggie, Jillian, Raine, Megan, and Princess. They're practicing their harmonies. I breathe out a sigh of relief. The girls sound fantastic.

High runs his hand over my breasts, squeezing. "Baby, your tits are half out of the goddamn shirt."

I try to ignore his glorious hands. *Think sound check with Cam.* I give High a mic. He groans.

"One...two...three...check...check...check," I say into the mic.

"You're good, Little Bit. Now, High."

"One...two...three...fuck...fuck...fuck," growls High, all his badassness in play.

Cam chuckles, "You're good, High."

Megan runs over to us. "Dad, hurry, rip my tee at the neckline. It needs to slouch off my shoulders."

I giggle at her request. Maggie, Jillian, Raine, and Princess are biker babes. Like rocker chicks, biker babes have wild hair, heavy makeup, and show a lot of skin. Megan is dressed conservatively: a cute pink tee, paired with dark jeans and black booties.

I grin, watching High rip his daughter's tee to her specifications. My badass biker is an excellent daddy when he's allowed to be.

Benny comes over with a tray of shots filled with JD. It's not surprising; most bands have a dose of liquid courage before they hit the stage. I've been doing shots for luck since I was fourteen.

We all take one. I hold mine up. "Here's to killing it tonight." Then we all clink and shoot the amber liquid back.

Cam, Woody, Lex, and Max jog onto the stage, taking their positions. I give each of the girls a hug, and then they're off, going behind their mics. Woody bangs his sticks together, the lights flicker, and the crowd roars.

High leans down and kisses me. "Go time, baby."

I bounce on the balls of my feet; my nerves buzz as they always do just before I go on stage. I take the mic; the first bars are played.

I run out on the stage, belting out Steppenwolf, "Born To Be Wild." The lights are hot and blinding. I can't see anyone except for the people directly in front of the stage: the Sinners, Al, Margo, and Willamena. The audience is pushing toward the stage. Mika, Cole, Tristen, Robbie, Tank, Joker, Buck, and Beau are trying to hold them back.

I point to Beau and then to the back of the stage. He nods, understanding I want Willamena, Margo, and Al in a safe place, backstage with Dana and Raven. The audience is young; they're drinking, and they're going to get rowdier as the night progresses.

Beau lifts Willy into his arms, moving toward the stairs with Al and Margo sandwiched between him and Tank.

Now, it's me, the music, and the crowd's screams. The adrenaline hits my bloodstream. I let loose, my body takes over, I'm all over the stage. Sweat starts pouring off me as if I got out of the shower without toweling off. I hit the hook and hold out the mic to the audience. The room fills with voices singing.

The song comes to an end, and Cam goes right into the next one, Aerosmith, "Dream On." I fly over to my girls, leaning into them. They are singing their hearts out with their arms swinging, their hips swaying. I grin and shout, "Give it up for Maggie, Jillian, Corinne, Raine, and Meeeegan!"

The crowd roars, their stomping vibrates the walls.

I sprint over to the guys, pointing. "Cam on lead guitar! Lex on bass! Max on keys!" I leap up onto the podium. "Woody on the drums." I lean way back and bellow into the mic, "I'm COOOOKIE!" I cross my legs, my forehead hits my knees, my arms spread-eagle; I bow before the crowd.

As I suspected, my antics energize the audience. The roar of their screams rattles the walls of the bar. They're college kids, not hard to read.

I quickly pick back up where I left off. At the hook, I drop to my knees; my shoulder blades hit the floor. I give it all I got, reaching for the stars. My voice repeatedly shreds the lyrics. Leaping to my feet, I finish the song to thunderous applause and ear-piercing whistles.

My heart's beating in double time, my breathing is accelerated after two powerhouse songs. I concentrate on slowing my breathing and jog over to grab an electric guitar. I strum it a few times. "For those of you who don't know, this song was written by Bob Dylan, not Axl Rose. But Axl sang the hell out of it. So we're going to do his version. Guns N' Roses, 'Knockin' on Heaven's Door!'"

Again the crowd roars their approval.

During the last few bars of the song, a woman screeches, profanity pouring from her mouth. I shield my eyes from the lights, looking over to where it's coming from. At the bottom of the stage's stairs is an older woman with short brown hair, dressed in mom jeans and sneaks. The woman is screaming at High. Three young men are behind her, ready for a fight. I can guess who the woman is—the moneygrubbing witch, Elizabeth Wheeler-Cooper. She has her son and his friends at her back.

I tap the volume control with my toe, and the sound of the instruments booms through the room. I need to raise my voice. Thankfully I drown her out. Then I dive into "Radioactive." It confuses the band and the girls for a few seconds; I was supposed to break after the third song, talk up the crowd—sell booze. But the band quickly catches up. I dig deep, bounce on the balls of my feet, work the stage, and push my voice. The crowd is eating it up. I catch a glimpse of Cam; he has his eyes pinned on me. He probably thinks I'm going to keel over. I don't know, I might. I haven't done a gig like this in more than four years.

I look back to High; he's tangling with the three boys, and those bastards aren't little. The witch is standing off to the side, still screaming like the lunatic she is. *Jesus, High.*

I end Imagine Dragons and launch into Creed, "What's This Life For."

I'm pissed, really pissed. I strut over to the edge of the stage, trying to judge if my foot will reach the witch or the boys' heads. *Damn, I'm too short. Where are the other Sinners?* I need to get High some help. My man could quickly take them out; his hands are registered as lethal weapons from his MMA days. Jail time is not in the cards. We're moving into the cabin.

I sing the hook adding, *"JOKER, TRISTEN, MIKA, ROBBIE, COLE!"* hoping they'll get the hint. Then, I sing louder, straining my voice to make them understand. They're way at the other end of the stage.

Cam comes over, looking down. He snarls, kicking one of the boys in the temple. The kid's head jerks back; he bellows out in pain. High looks up just for a second and takes a punch to the jaw. The hit doesn't rock him. *Non,* the little creep awakened the MMA fighter. Mafia Man, Joker, and Flame come jogging across the stage singing. It would be hilarious if my man wasn't about to be in a GD bar brawl. The Sinners leap from the stage, landing on the balls of their feet. They jerk their heads for me to leave. I clock Tristen, Cole, Mika, and Robbie, pushing their way through the crowd. I'm not sure the witch or boys will leave the bar breathing. Right now, I hope they don't!

I sing the last bar of the song and dart my eyes over to the stairs. I let out a breath, glad it's over. The witch and the boys are being dragged out through the back door.

One more song to give my man time to take out the trash. I raise my arms above my head. "Here's a little Queen!" I shout.

Stomp...stomp...clap...stomp...stomp...clap. The band and the audience start stomping and clapping with me. Woody bangs the beat out on the kit, helping the crowd keep the rhythm. I sing the lyrics to their stomps and claps. I get to the hook, holding the mic out to the audience. "Sing it, Butte!"

The room fills with a hundred voices singing Queen's, "We Will Rock You."

I feed off the energy of the room, pushing myself to work the stage and belt out the tune. Sweat drips off my chin, spreading droplets across the floor. My tee is pasted to my skin. On the last note, I drop my forehead to my knees, holding up the mic.

The crowd goes electric, screaming and pushing toward the stage. I hear Tristen shouting to the Sinners to hold them back.

I've been here before; I need to do one more song to calm the crowd down. I hold up my hand. "How are you feeling, Butte?" The audience roars. "I want to introduce someone very special to me. Give it up for my man, High!"

High comes jogging out on stage with a glass of Crown in his hand. "You need water, not fucking whiskey," he growls, handing me the glass. Then he yanks off his tee and wipes me down.

"My man is hot, with a voice angels swoon over," I shout, running my glass of amber liquid across his muscled chest. Then, I make a production out of taking a healthy gulp of my Crown.

The audience goes wild over High: girls and gay guys catcall to him, some of them very explicit about what they'd like High to do to them.

"Christ," barks High, hiding my body with his. He shoves his tee under my shirt, wiping down my chest and under my boobs.

That gets the guys and the lesbian girls revved up. They all want to take his place, and they make it known by pushing toward the stage. My eyes go to the Sinners, who are creating a wall between them and us.

Cam runs over, attaching a mic to my drenched tee. "Your fucking tits are on full display," he growls.

"No help for it," I murmur, taking another massive gulp of the Crown. I hand the glass to Cam.

"Butte," I shout, smiling up at High. "My man and I are going to sing Kings of Leon, "Beautiful War."

Again, they roar their approval.

Wrapping our arms around each other, we sway to the beat, looking into each other's eyes. I smile. High grins down at me. It's just High and I singing the words that define us.

On our last word, High lifts me into his arms, putting his lips to mine. He kisses me. I wrap my arms and legs around him, kissing him back.

I don't hear the crowd's reaction; I'm totally engrossed in my man.

Cam's beside us, making a come-here motion with one of his hands and pointing to me. Max is playing a solo on the keys, buying us time to get off the stage.

"Cookie doesn't need any fucking whiskey, Cam." High shouts, "Dad, bottled water!"

"The girls need water," I say as High carries me off the stage.

High looks over. "Brainiac and Patriot have them."

Cam chuckles into the mic, "After that performance, we all need to take fifteen. Save the dirty until you get home. Butte's finest is in the house." He turns off the mic and jogs over to us. "Christ, Little Bit, how's your voice?"

"She's not talking until it's time for her to sing," barks High. "I need to get her cooled down and into a goddamn dry shirt."

"What the fuck happened?" asks Cam in a gravelly voice.

"Elizabeth found out about Cookie and me. She's a crazy bitch. It's handled," growls High.

I want to ask, "Handled for tonight, or forever?" but I don't. I'm praying for forever. People are running around, working at a fevered pace to get ready for the next set.

Dana runs over to us. She lifts my hair and holds a cold, wet paper towel against the back of my neck.

Patriot jogs over. "The girls' voices are toast. Brainiac, Dev, Buck, and I are taking their places for the next two sets."

"Those sets need to be worked out—"

Rene interrupts me by tipping the bottle to my lips. "Shush and drink," he orders. Then he yanks his tee over his head. I get a glimpse of what my man will look like when he's seventy. Non, *I'm not going to be disappointed.* Rene has a six-pack young women would drool over, and young men would die for.

"Turn around. Make a wall," orders High.

Cam's averting his eyes, mumbling his wife would cut off his balls if she caught him looking. He rattles off the new sets, blindly trying to help High.

High laughs. "I got her, brother." He quickly strips me out of my tee, pulling his father's black tee over my head. It's a hundred times too big, hitting me three inches below my knees.

"Amour, rip it just below my boobs."

High chuckles as he does my bidding.

I pay homage to the legendary women for our second set: Tina Turner, "Proud Mary," complete with Tina's moves. Whitney Houston's version of Chaka Khan's, "I'm Every Woman." I need to grab Brainiac and dance with him on stage to keep from laughing at my badass bikers singing. Next came Alicia Keys, "If I Ain't Got You," Lady Gaga, "The Edge of Glory," Celine Dion, "My Heart Will Go On," and Adele, "Set Fire to the Rain." I end the set with Madonna, "Like a Prayer."

High comes jogging out on stage. Ignoring the audience, he lifts me into his arms and carries me to the wings. I giggle. Rene, Dana, and High have become a well-oiled machine with the cold compresses, wipe downs, and water.

General, Joker, Flame, Tank, and Tristen stalk over to us.

"We need to button this shit up," growls Tristen. "The animals are hyped up on alcohol and drugs. Their sights are set on Cookie." Then he chuckles, "The zookeepers want to shoot their asses."

I look over to the stage; Robbie, Mika, and Cole are throwing guys off it.

"Aye," says General. "We'll cause a riot if Cookie doesn't go back out. I think we should send High out with her. They'll sing as a couple. It's one thirty. We'll get Benny to do last call and shut down the bar."

"The bar shuts down now. Cookie and I sing one song, and then we're out of here."

I give High his mic and take his hand. "Rolling Stones, "Wild Horses," Amour." Then we walk out onto the stage hand-in-hand.

"It's been a blast, Butte! Everyone up here wants to thank all of you out there! The bar is closed. High and I are going to sing you out. Please be safe getting home. We'll see you at Callaghan's Bar in Pony next Friday!"

He grins, singing "Wild Horses" to me. I've lost my voice, mesmerized by my man. *Good lord, there isn't a sexier male on earth.*

High is a chameleon. Unlike me, he can fit into any culture: civilian, Sinners, or rocker. We're different in so many ways. Doubt creeps into my mind. In the end, I wonder if I'll be enough.

CHAPTER 19

TIRED OF WOMEN PULLING MY STRINGS — HIGH

Cookie has entirely shut down on me. I have no idea what in the hell is going on with her. It's two in the goddamn morning; we're packing up the equipment with Cam and the guys. I look over at Cookie; she hasn't spoken much. Maybe it's from the adrenaline rush leaving her body.

"Are you spending the night at your parents' crib?" asks Joker.

I nod, putting the speakers on a dolly. "Yeah, Meg, Cookie, and me. Catch a ride with Beau."

Joker smirks. "Beau took Willamena and Margo home. Judging from the vibe Margo was giving him, the brother is getting his wick wet tonight. Liam, Rocky, and Guard Dog split from doing surveillance on Elizabeth. They said Hinkle showed an hour after the bitch got home. He only stayed a half hour, and then he took off."

Elizabeth put on a great show, ranting about how I was her husband. She called me out for cheating on her with a girl the same age as my stepson. It was bullshit; Jason Jr. was recording Elizabeth on his iPhone. Things ramped up when I took his cell and smashed it beneath the heel of my boot. It would have gotten bloody if Cookie hadn't intervened. I'm sure my ass would be sitting in a cell right now. After Liam, Rocky, and Guard Dog dragged Elizabeth and the little shits out of the bar, they decided to hang outside of Elizabeth's apartment building to see if Hinkle would show.

Joker fist-bumps me. "I'll catch a ride with General and Raven."

Cam grabs Cookie, hugging her. "Awesome gig, Little Bit." He pulls a wad of cash from his pocket and hands it to her. "Your cut, eleven hundred bucks." He laughs. "It's the most money the Heartbreakers have ever made in one night. My wife is going to love you. The guys and I will be at Callaghan's on Monday morning to jam."

Cookie nods, staring at the cash as if there's been some kind of mistake. Her reaction makes me believe the bars in Quebec ripped her off.

I wrap her in my arms. "Baby, you earned every penny." I chuckle, "Benny's pissed as hell you're singing at Callaghan's."

She peels off a hundred bucks and shoves the rest of the money into my pocket. "For the girls, guys, and you."

"Baby, we don't want your green."

She shakes her head, pulling out of my arms. Cookie holds up the Franklin. "It isn't my money. This is what I get per gig." She walks away from me, trailing Mom, Dad, and Megan out the door.

On the way to my parents' house, Megan and Mom try to engage Cookie in conversation. Mom asks if her gigs were as crowded in Quebec. Megan questions why she never signed to a label. "Mama Cookie," she quips, "you're the bomb!" Then she breaks into, *"This girl..."* Meg grabs her throat. "Ouch!" Then she giggles. "How did you learn to dance like that? I'd dislocate a hip. You're Gumby on steroids."

Cookie doesn't need to say anything; Megan is chatty enough for everyone.

I pull into my parents' driveway.

Megan is still a chatterbox, going on about Cookie's eight-pack, sixteen-inch waist, and size C boobs. "How much weight do you think you lose per gig? I mean, it's the ultimate workout. I never realized how much work it is to be a rocker. My legs and arms are killing me."

My father chuckles, "Are you going to take a breather, Meg?"

Megan giggles, buttoning it, thank god.

As soon as we hit the foyer, Cookie drops to the floor. Her entire body trembles as she tries to remove her boots.

I don't know what the hell is going on with her. I'm exhausted and tweaked to be back in the house I grew up in. After Elizabeth's tirade, I don't have the patience to deal with whatever is in Cookie's head.

I throw our bags over my shoulder, lift her into my arms, and fly up the stairs. I kick my old bedroom door closed and drop Cookie onto her feet.

She glances around, shaking like a leaf. *What the hell?* Yeah, it's the typical teenage boy's room: posters of MMA fighters, football, and baseball players are on the walls. My trophies from boxing, football, basketball, baseball, prom pictures of Elizabeth and me, and our friends cover the shelves. *Cookie's a goddamn adult, she can deal with it and move the fuck on.*

"Cookie, I'm fucking tired. I don't know what has your panties in a twist." I toss a hand out to the prom picture. "Elizabeth was a part of my life. I can't change that. I've cut Fawn and Elizabeth's support. Now I'm in the middle of Margo Cooper's fight, and in my own battle over fucking money. Christ, woman, Elizabeth called me out at the bar..."

Cookie shrugs, grabbing her bag. "So don't cut their support if you don't want to, Christian. I didn't ask you to do that; no one did." She heads for the door.

"Where the hell are you going?!"

"Home. I don't belong here."

I know I should go after Cookie, but I don't. Fuck her! I'm tired of women pulling my strings, as if I'm a puppet they can play with at their leisure.

CHAPTER 20

YOU ARE MY HOME — HIGH

A week came and went. Cookie has been rooming with Jewel; she wants nothing to do with Megan, the Sinners, my parents, or me. To Megan's and my disappointment, we didn't go to the flea market or the cabin. Joker told me Cookie is jamming with Cam and the boys in the morning, and then she's driving to Butte to busk on Lexington Avenue. My father and Al have been keeping eyes on her.

Cookie and the Heartbreakers played at Callaghan's last night. Cam asked me to stay away from the stage's wings. "You mess with her head, brother. That can't happen during a gig." I stood in the shadows and watched. Cookie did three sets, vacillating between hard and soft rock songs.

The crowd went wild over Cookie just like they had at the Blue Heaven. She controlled the audience with the expertise she learned long ago. She downed tumblers of amber liquid as if they were water. Between songs she talked up the crowd, giving them tidbits about the legendary artists.

I wanted to go to her during the breaks. It scared the shit out of me: drinking like a fish, refusing water, and sweating out two liters of body fluid was makings for a disaster. But Cookie wouldn't let anyone near her. She stayed in the shadows, headphones on, waiting for Cam to cue her for the next set. There was nothing the Heartbreakers, Sinners, or I could do. She shut all of us out, even Jewel.

Cookie shredded the electric guitar on "Free Bird," and her voice was killer. "Man, I've been playing all my life, and I can't do what she does on a guitar," said Cam. "Max can't compete with her on the keys."

The Sinners sold more liquor last night than we ever had. It should have made us happy. It didn't.

It wasn't a surprise the vultures came out of the woodwork— record labels that had seen Cookie's performance at Blue Heaven online. Four of them showed up at Callaghan's last night. General and I kicked their asses out the door. We made it crystal clear what would happen if they crossed our doorstep again.

General drops two stacks in front of me. "Cookie wouldn't take the money from the two gigs. Toss the green into her shoebox for me."

"Shoebox?"

"Her stash of money she keeps in her closet." He takes a sip of coffee and sighs. "Merrill informed me Cookie received two letters this week. He said the return address on both was from a Sylvie Fayette, Quebec City, Canada."

"Cookie's mother!" I growl, "The bitch is fucking looking for green."

He nods. "Aye, that's what I thought. Merrill said Cookie was upset when he gave them to her. I let Merrill know: if she gets any more, they come to me."

I shake my head, balling my fists. "No, they come to me."

General takes another gulp of his coffee. "I don't know what's in the lass's head, but it's nothing good." He stares at me. "Your head is just as fucked up. Pick needs to know if you're paying the bitch or fighting back. If you're giving away half of your green, Corinne and Pick need to work out another strategy for Margo and Willamena."

I snort, taking a sip of my coffee. "Let Willy shoot Elizabeth's ass. That'll take care of the problem for everyone."

"That's not goddamn happening." General sighs. "Beau is flying

Megan back to Denver for the holidays. Faith doubts Megan will come back to Pony. Fawn ran her mouth and laid a guilt trip on her. According to Faith, Fawn wasn't too happy about Megan's relationship with Mama Cookie."

I roll my eyes. "It didn't matter how I felt about Ed playing daddy to my daughter for ten goddamn years. Meg's an adult. She can do what she wants; I'm not stopping her."

The bar door opens with a bang. Cookie comes rushing in. She doesn't notice General or me; we're in a booth in the back of the room.

"Shitty day, Cook," says Rex. "It's Sunday, sweetheart. The boys won't be comin' today."

Cookie shrugs out of her coat and unwraps her scarf. "*Oui*, I know. It's freezing rain; I can't go to Butte. I decided to come here and practice for a bit."

Rex nods. "I'll bring you your coffee with a double shot of Crown."

"Thanks, Rex."

It's nine in the morning, and she's drinking whiskey. I watch Cookie walk to the stage; she's thin, too thin. She's wearing a midriff white sweater and a low-slung pair of ripped jeans. Sexy as hell, but I can count her ribs.

Cookie runs up the stairs and over to the piano. Then she puts on a headset, fiddles with a few buttons, and stands with her small hands on the keys. Her fingers fly, her eyes are closed, her voice fills the room with Guns N' Roses, "November Rain."

Rex struts out from behind the bar with a steaming mug in his hand.

I jump up, cutting him off. "I'll take it to her, Rex."

He nods, handing me the coffee. "Good luck," he mutters, returning to the bar.

I take a sip of the hot liquid; the taste of Crown mixed with the bitterness of dark roast rolls over my tongue. I walk up the stairs and over to the piano. Cookie doesn't look up; she's engrossed in the song. I set the mug down and move her headset to the side.

Cookie's head jerks up; she just about clocks me in the chin. Her eyes go to the steaming mug of coffee. She hits a button on her head-set, pausing the instrumentals. "Thanks," she says, taking the mug. She blows on it and takes a slurp.

I grin. "It needs whipped cream and cinnamon."

"*Non*, I don't like sugar in my coffee." She takes another sip.

I pull over the piano bench. "Sit with me for a minute. I need to apologize."

Cookie drops down on the bench beside me. She sips her coffee and twinkles the keys with her other hand. "You don't have anything to apologize for." She stops playing and keeps her eyes to the keys. "I have everything I need, High. A roof over my head and a place to sing."

I nod. "Cookie, why were you tweaking at my parents' house?"

She looks up at me. For a minute, I don't think she's going to answer.

"Your parents' home is only the second house I've ever been inside of, High. Mafia Man and Maggie's was the first. It just reminded me of how different we are. Then, you said what you did, and that confirmed it." She takes another sip of coffee and sets it on the piano. "I need to get back to work."

I still her hands with mine. "I was screwed up about being back in Mom and Dad's house. I should have come back to the club with you."

Cookie shakes her head. "*Non*, you had your daughter and parents. You were right where you should have been: home. I'm right where I should be, too, High. In a bar, entertaining people. It's my home." She grabs her acoustic guitar. "Stevie Nicks wrote this song. The Dixie Chicks covered it, but no one does it like Stevie." Cookie starts singing me "Landslide."

I lunge forward, crashing our lips together. The force tips us back. I twist, taking the impact of our fall.

I turn us over, pinning Cookie down. "I fucking love you. I made a goddamn mistake, and you're going to forgive me."

I put my lips to hers. Angry kisses become hungry, hot, wet kisses mixed with love bites. Cookie claws at my tee, trying to get to my skin. I reach between us, undoing her jeans. I yank them down.

Blindly, I free my cock, not giving a shit we're in Callaghan's, on the goddamn stage.

"Rex," chuckles General, his heavy footsteps fading away. "The dining room is closed."

I cover Cookie's mouth with mine and surge forward, swallowing her scream from my quick entry. I'm sheathed to the root in her warm, wet pussy.

"I'm fucking home...in you...connected to you." I breathe into her ear, "You...are...my...home."

She puts her feet flat on the floor and lifts her hips, digging her nails into my lower back.

"Love you, baby," I murmur against her lips, giving her long strokes of my cock.

She has her blues pinned to mine.

"Tell me, baby. Tell me you fucking love me."

"I love you, Amour," she murmurs, her arms tightening their hold onto my back.

I grin, speeding up my hips. "Do you want to move into the cabin with me and make babies?"

Shit, I'm talking about making babies on Callaghan's goddamn stage. It's out there; I want a lifetime with her.

She laughs. "Babies, as in more than one." Tears are running down her temples. "*Oui*, I'll move into the cabin with you and make babies."

I wrap her up, one hand under her head, the other under her ass. I send my hips flying, anchoring my woman to take my powerful thrusts.

Cookie whimpers, speaking to me in French. Her pussy walls flutter. She lifts her hips, opening as wide as her jeans will allow.

I grunt, grind down, humping. "Go, baby. Milk me."

Cookie's pussy clamps down on me. She moans, putting her lips to mine. I groan, stay deep, giving her open-mouthed, hot, wet kisses. My cock jerks, bathing my woman's pussy with my jizz.

"We need to come off the pill." I smile onto her lips. "And you need to stop drinking at nine in the morning. You're going to get over your aversion to houses with white picket fences."

She giggles. "Are you going to build me one?"

I laugh. "Yeah, baby, this spring."

"Sorry, folks. The dining room is closed," says Rex, loudly. "Take a seat at the bar."

Cookie laughs. "Do you think Rex is trying to tell us something?"

"Baby," I drawl, chuckling. "We just had makeup sex on the floor of the goddamn stage." I run a finger down her cheek. "Your pussy missed me."

Cookie's arms tighten into a death grip around my neck.

"I'm not going anywhere, baby. It's you and me, partners for life."

Her blues are shining up at me: windows to her soul—she loves me. "Partners for eternity," she whispers.

"Yeah, baby," I say against her lips. I pull out, kissing her tit. "Come on, we have a cabin to clean and furniture to pick out."

CHAPTER 21

WE'RE PARTNERS – COOKIE

I am not a country girl. It's freezing outside, twenty degrees in the sun. The wind makes it feel like twenty below. I insisted on helping High put the chains onto his truck tires. They're super heavy to lift, and they need to be placed on the tires perfectly straight—a difficult friggin' task when you can't feel your fingers.

High leans over me, chuckling in my ear. He straightens out the chains I've been working on for the last ten minutes.

"Okay, baby, get in and pull forward."

"Get back," I yell out the driver's side window, waving him away.

"Babe, just pull the goddamn truck forward. You're not going to run me over."

Joker chuckles to Jewel, "How do you think Cookie's going to do living in the backwoods? High heats the cabin with wood. I want pictures of her swinging an ax."

"Oh, god," grimaces Jewel. "I hope he hides the ax. She'll cut off her leg."

I grip the wheel, cringing. I've never needed to use an ax. I recall the story General told about the ax handle breaking and cutting Istu's calf. *Good god, I hope I won't cut my leg off.*

I nudge the gas; the truck moves forward an inch.

High chuckles, "Give it some fucking gas, baby."

"I don't want to spin the tires and have the chains whip off and hit you, Amour! I love every part of you. Stand back!"

Rene laughs, Dana giggles, Megan snickers.

When High and I got back to the club, we talked about my fears. High held me and explained the facts of life: I was his, he was mine. Nothing and no one would come between us. Round two of makeup sex was more fantastic than round one.

After we took care of business, we called High's parents and daughter. I was vibrating with excitement. High and I were back on track to start our new life together. We were cleaning out the cabin. I asked them to come; I love Dana and Rene. Rene probably gets me more than High. Dana's an easygoing super-mom, so easy to love. "We'll be there shortly, darling," said Dana. I knew, the way Rene drove, she meant it. Forty minutes later, they were at the club, kissing me and hugging High.

Megan just got here. She's on her lunch break, so she'll need to return to the Reservation soon.

"You do know, Mama Cookie, it's kind of gross how much you love my father," shouts Megan, laughing. "Just push down on the gas."

I blow out a breath and give the truck more gas.

"Whoa, that's good, baby. Stay there; I'll get the chains linked together."

I leap out of the truck. "I need to know how to do it in case something happens." I say in my most serious tone of voice, "Amour, we're going to be living among the bears and mountain cats." Then I think about that for a second. "Oh, god, you're not going to get eaten while chopping wood or doing whatever badass mountain men do?"

That makes everyone roar in laughter.

"Dad isn't going to get eaten, Mama Cookie." She says under her breath, "You might. You're the one who kept a bobcat in the barn for four years."

I crouch down, shivering with my teeth chattering; I watch High link the chains.

He lifts me up, putting me back into the truck. "Keep your ass there."

Rene and Joker go around to the other side, hooking together the chains.

"We're partners, I'm all in," I yell out the window, needing him to know I won't be a loafer. I'm going to be the mountain woman he needs me to be. I cringe at the thought of applying chains I can barely lift, hooking up enormous snowplows, and using sharp objects that could cut my leg off.

High smiles, kissing me. "I got that, baby. You can be my partner by cooking our meals, doing our laundry, and cleaning our house." He kisses me again. "And romancing me between the sheets a couple times a day."

"Eeewww, Dad," whines Megan, scrunching up her face. "Grandpa, Grandma, and I don't need to hear about that."

I nod, giggling. "I can do that. And I'll add to our pot with my gig money."

Cripe, I didn't take my gig money. No worries, I'll take it next time. I need sheets to romance my man between.

"Meg," barks High. "You're going back to Denver for the holidays. So you won't be fucking hearing it."

Megan sighs. "Yeah, I wanted to stay, but Mom is freaking out. I sent her a video of Mama Cookie singing "I'm Every Woman." Mom loved Whitney Houston in *The Bodyguard.* She was all in a tizzy. She wanted to know why I was lying about you dating Mama Cookie."

"Why would you lie about that?" laughs Jewel.

Megan rolls her eyes. "If you saw Elizabeth and my mother, you'd know—thick waists, bubble butts, and no boobs. They're the total opposite of Mama Cookie. And, you know, Mama Cookie is twenty-two years younger than my mom...thirty years younger than Ed." Megan giggles. "Ed wants a signed poster to pin up on the wall."

Now I want to see a picture of Fawn. How do I ask that without sounding nosy?

"Mom said Dad couldn't possibly have a beautiful rock star for a girlfriend. So, I got ticked and sent her the video of Dad and Mama Cookie singing "Beautiful War." She said Dad was obviously having a midlife crisis. And Mama Cookie has daddy issues."

"What daddy issues do I have?!" I ask, irritated as hell I'm being discussed by Megan and Fawn. "I never had a father, so how could I have issues?"

"Christ," laughs Joker. "Chéri is coming out to play. Rene, she's all yours."

Dana is looking up at Rene. I scowl, staring at him, waiting.

"You don't have any, so you needn't worry about it," he chuckles.

"Good answer, honey," smiles Dana. "Very educational."

"Jesus, Dana," growls Rene.

Megan laughs. "Mom thinks Dad is taking Viagra."

Fawn sounds like a wickedy, witchy woman.

I jest, trying to hide my growing annoyance, "Are you taking the little blue pill, Amour?"

"Did it feel like I needed a goddamn little blue pill when I fucked you on the stage and in our room this morning, baby?" High growls, "Maybe we should have videoed that for nosy ass bigmouth mom!"

Joker snickers, glancing at Megan. "You might want to wipe that image from your head."

"No kidding," grumbles Megan. "I need to run, or I'll be late." She blows kisses to High, her grandparents, and me.

I wave. I like Megan, but she's very close to her mother. I'd rather stay out of High, Fawn, and Ed's triangle of parenting. Megan is a civilian girl, raised in mainstream culture: she doesn't have a filter. I don't need Fawn to know all my business.

"Baby, you need to line the truck up with the plow."

I leap out of the truck, running to the front. I examine the front end of the Ford and the plow.

"Babe," chuckles High. "You need to pull the truck forward."

"I know that, High, but you need to explain to me how I'm supposed to hook them together. I can't just drive the truck"—I make a sweeping motion with my body—"into the plow and hope they connect."

"Baby, the truck has two male connectors, and the plow has two female connectors. They go together like you and me. Just like I line up, the truck needs to line up. Once the male connectors slide in, the female connectors clamp down." High runs his tongue over my lips, parting them and thrusting in, giving me the most deliciously erotic kiss. "The perfect marriage," murmurs High, running a finger down my cheek. "Both connectors are snuggled up, tight and happy."

I look up at him dazedly. Right now, I'd like my man to show me how our connectors snuggle up, tight and happy.

"He did not just use sex as an analogy for hooking up a plow," laughs Jewel.

Dana nods, laughing hysterically.

Jewel adds, "He made it sound so freakin' hot, I'm going to dream about plows and trucks connecting."

Joker is bent over, his hands on his knees. "The truck, plowing the plow," he wheezes, trying to catch his breath.

Rene guffaws, "I'll drive the truck. You can watch them connect and become happy, Chéri.

Thirty minutes later, Dana, Rene, and I bounce around in the truck as High plows our two-mile driveway. The snow is unusually deep for the beginning of October, at least six feet. Our driveway is steep; High needs to make several passes.

I've given up on the idea I can plow our driveway—too many buttons and levers to keep track of. I need a shovel.

I have my ins and outs notebook open to the needs page. I write in bold letters, SHOVEL.

Dana's holding on to me so my temple doesn't smash against the window. She looks at my book, smiling. "Have you ever shoveled before, Chéri?"

I shake my head. "*Non*. Quebec gets lots of snow, but the city takes care of the streets and sidewalks. The brothers take care of it at Sinners Compound." I pull my iPhone from my hobo bag, showing Dana. "Look, no cell service. Here it's just High and me." I bite my lip, staring out the window. *There is a lot of snow.* "It's a matter of scooping and tossing it aside."

High chuckles, "Baby, the cell service is spotty because of the weather. You don't need a shovel. I have two in the bed."

He pulls up in front of the cabin. It's so cute, a one-story log structure with a porch running the building's length—it has a massive stone chimney on the right-hand side.

Excitedly, I swing open my door and leap out of the truck. To me, it's a beautiful home, and it's going to be High's and mine.

"Needs new windows, son," comments Rene.

High snorts. "I'm tearing the shithole down in the spring."

My eyes widen. He can't tear down our first home. "Non!"

High gets out of the truck and wraps me in his arms. "A house with a white picket fence is what I need for you and our babies." He points to the left. "Over there, by the lake."

I inhale the crisp, pine-scented air, looking from the cabin to the spot he pointed out. Then I nod, conceding. Families live in houses with backyards filled with family, friends, playsets, and barbecue grills. Our children won't be raised by civilian norms. They'll be brought up in the Sinners. The brothers have an open door policy— our home is their home.

I smile up at High. "I'll help you knock it down in the spring."

High chuckles, "Are you going to swing a sledgehammer, baby?"

"*Oui,*" I laugh, pulling out of his arms. Then I laugh louder when I can't lower the tailgate to get my cleaning supplies.

High and Rene have thrown out all the beds, dressers, and nightstands. Now they're tossing out the broken kitchen table and chairs. I didn't need to ask; the evidence said it all. Fawn was destructive when she got mad. My mother was the same way. I used to hide in the closet until the cyclone passed. Sometimes it was one or two broken things; other times, it was mass destruction. The signs of an unhappy, frustrated woman.

Megan is right; I'm the total opposite of her mother. I cherish my possessions.

Dana hugs me. "Are you ready to tackle this old recliner?"

I frown down at the broken leg rest—too bad. It's a waste of a perfectly good piece of furniture.

Rene's rumbling laughter floats into the living room, followed by the same rumbling laugh from High. They've been working together all day, enjoying each other's company.

"Dana, will you sit with me a minute?" I ask, dropping down on the dirty old recliner. I scooch over, giving her room. "I need to tell you about my life."

"Baby, no," says High, coming into the room, his dad on his heels.

"Amour, it's time. If Dana and Rene think less of me…"

"That won't happen, Chéri," assures Rene. He drops down onto the dirty floor by the recliner and takes my hand. "The four of us are family. Like the Sinners, we do not judge each other." He chuckles, "Dana and I are all in."

"If we're going to do this, I'm going to hold you," growls High. He lifts me out of the chair, plops down on the floor next to his father, and settles me onto his lap.

Dana drops into Rene's lap. She reaches over, taking my hand.

In a monotone voice, I tell them about my life as if someone else lived it. High needs to help me with Brian Stratton; the rape is still too fresh in my mind.

Dana is crying, still holding my hand.

Rene is raging; I know this because he growls, "Stratton is a dead man walking."

"Dad, I dealt with Stratton. He's six feet under," assures High.

"Good, son, as he should be," nods Rene, blowing out a breath.

"High, Jewel, and the Sinners have changed me. They're the family I never had, and now I have the two of you. I'm thankful for that." I wet my lips. I'm nervous to ask, but I do it anyway. As Maggie would

136

say: nothing ventured, nothing gained. "Mafia Man and Maggie live with their family, and so do Flame and Princess."

"Baby," drawls High. "Dad and Mom's lives are in Butte. Dad has a business."

"Do you want us to live here, in the cabin, with you and High?" asks Rene, chuckling.

I nod, looking at Dana's hand holding mine. "I want that for High, me, and our kids. High said he was building us a big house with a white picket fence. We'd only need to live in the cabin for a year."

Dana tips her head down, smiling at me. "I'd love that, Chéri. Christian is our son. Rene and I have been lost, living in a vacuum without him. And now, we have you." She giggles. "We're very compatible, aren't we?"

I laugh. "*Oui*, very compatible. We both love High and Rene. I'd do the cooking, cleaning, and laundry." I scrunch up my nose, thinking about how Istu cut his leg. "I'll give chopping wood a go…"

High and Rene throw their heads back, laughing.

"Baby, you're not going to chop wood," growls High, hugging me.

Rene looks at High. "I've been talking to your mother about selling the business. The house is too big for just the two of us. Knowing your mother, she's going to want to spend most of her time in Pony with Chéri."

High rubs circles onto my back. "Put the house on the market. I'll talk to the brothers and see if they're interested in the business. We'll do the holidays at the club; Cookie won't leave Jewel."

I smile up at High, running my fingers over his lips. "You're happy, Amour."

He kisses my fingers. "Yeah, baby, it's been a long time coming, but I'm over the moon happy."

CHAPTER 22

LIVE BY THE CLOCK – HIGH

The alarm goes off. I moan, "Dammit, baby, it's Friday. Our sleep-in morning." I reach over her, yanking the plug from the socket. I don't live and breathe by the clock. Cookie is a different story; every minute of her day is planned out. For the last two months, no matter how many alarm clocks I smashed, another one turned up to take its place. My woman keeps to her schedule.

Chuckling to myself, I tighten my arms around my woman, thinking about all her adorable quirks.

Monday through Thursday from 7:00 to 8:00 a.m., we get our groove on, and then she's in the shower and off to Callaghan's. Cookie jams with Cam and the boys from 9:00 a.m. to 1:00 p.m. If the boys are late, she doesn't mind. They have young kids; she gets that. Cam laughed, telling me, "She starts without us, High. Then, at one o'clock, she's done…gone, brother. Out the door."

I give Cookie a gentle squeeze, grinning. My little speed demon zooms up the mountain at a whopping twenty mph after her jam sessions. Cookie needs to "work" on our cabin—her labor of love.

Cookie was all over the cabin's renovations. I smirk; my tiny biker babe has scrubbed every inch of the place while singing "Love Shack." It was funny as all hell. Then she painted the cabinets "French Vanilla," a color she'd found on the "oops" rack at the big-box store. According to her, at five bucks a gallon, it was a steal she couldn't pass up. My woman has a cute quirk when she finds her "deal of the day": she dances out to the car singing "I Feel Good." And she usually gets a round of applause from the passersby. Maggie has idioms, Cookie has songs.

Cookie had me bend sterling silver spoons and forks she "rescued" from Mom's Salvation Army bin. She shined them up and told me she was going to use them for cabinet pulls. She needed to "borrow" a drill. I chuckled, "We're partners, baby. I'll work the power tools." Christ, I didn't need her drilling a hole through her hand.

It took me a day. I modified the silverware's bend, attached them to silver cylinders, and then affixed them to our cabinets for pulls. They look cool as shit.

Cookie went to work polishing *all* the wood surfaces with a concoction of olive oil, lemon, and water.

Then I got a call from Max: "It's none of my business, brother, but you did say you and Cookie are trying for a baby. Some guy just dropped off trisodium phosphate to Cookie. She told me she's going to use it on your stone fireplace. The shit is lethal; I used it to clean my foundation. It's not a good idea for her to touch it. Your kid might come out with six fingers." Yeah, I beat feet to the cabin in record time. I kicked Cookie out and needed to open all the windows just to breathe. But the shit worked; the fireplace turned out fantastic. It brought out all the nuances of the rocks.

My woman didn't stop there—she needed a mantel. Cookie found a giant oak tree that had fallen next to the lake. She showed Dad and me a YouTube video on how to make your own mantel. Could she *"borrow"* a chainsaw? She wanted to give it a *"whirl."* Dad almost pissed himself from laughing so hard. Christ, that wasn't happening. It became a father/son project: Dad and I cut a mantel from the oak. The two of us worked for days sanding, torching, and varnishing the piece of wood. It was good; it gave Dad and I the alone time we needed to work out some of my old issues surrounding Elizabeth, my drug addiction, and the end of my MMA career. Mafia Man's woman, Maggie, claims love knows no boundaries. She's right; by the time Dad and I were done, we were closer than before all the bad shit happened.

We both laughed when we tried to lift the mantel onto the fireplace mounts. I needed to recruit Joker to help us hang the heavy-as-hell slab. It looks fucking awesome.

Cookie wasn't done; she came home with ten boxes of discontinued antique square terra-cotta tile she'd found at a home improvement tent sale. My woman was on-top-of-the-world happy and removed all the old laminate from the kitchen countertops. Then she asked Dad and me to lay the tile for her; there was just enough, and she didn't want to mess it up.

Dad laughed, whispering to me, "The tile is porous; we need to find a way to seal it." We didn't tell her the cutter, grout, and sealer cost a bundle. It was worth it; the countertops and backsplashes are the fucking bomb.

Between the time we built the mantel and tiled the countertops, Dad and I installed ten new double-pane windows and electric baseboard heat. It's not the most economical heating system, but it was the quickest and easiest to install. An added bonus: Cookie won't smoke us out by forgetting to open the fireplace damper.

Joker and I took Cookie to pick out a stove, fridge, dishwasher, washer, and dryer. We laughed our asses off when we found her ass-end-up in a washer. She wanted to know how the clothes came clean without an agitator. The sales guy didn't know what to make of her.

Joker needed to distract Cookie while I paid for the KitchenAid appliances. She was all worked up over the "sale" prices. Joker lied; he told Cookie I got the scratch-and-dent prices. She was happy as a pig in shit.

My woman isn't cheap; she worries. We have Elizabeth hanging over our heads, and every time we turn around, Megan needs a fifty for clothes, makeup, books, the list is endless. Cookie never asks me for a dime, nor has she asked how much bank I have. Yet I'm always finding an extra Franklin in my wallet. It's not hard to figure out how it got there. All I need to do is look in Cookie's spiral notebook. I'll find, "Amour, $100.00" in the outs column.

I laugh every time she does her checks and balances. Her shoebox of green is double the balance she has written down in her notebook. It drives her crazy in the right way.

Cookie ends her "work" day at the cabin at 7:00 p.m. Then she makes her way down the mountain to help Merrill and Jewel cook dinner for the brothers. It's Cookie's girlfriend time; yeah, Merrill is one of the girls. He's a Vietnam vet that got entirely screwed up by the war. Years ago, Sinners took him on as a cook and gave him a place to live. The Sinners' women are his "besties"—his word, not mine. Though I do believe he'd shoot Marshmallow, given a chance. He loathes her lazy ass almost as much as I do.

At 10:00 p.m. sharp, Cookie calls my mother and father to "check" on them. Cookie worried about my father driving home after working on the cabin. "He's tired, Amour, and he drives too fast." I'm Cookie's go-to guy, but Rene Fontaine quickly bumped General out of second place.

On the weekends, Cookie changes things up. Mom and Dad come to Pony for Cookie's gigs. Cookie and the Heartbreakers play at Callaghan's Bar every Friday and Saturday from 9:00 p.m. to 2:00 a.m. We need to be there at 7:00 sharp for the soundcheck. It's not unusual for the Sinners' kids to show up then. JJ, Keeley, JT, Brie, and Anna love to sing on stage with their Aunt Cookie. By 8:00, the kids are taken home, and people start rolling in, wanting the closest spot to the band. Cookie packs the house to the rafters. For the Sinners and Native Americans, it's all-hands-on-deck. The alcohol flows freely, making security a bitch.

I laughed when my father became Callaghan's third bartender. During the breaks, Rex, Tristen, and Dad are the entertainment: flipping bottles to each other, making a show of shaking their asses, and coming up with foo-foo drinks for young women. Pop Rock Explosion is one of the favorites: a double shot of bottom-shelf vodka in red fruit punch, with Pop Rocks candy rimming a martini glass. Rock Hard Heaven is another: blue fruit punch with a double shot of cheap whiskey and a blue rock candy stick. They'll give you a toothache and the hangover from hell. At twelve dollars a drink, they're moneymakers.

My mother became the self-appointed "stage mom" for the band: Cam provides her with a schedule of their sets, and she makes sure each member's preferred drinks and their instruments are in the proper order.

In church, I had told the Sinners' brothers my parents were selling their house, the business, and moving in with us.

General nodded. "That's no surprise, High. Rene is in Pony more than he's in Butte nowadays."

Flame chuckled; his eyes twinkled with mirth as they moved to Pick. "Be prepared for how often your parents need to *express their love*, brother."

Princess's father, Pick and Flame's mother, Hialeah fell in love. And according to Flame, they don't hold back when they do the dirty. I smirked, recalling Flame beating feet to Sinners and begging for help to build a wing onto their house.

Crank's eyes lit up. "You said the house and business are in Butte? My wife's parents live in Butte."

General and I looked at each other; Crank has been a Sinner for ten years. Was he thinking of leaving the club?

Crank explained: "My father-in-law was diagnosed with prostate cancer. My mother-in-law is having a rough time. She needs our help."

Shitty news, but totally understandable. Crank needed to move his family to Butte.

I called my father and put him on speaker. The deal was cut; my parents sold their home to Crank. Dad gave the business to Sinners for a weekly paycheck. Crank has a head for business; he'd handle the day-to-day bullshit. It worked out for everyone.

My father laughed. "Does this make me a Sinner?"

General looked at us, chuckling. "Let's vote."

It wasn't a surprise the vote was unanimous. Mom and Dad already had a room at the club; they'd been with us every weekend since Cookie walked them through Sinners' door. The brothers love my parents. Dad was grandfathered into the Sinners as a full brother.

For the last week, I've been packing my parents' house. Mom and Dad asked Cookie and me what we wanted for the cabin. Cookie did a happy dance and ripped up her needs page. "You pick, Amour, I'll make it work."

Everything in my old room went to the dump. That life is done. At thirty-nine, my screwed up head is finally straightened out; I'm the man I should have been years ago.

In the end, it was Mom and Cookie who chose what to keep and what to store. Cookie wanted everything in the kitchen. Dad's den had the *"perfect"* brown leather sofa. Cookie insisted on Mom and Dad's recliners: "Your parents sit in them every night, Amour. I'll make them pop with colorful throws and a few decorative pillows."

Mom chose to keep their bedroom set for their room. The spare bedroom furniture Cookie is going to use in Megan's room. Everything else, I brought back with me, including my father's Harley. It's all stored in Sinners' barn.

I insisted on a new bedroom set for Cookie and me. Together, we picked a rad, rustic oak four-poster bed, two dressers, and nightstands. Then, Cookie chose a white goose down comforter with rust-colored sheets. I saw her eyes continuously going to a coffee table and two end tables. I knew she wanted them; they matched our mantel. I laughed and added them to the cart. Finally, I chose a new seventy-five-inch flat-screen TV. Cookie giggled wildly when I covered her eyes. "Don't look, baby," I laughed as I clicked the purchase icon.

After two months of nonstop work, things came together. Today we're making our life-changing move without Megan. She caved under

Fawn's pressure; Beau flew her back to Denver yesterday for the holidays. In some ways, I was relieved; Cookie has enough anxiety over leaving Jewel at the club. My woman doesn't say it, but I know Megan adds to her stress. Megan's mouth runs like a whippoorwill's ass to Fawn.

Jewel calmed Cookie down. "You're not moving across the country, sister. We'll see each other all the time. Besides, I'm busy designing for Sinners Biker Babe Boutique. It's all good."

Dad and Mom arrived late last night with the U-Haul. I was worried my parents would have regrets or sadness over leaving Butte. Nope, Mom was as excited as Cookie to move into our new home. Jewel, Cookie, and Mom opened a bottle of wine and started gabbing. Dad slid onto a barstool and shot the shit with the brothers over a beer.

Mom laughed, telling Jewel, "Christian wants to build us a house in the spring? I don't know why? Cookie made us a gorgeous home." Then, she pulled out her iPhone, showing Jewel all the pictures she'd taken throughout the restoration of the cabin. Jewel oohed and ahhed over them as if she hadn't seen the transformation. Cookie had Face-Timed her throughout the entire process.

Four adults living in a tiny cabin isn't doable for the long term. Cookie and I are planning on kids. Mom was correct: Cookie did turn our shack into a beautiful home. I'm not knocking it down; one of the brothers will want to live in it.

Cookie gives me a soft kiss, yanking me from my thoughts. "Hey, Amour," she whispers, running her finger around my lips. "You look intense. Are you sad Megan isn't going to be moving in with us today?"

"Nope, Megan needs to deal with her mother in her own way," I murmur, wrapping her in my arms. "I was thinking about everything that we've done in two months."

Cookie smiles. "Are you ready to move into the cabin with me and make babies?"

"Hmm," I hum, grinning. "Are you ready to become a Fontaine?"

Cookie's head pops up. She stares down at me. "Are you asking me to marry you?"

I laugh. "Baby, I'm not fucking adopting you, so yeah, I'm asking."

"*Oui*, I'll marry you," she squeals, smothering me with kisses. "Amour, we need to get dressed and start our new life. Babymaking will need to wait until we're in our new bed." She leaps off the bed, does a happy dance, and runs to the bathroom.

No doubt, forever with Cookie is going to be a fantastic ride.

CHAPTER 23

DAUGHTER – COOKIE

Dana and I dash out to High's truck. The weather is crappy for our moving day. Big white fluffy snowflakes are falling rapidly from the sky, and the wind is whipping. High jumps into the driver's seat of the U-Haul. Rene climbs into the passenger seat.

Joker is driving my Cayenne filled with our must-haves from the club: most of our clothes, toiletries, makeup, and hair products, High's weapons, my keyboard, guitar, songbook, ins and outs notebook, and my shoebox of money. The other stuff, we left. It's still our room, and we'll be using it.

"Baby," yells High over the wind. "We'll follow you. Drop the plow when you get to our driveway."

I cringe. Lord, have mercy, drop the plow. I look at all the levers and buttons. *You can do this; you're High's biker babe...a mountain woman.*

I wave, yelling back, "Okay, Amour," as if it's no big deal.

Dana gives me a sideways glance, giggling. "No worries, if we get stuck, they're right behind us."

"Right," I nod, putting the Ford into gear. I take a deep breath and push on the gas.

"Oh, my god!" I shriek. The tires of the U-Haul spin; the entire van is sliding right, trying to gain traction.

Dana pats my knee. "Christian is a good driver. They'll be okay."

When we get to the gate, I blast the horn, not wanting to stop.

Rascal bellows, "Put it into four-wheel drive, Cookie!" as he opens the gate.

Oh, right, four-wheel drive.

I jab the button and take the truck up to twenty mph. It's faster than I want to go, but High said he needs speed to make it up Diva Mountain Road.

"Dana, keep your eyes on High," I order, gripping the wheel tighter. I give the truck a little more gas, praying we don't slide off the mountain.

My heart is pounding, I scoot closer to the steering wheel, trying to see through the flurries. I don't dare look into my rearview mirror.

"Christian is doing great, darling. Give it some more gas, so they'll make it up the mountain."

I swallow, forcing my foot to press down on the accelerator.

Lord, if we make it to the cabin, I swear I'll be the best wife and mother. I won't ask for anything for myself. Please just let us make it to the cabin. Amen.

Thirty minutes into the drive, I pass the two massive twin oaks. I squint, looking for our driveway. *There!* I pump the breaks and make the right-hand turn. *Merde-merde-merde, which button lowers the plow? Think!* I glance down and push in the button that has an arrow pointing down. *Bang!* The plow drops onto the driveway.

"Hold on, Dana," I yell, white-knuckling the steering wheel. We're bouncing around like popcorn in a hot pan. Snow is flying in a sheet of white on both sides of the truck—the noise of the plow scraping is deafening.

"Dana, can you see Amour?!"

"Amour?" she shouts back.

"Christian! Is he behind us?!"

She grabs the oh-Jesus handle and turns, looking out the back. "Noooo! Can't...see...a...thing. Keep gooooing!"

Two feet in front of us, a moose darts out of the woods running across our driveway. Dana screeches at the top of her lungs.

"*Merrrde!*" I scream, forcing myself to keep my eyes wide open and not hit the breaks or swerve for fear I'll kill Dana, Rene, Joker, or High.

I let out a huge breath when the cabin comes into view. Hitting the brakes, I jam the truck into park and fall against the steering wheel, breathing erratically. Black spots dance behind my eyelids, my head whirls in dizziness. My heart is thudding and my ears are buzzing. Goosebumps pop out all over my skin.

I hear voices, but they sound as if they're far away, underwater. Someone's hand is on the crown of my head; it tingles from their touch.

"Baby, you're all right. Slow down your breathing; you're hyperventilating."

I turn my head, my temple resting against the wheel. High leans into the cab; his grin lights up my world. My head clears.

He chuckles, giving me a soft kiss.

I smile against his lips. "We're home. I plowed the driveway for us."

His deep, rumbling laugh fills every part of me, making my girly parts dance in delight.

"Yeah, you did, baby."

He lifts me out of the truck. I look over his shoulder. Squinting my eyes, I look through the flurries. "Is that Dish TV, and Montana Furniture? I thought they'd both cancel due to the weather."

High chuckles, trudging through the three feet of snow to the porch. "We live in Montana, baby. Snow is part of the deal." He sets me on my feet, giving me a lip touch. "Get inside with Mom and Dad. Joke and I will unload."

Rene comes out of the cabin. He grabs the shovel, giving me a kiss on the forehead. "Great plowing, daughter."

Daughter. Rene just called me, Chéri Fayette, *his* daughter. I look up into the sky, blinking back my tears. *Merci.* It may be entirely screwed up, even psychotic, but at this moment, I know everything I've been through in my life has led me right here. And I'd do it again and again to have my wonderful family.

"Cookie, fucking fantastic, Rene took you on as his daughter. Process it inside the cabin," chides Joker. "This shit is goddamn heavy."

I blink, getting ready to lambaste Joker in French. I mean, god, this is the best day of my entire existence. I'm moving into a new home, High asked me to marry him, and I got a father.

He tilts his head, grinning at me while holding a huge box. "Got something to say, Chéri?"

I laugh, shaking my head. Chéri is what Joker calls me when I blast my Frenchwoman's attitude.

I hold open the door for Joker and follow him inside. The cabin is warm with our new heating system and windows. I inhale deeply, filling my nose with the fragrance of lemons. I walk over to the mantel, running my hand over the glossy smooth surface. Dana whizzes past me, showing the delivery guys where our new bedroom will be set up. My eyes go to the backyard. The Dish men are setting a ladder against the cabin: High is getting his one hundred ninety channels, high-speed internet, and landline.

I go to my knees in front of the hearth. Nothing says home like a crackling fire.

High kisses the top of my head, chuckling, "I'll start the fire for you, baby. Go set up your kitchen."

I giggle, aware he doesn't want me to burn the place down. *Oui,* I forgot to open the damper once. High caught it before the entire cabin filled with smoke.

I kiss his lips, pull off my boots, and shrug out of my coat. Leaping up, I text Jewel about everything that happened and our near miss with the moose.

Jewel: Enjoy every moment, sister. You deserve all the happiness life has to offer. Take pictures. And stay away from the wild animals! Love you!

Me: Love you a million times back.

I snap a picture of High starting the fire and hit send.

I laugh; my man's fine ass is worthy of a butt pic. Maybe I'll have it blown up and hang it on our bedroom wall.

CHAPTER 24

DOMESTIC BLISS – HIGH

Flame slaps me on my back. "Are you still in domestic bliss?" he laughs, setting a beer on the bar in front of me.

The Sinners and Native Americans' businesses keep everyone hopping during the week. There isn't any time to relax and hang out. So, Cookie and the girls decided to make Sundays Sinners Family Day —all of us kicking back at the club with a late lunch and chilling over a few drinks.

I glance over my shoulder—Cookie's with Mom, Merrill, and the girls, drinking wine. The girls are gabbing; per usual, my woman is the listener of the group. Dad's by the pool table, nursing a beer. He's talking with the older brothers, making plans to go hunting with them. I grin, hearing the kids' loud giggles coming from the war room —their playroom. Raven had Sly put their toys, a TV, a DVD player, a gaming system, and beanbag chairs up there for *her grandbabies*. Then she had Cue Ball install gates at the top and bottom of the stairs. Raven feared the little ones would take a header. That awoke the dragon; I thought fire was going to shoot from General's mouth when he roared, "It's my war room, Raven!"

In the end, Raven soothed the dragon and got her way. In church, General didn't ask; he told the brothers, "We're building a goddamn addition for the kids this spring."

We all chuckled, knowing it was General's way of taking back control. He loves his wife, but it annoys the hell out of him when she puts her nose into the Sinners' business.

I take a pull off my beer. "It's been a week; everyone is still breathing." I chuckle, "Cookie and my parents are in sync. Cookie does the laundry, Mom cleans, and they cook together. Dad does Cookie and Mom's bidding." I smirk. "He's making shelves out of oak for my mother's teapot collection."

Flame takes a swig of his beer. "Have you heard from Megan?"

I nod. "Cookie FaceTimes with her every night. Fawn gets Meg to pump Cookie for intel about Mom, Dad, Cookie, and me. Fawn is a nosy bitch. She doesn't know my woman is the queen of evasion. If Fawn was any other woman, I'd snap her goddamn neck. But I can't; the bitch is my kid's mother."

Flame chuckles, taking another hit off his beer. "High, we've come to a fork in the road. Elizabeth is turning up the heat on Margo and Willy. Beau is fucking around with Margo; he's not going to let the bitch take her property. I need to know if you're in or out. I'm heading to Butte tonight." He laughs, "Corrie's getting down in the mud. It's going to be goddamn ugly, brother."

I exhale. Eliminating Elizabeth would be a massive weight off Cookie's and my shoulders. I contested the divorce based on the fact we were never married. The goddamn cunt had her attorney set a court date for a judge to rule on our nonexistent marriage. It sent Cookie over the edge. Since my parents have arrived my French has returned; I understood every word of Cookie's rant. The leech was sucking off *her* Amour. I grinned at my woman, wanting to douse the parasite with salt so that she'd shrivel up and die.

I tip back my beer, guzzling the rest. "I'm in. What time are we leaving?"

"Nine. Joke and I will pick you up at the cabin. Joker and Crank are covering the street. We need to get into the bitch's apartment and find the dirt."

I nod, glancing at the clock—it's five. Cookie and I have time to get romantic between the sheets before I need to leave. "Baby, let's make tracks. We have shit to do at home."

CHAPTER 25

WANTING A MINI-ME OF MY MAN – COOKIE

High told me he needed to go to Butte tonight. I knew it was about the parasite. I didn't question him; High will do what he needs to do to end this nightmare for us. My job is to support him so that he can get the job done.

My man has his back to the headboard, his knees bent and spread wide. I moan as his two fingers penetrate my pussy; his thick thumb pushes into my ass. My two fingers pierce his hole. He growls in a low rumble, "Fuck." I speed up, sucking him to the back of my throat. My man's cock is ginormous, hard as steel, yet silky against my lips. The scent of his musk intoxicates me; the taste of his precum is my drug. I push down, sliding his bulbous head past my gag reflex, squeezing my lips, and massage his shaft with my tongue.

"Jesus Christ," he snaps. His hips come off the bed.

I quicken my fingers, fucking his ass. He'd only admit it to me, but High loves when I fuck his ass while sucking his cock.

His magical fingers are working me into a frenzy. I buck my hips and grind down, needing a release.

"Enough," he barks. "Reposition, baby. Ride my cock."

I slip his cock out of my mouth with a pop and slide my fingers from his ass. Then I nuzzle his balls. Murmuring softly in French, I encourage them to do their job and make us a baby boy—Christian Rene Fontaine Jr.

High chuckles. "They'll do their job when my cock is in your pussy, baby."

I turn, swinging my leg over High's hips. Running my tongue across my swollen lips, I pin my eyes to my man's massive erection. My pussy drips at the sight of his enormous purple head peeking out of his foreskin. My breasts tingle, wanting High to suck on my nipples.

My man holds his cock in one hand, my butt cheek in the other. His eyes are dark as a stormy sea, watching me stretch around him. I hiss at the sensation of my pussy, accommodating his wide girth. *Sooo fantastic!* I pant to keep from climaxing.

I glide down, digging my nails into High's muscular thighs. I love the feel of him inside me, growing, lengthening, and thickening, filling me. I get to his root and circle my hips, grinding onto him.

"Feed me your tit," he growls, nuzzling his face between my breasts.

Oui, merci, Lord Jesus!

I hold my boob up to his mouth, running my hard nipple over his lips. The tingling intensifies, sending a quiver throughout my body. My man growls, latching on, sucking.

I whimper, my toes curling from his glorious mouth loving me. I wrap my arms tightly around his head, muffling my cries into his hair.

High grips my butt cheeks, helping me to ride his cock. His curses are smothered by my breasts.

"Oh, god! Amour!" I scream, grinding down and gyrating. My body is taut; my pussy needs to feel his release.

He makes a feral growl, taking my mouth in a rough, wet kiss. "Go!" he orders.

And I do, screaming out his name and my love for him.

He growls, following me. His cock jerks, sending me into another mind-blowing continuous orgasm. I fall limply against his chest, reveling in the aftershocks of our lovemaking. Both our breathing is labored; we're slick from sweat. High wraps me up and scoots down the bed, lying us face-to-face. He stays deep inside me, his hands running up and down my back and butt.

After a few minutes, I find my voice. "Are we pregnant, Amour?"

He chuckles onto the crown of my head. "We'll know in a few weeks, baby." He kisses my temple. "But yeah, I think we made CJ. No more drinking."

I nod against his chest, snuggling into him. I pray that he's right: I want a mini-me of my man—a little boy with sky-blue eyes, black wavy hair, and a smile that lights up my world.

CHAPTER 26

SEXY BUNS – HIGH

Cookie buttons my jeans, her forehead resting against my chest. I put my cheek against her crown and finish giving her the details of what's going down tonight.

She looks up at me; worry is in her eyes. "Amour, I know you need to do this for the Coopers and us. I also know you're the strongest badass among the Sinners."

I chuckle at that; all the biker babes think their man is the strongest badass of the Sinners.

"But don't get caught, Amour. CJ and I need you here with us. And for god's sake, don't get hurt." Her eyes brim with tears. "Or killed."

I run my thumb underneath her beautiful blues. Leaning down, I put my lips against hers. "I won't get caught, hurt, or killed. I'll be back in the morning. No more worrying." Then, I give her belly a rub. I'm hoping we made our child, too. "Christian Rene Fontaine Jr. will have me around until I'm farting goddamn dust, baby."

Cookie giggles, putting her hands over my ass.

I chuckle, "Jesus, woman, you love ass play."

Cookie leaps onto me, wrapping me up. "*Oui*, I do!" she admits, giving me a wide grin. "Amour, you have *very* sexy buns."

"Yeah," I murmur against her lips. "Open," I command, giving her a kiss—our tongues tangle into a lust-filled dance. My woman's breathing accelerates, the heat of her pussy penetrates my tee. My cock responds, becoming hard as stone. I groan, deepening our kiss.

"High! Carry your sexy buns out here," laughs Joker from the kitchen. "Babymaking is over. We need to hit the road."

I set Cookie onto her feet, giving her a chaste kiss. "To be continued," I chuckle, taking her hand and walking out the door.

Joker and Flame are sitting at the table. Flame smirks at me and tips back his beer, guzzling down the rest. Joker's chowing down on a triple-decker sandwich. I roll my eyes—the brother's an empty pit.

Dad sets three travel mugs of coffee onto the table. He's edgy; he knows the score. Dad wanted to come with us. I insisted he stay at home with Mom and Cookie.

Mom is her typical self: she's jetting around the kitchen, making Joker a snack for his long night of surveillance. She has faith that her "boys" will do what needs to be done.

Cookie is a different story. My woman has witnessed the wars between the Sinners and the South American Cartel, the Italian Mafia, and Dyson's torture. She participated in the Diamondbacks' demise. Cookie was there for Josie's betrayal and subsequent death, and when Heaven's Portal kidnapped Princess. She mourned Mama Cass when she was murdered by Jerome Reed's men. My woman's aware that the most uncomplicated mission can go wrong within a snap of two fingers. She knows when her man walks out the door, he might not be coming back breathing.

Joker jumps up, kissing my mother on her cheek. "Thanks, Mama Dana." He struts over to Cookie, pulling her into a hug. "Stop worrying. Nothing is going to happen to"—he rolls his eyes, grinning—"your *Amour* or his sexy buns. He'll be home by 0900 to commence babymaking."

Cookie hugs him back tightly, murmuring in French, "Don't take any unnecessary risks, and don't get caught. Jewel loves you."

Joker chuckles, releasing Cookie. "I don't know what the hell you said, babe."

No, I won't be translating that for Joker. It would end Joker's nightly visits to Jewel's bed. To him, relationships and babies are endless money pits that drain a man's wallet for life. According to Joker, love is a poison pill he'll never swallow. It's ironic; his actions toward Jewel point to him swallowing that pill years ago.

CHAPTER 27

RAUNCHY KINK – HIGH

Flame pulls over, parking on the side of the street outside Elizabeth's apartment building.

"Christ, brother, you've been paying for the bitch to live here?" asks Crank, his eyes on the building. "Robin and I checked the place out before we bought your parents' crib. Four thousand dollars per month for a two-bedroom, no utilities included. Fuck that."

I ignore the rhetorical question, watching a guy in a black overcoat rush by us. His baseball cap is pulled low, hiding his face. Yeah, I recognize him—Elizabeth's attorney, Lewis Hinkle. I growl, "A bit late for an attorney house call. Let's move."

Flame, Joker, Crank, and I attach our throat mics, insert our earpieces, and then pair them with our burner phones. Flame does roll call, making sure we're all connected.

I leap out, steeling myself against the ten-degree wind howling around me. The sky is pitch black—no moon, not one twinkling star. Light, icy snow falls at a steady pace, making the night miserable. I glance up to the tenth floor; the lights are on in Elizabeth's apartment.

Flame hands me a hook with an enormous coil of rope attached to it. "Of course it's on the fucking tenth floor," mutters Flame. "The bitch wouldn't have a view from the lower floors."

The apartment does have incredible views: the front is Butte Central Park, the back has the Rockies. It was Jason and Elizabeth's home. I was the dumbass who picked up the tab after he died, not knowing Elizabeth was double-dipping. I still can't believe the bitch was getting a check for three grand a month from the Coopers.

"Let's make tracks before my balls freeze off," I bitch, irritated as hell I need to be here.

Flame smirks. "Cookie let us all know she loves your ass. Your balls didn't make the list."

I know he's trying to lighten my mood; I appreciate him for it. I grin. "No worries, my boys made the list, brother."

He chuckles as we jog side by side through the ankle-deep snow-drifts to the back of the building. There is a balcony that spans the length of the apartment. It has two sliding glass doors: one off the bedroom, the other off the living room. Elizabeth never locks them.

Flame opens a case containing two surveillance cameras with audio. He hands me one, giving me a quick tutorial on how to work the equipment. Right now, I could kiss the kids for making me play video games with them. The wand works just like the controller on the Xbox.

My anger rises as my eyes go vertical, taking in the ten-story apartment building. It's bullshit that I got tangled up in the web of Elizabeth's deceit. Now Flame and I are looking at an eight-foot climb to the wrought iron ladder's icy rungs. From there, wind and ice will make our nine-story climb dangerous as hell. Once at the top, we'll need to jump three feet to the balcony, which appears equally as icy. I snort. The "fire escape" was designed more for aesthetics than func-tionality. God fucking forbid the assholes attached the damn thing to the balconies. No, that would destroy "the look." How the apartment dweller is supposed to access the ladder in an emergency is beyond me. At least dodging the security cameras on the sides of the building won't be an issue; they're all pointed in the wrong direction.

"Dogwalker, six o'clock," whispers Joker through our earpieces.

Flame and I step into the shadows and wait for the guy to pass us.

The goddamn dog makes a hundred circles as its owner shivers, waiting. Finally, the damn animal squats, taking its dump.

"Clear," murmurs Joker.

I swing the rope in giant, tight circles, letting it fly. The hook makes a clatter against the wrought iron—it's a wringer. I tug on the rope, motioning for Flame to go first. He's Native American, an ex-major in the Army's special forces, and Sinners' Sergeant of Arms. Now he's Spiderman, zipping up the rope as if it's another day at the office.

I get three-quarters of the way up, waiting for Flame to make the three-foot leap to the balcony. Like a mountain cat, Flame lands soundlessly onto the icy railing and hops down.

It's my turn. I have excellent balance from my MMA days, but I'm not an acrobat. I take a deep breath and push off with my legs. My hands catch the railing. Quick as lightning, Flame's hands dart out, making iron bands around my wrists. I pull myself up and over.

Flame snickers, "You needed to jump up and out."

I roll my eyes, chuckling low. "Yeah, fuck you, brother."

Flame and I drop to our bellies, crawling along the snow-covered balcony to the living room's sliding glass door. We extend the telescopes, attach the mic to the glass, and hit record. Jason and Hinkle are on the couch, Jason's head resting against Hinkle's shoulder. They're looking damn cozy.

"Dad, I need five Bennies for tonight," says Jason, fiddling with his cell. "The guys and I are playing poker at the Indian casino over on Grizzly Trail. They comped us a room."

Huh, that's interesting: Jason knows Lewis Hinkle is his biological father. When did he find out? A year, a month, or a week ago? Or did the little shit know from the day he was born? By the way Jason is cuddled up to his dad, my guess is he's always known. Flame and I need a date. Speculation isn't good enough; we need evidence Elizabeth played Jason Cooper.

Jason continues: "Did you get the deposit for my Jeep from your money-honey? The dealership won't hold it forever."

"Jay," sighs Hinkle, "things are tight right now. As you know, Christian has yanked his support from your mother. We're in a pickle with the apartment manager and the utility companies. Your mother and I are working it out, but you'll need to wait until she gets the settlement from Christian."

My anger flares, making my grip crushing; it's a wonder the hand-held monitor doesn't disintegrate. *Un-fucking-believable!*

"Mom isn't going to get shit from Christian, Dad. He told Mom he'd snap her neck if she even looked in his direction again, and he meant it."

That's motherfucking correct. I'll put the bitch to ground before she ever sees another dime from me.

"The Sinners are real bad dudes, Dad. The bikers snapped Julius's arm like a twig. The other Sinner crushed one of Carl's nuts with his bare hand. He needed surgery to have it removed. Carl calls himself the one-nut wonder," laughs Jason.

I bare my teeth, suppressing a growl. The little fuckers deserved it. Outside Blue Heaven, they pulled knives on Liam, Guard Dog, and Rocky.

"Good lord, Jay," grimaces Hinkle.

"I told the guys to run, but Julius and Carl decided to square off with the Sinners. I grabbed Mom and got the hell out of there."

"Uncivilized thugs," sneers Hinkle.

"Christian is into the lead singer of the Heartbreakers. I'd like to know how he landed her; she's my age and smokin' hot." Jason holds his phone in front of his father's face. "A golden piece of ass."

Hinkle's brown eyes widen, staring at the cell. "That's Christian Fontaine's girlfriend?"

"Yup," nods Jason. "I don't think you and Mom have a chance of squeezing Christian out of his dough. Julius's mother said Corinne Hunter is cutthroat in the courtroom. The Coopers are our best shot. Mom had better hurry. Grandpa Wheeler called today; they got the foreclosure notice on their house." He looks up at his father. "Papa Wheeler asked me about my trust fund. I think he's getting Alzheimer's or something. I don't have a trust fund."

Fuck, Elizabeth never told her son about his trust fund. The bitch stole from her own kid.

Elizabeth comes rushing through the front door. "It's not fit for man or beast outside." She looks at Hinkle. "Have you been here long, Pooh Bear?"

Pooh Bear. Hinkle looks more like Ichabod Crane. At six feet tall, he's stick-thin. My guess is his orange-colored skin is the result of a spray tan gone bad. His comb-over is an attempt to hide his male pattern baldness.

Elizabeth strolls over, giving Jason a kiss on his forehead and Hinkle a kiss on the lips.

Okay, that's evidence they're still having an affair.

Jason slides off the couch, holding out his hand. "Dad, I need to meet the guys at the casino."

Hinkle pulls out his wallet, thumbing through his bills. "Jay, all I have is two hundred until I get my allowance from Virginia."

I pull in the telescoping lens and back away from the glass door. I motion to the bedroom. We belly crawl over to it. I reach up, sliding back the door soundlessly. The room hasn't changed in the last ten years. It's painted white with the same ugly-as-hell, provincial white and gold furniture. Unlike Cookie, Elizabeth has never been a neat, organized person. The laundry hamper is overflowing with dirty clothes, the wastebasket is brimming with dried-up old wet wipes. My eyes dart to the two dressers; they're piled with a foot of papers. Some have found their way to the floor.

I chuckle at Flame, murmuring, "Fucking pig," as he makes his way into the room, me on his heels.

Flame's wife and mother are equally as neurotic as Cookie and my mother over keeping a clean house. If the girls saw this, they'd yank on their rubber gloves and arm themselves with Pine-Sol, Lysol, and fifty-five-gallon garbage bags. Goodbye dirt, germs, and clutter; hello sparkle and spotlessness. The room would be fucking spick-and-span within an hour.

Flame takes the highboy closest to the bathroom. That leaves me the bureau near the closet. I rifle through old receipts, grocery lists, past due bills, warnings of eviction, multiple bounced check notices, Post-it Notes with dates to remember, and copies of the lawsuits Hinkle has filed. Nothing that I would consider dirt worthy.

"Let's bring our drinks into the bedroom, Lewis. Where did you tell Virginia you were staying tonight?" asks Elizabeth, coming down the hall.

I dive into the walk-in closet. Flame flies into the bathroom.

"I told her I have an interview in Helena early tomorrow morning. Jay said he and the guys are staying at the casino. We have the entire night...alone, Mommy."

I cringe. *God no.* There isn't any escape short of killing Elizabeth and Hinkle. Right now, that sounds like a viable option.

Joker chuckles in my ear, "Willamena is going to get her porn video."

I grimace. *Jesus.*

"Is my duffel in the closet? *I need to prepare* for *our night of pleasure,*" says Hinkle, like a bad actor in a B movie.

"What the fuck?" growls Flame through my earpiece. There's rustling, as if he's moving plastic containers around.

"Where the hell are you?" I murmur, scooting deeper into the closet to hide behind some of Elizabeth's tent dresses.

Flame stifles a sneeze, sneering, "In the goddamn utility closet. There's enough dust in here to grow fucking mushrooms. I'm telling you, brother, I'm killing these fuckers if they don't give us something useful."

Flame's pissed. He'll kill them without losing sleep over it. Nope, I won't lose sleep over it either.

"Get the assholes on video doing the dirty. Princess is right: Hinkle won't want that exposed. He'll lose his"—Joker chuckles—"money-honey."

I grimace. "Christ."

"Your duffel is right inside the door, Pooh Bear. Your little blue pills are in the zip pouch. I'll be out in ten," sings Elizabeth.

The closet door opens, and the light turns on. I hold my breath, feeling for the butt of my Glock.

"Did you wash my diaper?" asks Hinkle, grabbing the duffel.

"Yes, in Dreft baby detergent," yells Elizabeth.

What the fuck? Diaper? What in the hell are they going to do?

I move to the front of the closet and push the telescoping lens under the door. Using the wand, I scan the room. Hinkle is popping a pill and pulling out a large white cloth from his duffel bag, along with two supersized safety pins.

I hear Flame moan through my earpiece, "Fuck me, I had to take the damn bathroom."

"What's wrong?" whispers Joker.

"Elizabeth is goddamn douching. I'm going to fucking puke," whispers Flame.

Crank and Joker crack up laughing.

"I take it she doesn't have a pretty pink pussy," chuckles Crank.

"Fuck no," whines Flame. "How in the hell did you fuck her?"

"I haven't fucked the bitch in over ten years, so I have no idea what her pussy looks like," I whisper in disgust.

Now I'm the one moaning.

"Speak!" demands Joker.

"Hinkle is putting on a diaper," I whisper.

"What? I thought I just heard you say Hinkle was putting on a diaper," mutters Crank.

"I did," I sneer, squishing up my face. "A goddamn white cloth diaper and baby pins."

"I'm glad I'm out here and not in there. It's going to get raunchy," chuckles Joker.

"This coming from the guy who has his cock pierced," I snicker. "Jesus, you're more equipped to handle this shit than Flame and me."

"Wah...wah! Mommy! Mommy!" cries Hinkle, rubbing his eyes with his fists. "I'm hungry, feed me."

I can't help it; I snort. It's super-bad kink, the ultimate shitshow. I quickly cover my mouth, trying to keep from guffawing aloud.

"Keep it in, don't fucking laugh," chides Flame. "We need to capture it on video."

"Mommy's coming, Pooh Bear," coos Elizabeth sweetly.

Elizabeth skips out of the bathroom with a frilly white apron tied around her thick waist. *Christ, my eyes!* Elizabeth's rolls are jiggling, her dimpled ass is wobbling, and her tits are flapping.

I snap my eyes shut for a second, needing to remind myself I'm doing this for the Coopers, Cookie, and me.

Elizabeth hops on the bed, cradling Hinkle's torso like a baby. She rubs her nipple against his lips. "Mommy's here. Suckle my breast, darling," coos Elizabeth.

Hinkle latches on, making loud snuffles, snorts, and slurps.

"You had better be videoing this shit. This is your ticket to freedom," chuckles Joker.

Hinkle's diaper tents. A large yellow stain soaks the front—the smell of shit assaults my nose. Bile rises in the back of my throat. I quickly swallow, stifling a gag.

Flame whispers, "Did he just piss and shit his diaper?"

I groan, "Yeah."

There is a roar of laughter coming through my earpiece.

Flame growls, "Keep it down. We can't hear."

"Oh, Pooh Bear, you pee-peed and poopied your diaper," coos Elizabeth. "Mommy needs to change you."

Whatever people do in the privacy of their bedroom is fine by me. But this is the ultimate freak show—one I'd rather not bear witness to.

Elizabeth unpins the diaper and cleans Hinkle's hard-on and ass with baby wipes. "There there, all better," she purrs, blowing over his hard cock as if she's trying to blow dry him.

"If she goes down on him, I'll spew," I groan.

"She's going down on him," snickers Flame. Then, the ballbuster decides it would be a great idea to give us the blow-by-blow details: "Miss Piggy has her nose right in there, sniffing out the truffles."

"Oh, fuck," roars Joker and Crank, laughing.

"She is taking him in the cowgirl position," informs Flame.

"A hundred bucks Hinkle doesn't last two minutes," whispers Crank.

Joker chuckles, "One hundred and twenty seconds. I'll take that bet."

There are a few grunts and groans—a second of heavy breathing.

"Bounce...bounce... and bingo! We have the fucking finale," chuckles Flame.

Hinkle makes a high-pitched, girly squeal. Elizabeth falls, sprawling her large body onto his chest. He grunts, trying to pull air into his lungs.

"Shit, that was exactly one minute and forty-six seconds. That has to be the record for the quickest fuck in all of mankind," bitches Joker.

Elizabeth rolls over and turns out her light.

"Christ! Is she leaving the shitty diaper on the nightstand?" asks Flame in disgust.

"Yup," I confirm, grimacing.

Hinkle flips over; they're back-to-back. "Good night, Mommy. I love you."

"Good night, Pooh Bear. I love you, too. Don't forget to make the coffee in the morning," reminds Elizabeth.

I retract the telescope and put the surveillance equipment inside my coat. Loud snoring comes from Elizabeth and Hinkle.

"I'm going out the front door. If these two assholes wake up, I'll show them the perverted video we just made," I growl.

Joker laughs. "Buzz me in. I'll make sure the lobby is clear."

Flame and I come out of our hiding places. I look at the two sleeping figures in disgust. Not because they like kinky sex. They've hurt people, used their son as a pawn, and caused Jason Cooper to commit suicide. I stalk through the living room with Flame at my side —the security pad is at the right-hand side of the door. I punch in the old code, not giving a shit if the alarm sounds. I'm beyond pissed. The security pad blinks green. I jab the button to the lobby door and walk out, leaving every warm emotion I'd ever felt for Elizabeth in my wake. All I have left is a deep-seated loathing for the woman.

"You're clear, hurry," whispers Joker. "Crank is grabbing the hook."

Flame and I take the stairs at a run. We get to the lobby; it's 1:00 a.m., no one is around. Crank and Joker are hopping into the back seat of the Cayenne. Flame and I jog out of the building. Flame leaps into the driver's side as I jump into the passenger seat.

"Jesus, I need to go home and fuck my woman. I need to make sure I have a cock and a set of balls between my legs after seeing that shit-show," I jest, making light of what we just witnessed.

"Christ, that was bad," chuckles Flame. "I've seen a lot of kinky sex, but that wins the prize."

"Bro, did you have—"

I cut Crank off, glaring at him. "Fuck no. Elizabeth was as vanilla as a woman comes. I don't know what the hell happened to her."

Joker laughs. "I hate to tell you, brother, that didn't just start. She was a goddamn pro."

"Christ." I laugh, pulling the surveillance equipment out of my coat. I hand it to Joker. He cues up the video.

"I knew it was going to be raunchy," chuckles Joker. "But this shit is just fucking nasty."

Crank's eyes are pinned to the video. "Hinkle is a submissive with a mommy fetish. It's not that unusual. I've been to a few underground alternative clubs that got a lot kinkier. I bet there is one or two in Butte Hinkle and Elizabeth frequent. I'll check around. Owners of fetish clubs do not want their shit swung out there."

The kink video and Jason's acknowledgment of his biological father is the dirt we needed to shut Elizabeth down. If she refuses to drop her lawsuits, things will get ugly for Hinkle, Jason, and her. Copies will be sent to Hinkle's father-in-law and wife. Princess will demand a paternity test, and then she'll tear Elizabeth, Hinkle, and the Wheelers apart on the stand. Cookie and I will need to brace ourselves. No doubt I'll be dragged into it.

CHAPTER 28

MY RELIGION — COOKIE

"Take me to church with the beat of your heart. Let me rejoice in the warmth of your skin. Let me bask in the glory of your passion. Your body is the absolution of my sins. Amen...Amen...Amen."

"Okay," I murmur to myself. "Now, the second verse. Your light is my religion. Your body is the Church of my salvation. My soul is yours to keep. I worship at the altar of you. Amen...Amen...Amen." I furrow my brow and strum my guitar, trying to find the right notes. Closing my eyes, I put my nose to my shoulder, and inhale. The scent of High fills my lungs, infusing every cell of me with his light. Just like that, the notes pop into my head.

"Beautiful song, baby, but what are you still doing up? It's two in the morning."

I look up from my beanbag chair. High's looking down at me; worry is in his blues.

I smile, setting my guitar down in its stand. "I couldn't sleep without you," I confess.

Our bed is a cold, vast, empty space without High. *Non*, I'll never sleep in it without him. He is my light...my warmth...my religion.

"Hm," he hums, lifting me into his arms. Then his eyes become soft, staring at his tee on my body. I don't need to say anything. High knows his scent brings me comfort. It chases all my demons away. "Yeah, baby, I get that." He grins. "I'll take you to church with the beat of my heart. You worship at the altar of me. That shit will give your man a goddamn toothache."

I giggle. "Too sicky sweet for you, Amour?"

"Nope, throw a heavy beat onto it."

"Huh, a four chord riff in three-quarter time."

High chuckles, setting me on the bed. "Babe, I have no clue what that means. Dirty it up; it'll take the sweet out of it." He slips his hands under his tee, squeezing my breasts.

I inhale. Glory be to my religion.

"I'm totally down with you worshiping my body. Though, baby, you don't have any sins, so you don't need absolution."

"Amour, hurry," I say breathily. "I want to bask in the glory of your passion."

Certain things set my girly parts on fire. High undressing is one of them. The way he rips his tee over his head. It makes every muscle in his abs ripple. I go right for his belt buckle, quickly undoing it. Then I unbutton his fly, pushing his jeans and boxers down to mid-thigh. I run a light finger down the valley of his cut man V and up the length of his cock. It's long, thick, and so beautiful. A pearl of precum is at the tip; I dart my tongue out, licking it away. I love the way his huge mushroom head peeks out of its sheath at my merest touch. I cup his balls, loving the silky weightiness of them. I run my hands over my man's butt globes. *Oui*, I love my man's ass. *"La perfection."*

High chuckles, "Baby, are you done worshiping my perfect junk?"

I smile. *"Non*, I'll never be done, Amour." I push his jeans and boxers down his long legs, loving the feel of his fuzz-covered cut muscles. I nuzzle my nose into the tuft of hair surrounding his thick cock, dragging in his musk. I fill my lungs with him, thanking all that's holy High came back to me in one piece.

High kicks off his clothes and leaps into bed. "Arms up," he commands. *Woosh*, he rips the tee over my head; it sails across the room. My man hefts me to the middle of the mattress. He reaches over me, opening his nightstand. Without ceremony or flowery words, High slips a ring onto my left finger.

I inhale sharply, staring at my gorgeous engagement ring. It's a platinum treble clef with a two-carat round black diamond in the center. Smaller inlaid pavé black diamonds cover the clef and the band.

Through my tears, I babble in French, "My ring is the most gorgeous thing I've ever seen." I trace High's face, his forehead, the bridge of his straight nose, his eyes, and his laugh lines. I run my thumbs over his soft lips, memorizing every beautiful detail of him with my fingertips. "*Non*," I whisper, staring into his sparkling blues filled with humor. "You are the most gorgeous thing I've ever seen." I place my hand over my man's heart, feeling its steady beat against my palm, reveling in the heat of his skin, glorying in the rise and fall of his chest. "You are my miracle."

"Baby," drawls High, rolling on top of me. He takes most of his weight onto his left forearm; his other hand snakes between us. Gripping his shaft, he runs his head between my folds.

A low groan rumbles through his chest as he wets his tip. "Jesus, so wet and slick for me. I smell your pussy perfume, babe."

My nerves hum with excitement. "Amour, hurry," I beg, my legs circling his lower back. I dig my heels into his cheeks, my encouragement for him to speed up.

High puts his mouth to mine, giving me a heated, hot, wet kiss as he pushes into me inch by inch. He seats himself to the root, lacing our fingers together, then brings my ring to his mouth, placing a soft kiss over it. Then my man gets romantic between the sheets. Staying deep within me, he says, "Never doubt, down to my soul, baby, I will love you beyond my last breath. No matter what life brings or the challenges we face. You are my one and only; my heart beats for you."

My heart beats for you. Oh, god, I'm going to cry. These are my man's wedding vows to me...Chéri Fayette.

I cup his beautiful face. Tears spill down my cheeks. "You are my magnificent miracle, my protector, my lover, and my best friend. Your light fills me to the brim…"

High chuckles, pushing in his cock as deeply as it will go. "I don't think it's my light filling you to the brim, baby."

"Christian," I scold, giving him big eyes. "I'm saying my vows."

"I got it, baby. I'm your religion…your miracle. Now, I'm going to get real religious and fuck your pussy."

And he does, in deliciously long, slow strokes. My walls flutter, my toes curl. I whimper, "Amour," and dig my nails into his back. I breathe out in French, "I love you more than life." Then I repeat his vows: "You are my one and only; my heart beats for you."

High grunts, quickening his hips, giving me what I love: his humongous cock pounding me through my orgasm. And I reciprocate, giving him what he loves: my arms tightly around his neck, my knees at a ninety-degree angle, open as wide as my body will allow, my hips tilted up to take his wild fucking. I should be embarrassed at the loud, wet squish coming from my pussy. I am not; my man loves hearing it. I know this by his growls, snaps, and moans in my ear…by his cock elongating and thickening inside me.

I moan, "Oh, god," and tighten my limbs.

"Fucking go again, milk me," roars High into my neck.

I scream his name, thrash my head, my pussy clenches. High bares his teeth, keeping his cock planted to the root. He holds our pelvises snuggled tight as he spills his seed deep inside me. After, my man doesn't glide. *Non*, he stays deep, giving me tiny humps, which makes my body quiver. *Excellent!*

I take his weight, his face nuzzling my neck. *Oui*, I love that, too. In a few beats, he pulls back, smiling down at me. High chuckles, gently swiping my hair from my face. I'm languid, entirely sated, feeling as if I'm floating on a pillowy cloud of goodness.

"Baby, roll," orders High, moving us to our sides. Face-to-face, he keeps us connected. High pulls the sheet and comforter over us. He places soft kisses over my lids. "Sleep. I'll clean you up in a few."

I can live without most things…though I'd be heartbroken, even babies if that is what God decrees for me. But I could never, not for one day, live without High. I snuggle into his body, place my palm to my man's heart, and drift.

CHAPTER 29

HINKLE'S CONFESSION – HIGH

The sisterhood's phone tree was activated this morning. I swear, as soon as Cookie was caffeinated up, my woman was on the phone with Jewel. Dad and I laughed at Mom, Cookie, and Jewel squealing over our engagement. Jewel called Maggie, Mom called Raven, and it rolled on from there. The biker babes don't mess around when it comes to parties—hence, our engagement bash took the girls approximately five minutes to plan. "It's all set, sister," said Jewel to Cookie excitedly. "Four o'clock, here at the club. Raven had General call Cam. He'll be here with his wife and the band. Beau is bringing Willy, Margo, and Al."

Al, owner of Happy Hot Dog, made his way into our family. Mom and Dad have known him for years. Mom claims Al is Jeff Bridges's double—handsome in a rugged way. I learned from my father Al is a Vietnam vet. According to Dad, unlike Merrill, Al wasn't screwed up by the war. He accepted it as one massive government clusterfuck that three million Americans were dragged into: "Al is a proud American, son. He believes strongly in liberty and freedom for all people. He did what his country asked of him."

After Al was discharged from the service, he and his wife opened a diner on Montana Way in Butte. They opted not to have kids due to the horror stories of Agent Orange—an herbicide and defoliant chemical used by the US military as part of its chemical warfare program. Al's wife dropped dead at fifty-five years old—a brain aneurysm. He sold the restaurant and bought a food truck. "He's a good person, son. Solid in his beliefs."

I hold the door to the club open for Mom, Dad, and Cookie. The game room is filled with our family and friends—the music is playing low, kids are running around, giggling. The adults are talking, drinking, and munching on the snacks the girl posse whipped up. A huge banner is hanging over the bar: CONGRATS, COOKIE AND HIGH! There's a mammoth cake decorated with a picture of Cookie and me sitting on my bike. Horse's wife, White Dove, is the Sinners' self-appointed baker. How she managed to bake that cake in five hours is beyond me.

JJ comes flying up to Cookie, an acoustic guitar twice as big as he is bouncing on his back. My woman found it at the flea market and instantly thought of him—JJ's four years old, brilliant like his mother, and all about the rock star vibe. And like his adopted cousins, JT and Brainiac, the kid can sing. His father, Flame, laughs over him vacillating between wanting to be a Sinners' cowboy or rock star when he grows up.

"I want to thank you for the freakin' guitar, sister. He's only wakened the babies a hundred times over the last week," bitches Princess, grinning at Cookie. Princess isn't pissed; she's just giving Cookie shit.

My woman runs her hand down JJ's crown. "Practice makes perfect."

JJ takes Cookie's and my hands, dragging us to the dance floor. All the kids come flying over; they grab mics and stand behind Brainiac.

Brainiac holds up his beer. The room quiets. "To Cookie and High!" he shouts. "May they ride the open road to happiness!"

The brothers hold up their bottles and glasses. "To Cookie and High!"

"Show us your bling, Cookie," shouts Merrill, laughing.

I bring Cookie's hand to my lips, kiss her ring, and hold it up for everyone to see.

"High outdid Mafia Man, the master of bling!" bellows Tank, guffawing.

I smirk. Mafia Man, Rocky, and Brie helped me design the ring. But I'll keep that to myself. I need the cred more than they do.

"JJ and Uncle Flame have been working on a tune for the two of you," chuckles Brainiac.

"Daddy," whisper-yells JJ, motioning with his hand for his father to come.

"Jesus," breathes out Flame, shaking his head, laughing. He slides onto a chair, sets JJ onto his lap, and positions the guitar. "Cook, we're not you—"

"No one is her," snickers Cam, jogging to the dance floor with his acoustic guitar. "I'll help the two of you out."

Before Flame can get out a thanks and let Cam know what song he needs to play, JJ is shouting, "One and a two and a three."

Flame's left-hand fingers move across the neck; his right-hand fingers are plucking the strings at the bridge. "Strum," he whispers to JJ.

I laugh low, recalling Flame bitching about the YouTube videos he's using to teach JJ and himself how to play. "There are hundreds of them, brother, and half of them are shitty." That's Flame: a badass biker who would do anything in his power to make his wife and kids happy—even learn to play the guitar.

JJ strums, singing, "In My Life," bobbing his head to the beat. The kids jump in, singing in unison.

Cam grins, shaking his head. He picks up the Beatles' song quickly, covering up Flame and JJ's missed notes.

Cookie looks up at me, full of pride. Happy tears stream down her cheeks. "Awesome."

I wipe my woman's tears away and kiss her forehead. Wrapping my arms around Cookie, I sway her to the music. Yeah, our family is fucking awesome.

Flame points to Cam for the acoustic guitar solo. JJ jerks his head up, giving his father a what-the-hell look. Cookie, the brothers, their women, and I laugh; Flame just blew up JJ's solo. I'm sure he'll hear about it. Cam is a boss on the guitar, second only to my woman.

At the end of the song, the kids yell, "We love you, Aunt Cookie and Uncle High!" Then, they're all giggling, thrilled with their performance. JJ's bitching up a storm at his father for giving *his* solo to Cam. Flame snickers, looking at me.

The girl posse does precisely what I knew they'd do: go wild over the kid's concert. That's them; their love knows no boundaries.

Cookie is jumping up and down, devil horns flying. She jabs me with her elbow. "Whistle, Amour."

I chuckle, knowing that my woman can't whistle without putting her fingers into her mouth. And so, I whistle for her.

General sidles up beside me. "Sorry, brother, Pick and Corinne want to meet in the war room before you and Cookie get shitfaced."

I nod. "We'll be right up."

The last three months have been a rocky road for Cookie and me. Cookie's gigs at Callaghan's get millions of hits on all the social media sites. Some of the comments liken her to Van Styles in looks and tone. I had never heard of him, and neither had Cookie. Cam told us the guy was an American rocker from the eighties. "Van had the world by the balls. Phenomenal voice, a boss on the guitar. He was slated to make it big in the industry until he got hooked on drugs. Van couldn't beat the junk. He finally blew out his vocal cords, ending his career."

Cookie's mother, Sylvie, is all over the social media shit. My woman receives weekly whine letters from Sylvie: bottom line, she wants my woman to send her money. Cookie loathes her mother. All of Sylvie's letters now come to me. The woman is a barnacle I need to scrape off. Then there are Elizabeth's threats, a shackle around my neck. I can't marry Cookie until they're resolved.

I had asked Pick to put the Diva Mountain property into Cookie's name. I wanted her to have protection; her home would always be hers. Pick, like General, isn't a fan of Fawn. Pick also knows about Sylvie's letters. Elizabeth, Fawn, and Sylvie made it to Pick's fuck-you list. It's not a list anyone wants to be on. He'll use the law to take them out. If that doesn't work, a bullet is just as good.

I hold Cookie's hand and walk her up to the war room. General and the brothers are at the table. Princess is sitting on Flame's lap next to Pick. The three of them have their heads down, looking over documents.

Christ, this isn't just about the transfer of the land.

I take my seat, settling Cookie onto my lap. Dad takes the chair next to us.

"Pick, you're up," says General.

Pick pushes several documents and a pen toward Cookie and me. "The deed to the cabin and the land have been transferred into Cookie's name."

I glance down at the papers and nod.

"If something unthinkable happens to her, the property will go to Megan as per Cookie's request."

I'm getting ready to tell him that's unacceptable. If the unthinkable happens, the land will go to any children Cookie and I have, not Megan.

Pick holds up his hand palm out. "Let me finish. The day you marry Cookie, everything changes, High. When the two of you have children, it changes again. This is just a security measure Cookie wanted so that her mother won't sue her estate for the land."

"This is fucking ridiculous. Cookie is twenty-two and healthy. Nothing is going to goddamn happen to her."

"Yeah, I know all that. I've also lived through the ridiculous shit that did happen," retorts Pick. He points to Godfather and then to Mac. "And *they* lived through the ridiculous shit that did happen."

Thirty-four years ago, Pick's young, healthy wife was murdered by a stalker outside their Manhattan apartment. Godfather and Mac's wives died of cancer; they too were young. It makes sense why Pick's dotting all the i's and crossing all the t's.

Dad reaches over for the documents. He scans them. "Pick, the changes you referred to when my kids marry—"

"Standard will. When one spouse dies, the other gets all of the assets," he explains.

Cookie pipes up. "*Merci*, but I won't be needing that. When High dies, I'm going with him."

The entire room goes silent; all eyes are on her.

"Baby, that isn't how it works," I murmur, kissing her temple.

"That's how it works for me, Amour." She puts a finger into my chest. "Where you go, I go. We're partners in all things, including death."

"Baby, we'll leave it in God's hands."

Cookie smiles up at me. "All right, High, but he'll agree with me."

"Alrighty then," says Princess airily. "We have that established… we're all dying together."

"Jesus, baby," chuckles Flame.

General sighs, rolling his eyes. "No one is fucking dying. Sign the goddamn papers."

I laugh, handing Cookie the pen. "Sign, here, here, and here, baby."

She kisses my neck, gives me a squeeze, and signs the documents.

"Corinne and I sent the video to Hinkle this morning," announces Pick. "We made it clear if Elizabeth didn't drop her lawsuits against High and Margo, it would be made public. We also informed him we would get a court order for a paternity test."

"The video wasn't legally obtained. Hinkle knows it won't be admissible in court. But"—Princess gives us a shit-eating grin—"thanks to Crank, we have video footage of Elizabeth and Hinkle together in a public place. The two of them were laying a hot one on each other before entering Fantasyland. It's a fetish club in Butte, where Hinkle and Elizabeth have been members for the last twenty-three years."

"Twenty-three fucking years," I say through gritted teeth. *Christ, I want to puke.*

"Yeah, brother. I had a sit-down with the owner. He's not happy his club is being dragged into Hinkle's mess. Fantasyland is upscale, caters to an elite clientele. The membership costs a bundle," says Crank. "To avoid a subpoena, he's willing to cooperate."

Princess's cell vibrates on the table. Flame picks it up. "Hinkle." He jabs the answer and speakerphone button. Then he nods to Princess.

She sits up straighter. In her lawyer's tone of voice, she says, "Mr. Hinkle."

"Hello, Mrs. Hunter. I...ah," Hinkle blows out a breath. "I need to ask you to not make that video public."

"Mr. Hinkle..."

"Please. I love my son, Mrs. Hunter."

"Mr. Hinkle, you allowed Jason Cooper to believe he was your son's father. You allowed Christian Fontaine to pay for your son's care. And, sir, you knew Elizabeth was receiving trust fund disbursements for said care."

"Yes, Mrs. Hunter. When we found out Elizabeth was pregnant, I was in debt with student loans and living on ramen noodles. Elizabeth's father strongly suggested that Elizabeth find a man who could take care of her and the baby. I was against it. I wanted my son. Elizabeth convinced me we could have both and give our son a good life. She started dating Jason and introduced me to her best friend, Virginia. Jason Cooper was a good man, Mrs. Hunter. What we were doing to him messed with my mind."

I bare my teeth, flipping the phone the bird. It's a guilty man's bullshit.

"Mr. Hinkle, it's been twenty-three years—"

"Yes, it has, Mrs. Hunter. I'm tired and unburdening my soul to you with the hope you'll leave my son out of the mess."

"Continue, Mr. Hinkle."

"The Coopers eventually cut Jason off. Elizabeth was enraged because he wouldn't sell his grandfather's property, so she had me file for a divorce. She wanted half of all Jason Cooper's assets. The night of his car accident—"

Princess cuts him off. "It wasn't a car accident, Mr. Hinkle. Jason Cooper committed suicide because of Elizabeth's and your devious, despicable lies. The night Jason took his own life, his father, Tobias, had a fatal myocardial infarction—a heart attack on their living room floor. Their deaths are on you, Mr. Hinkle."

"I"—Hinkle clears his throat—"I was unaware of that, Mrs. Hunter." He blows out a breath. "Jason had found Elizabeth and me in bed. Elizabeth told him she had only married him for his money, and that Jason Jr. was not his son. Jason was devastated…distraught. I followed him to his parents' home to ensure he made it. The next day, Elizabeth received a phone call from Hugo. He informed Elizabeth, Jason had died in a car accident. I was shocked."

I ball my fists, growling low in total revulsion. Jason Cooper went to his childhood home; wrote his father a suicide note and then he left on his suicide mission. At one hundred mph, the man crashed his car, head-on into a goddamn tree. Shocked my ass; Hinkle had to have known Jason killed himself.

"Hugo said if Elizabeth agreed to leave the Coopers alone, Margo would set up a trust fund for our son. Jason didn't have any assets of his own. Mr. Wheeler burned through them. His grandfather's property was willed back to his mother. Elizabeth took the deal. A week later, she told me she was having drinks with Christian Fontaine. You know how that went."

"Mr. Hinkle, you are not innocent."

"No, Mrs. Hunter, I am not blameless, but my son, father-in-law, and wife are. I have told them nearly everything. As you can guess, my wife wants nothing to do with me. My son wants nothing to do with his mother or his grandparents."

"I'm sure that was a difficult conversation, Mr. Hinkle," sneers Princess.

I smirk. If Hinkle's looking for empathy, he's not going to find it here.

"Yes, it was, but I knew I had no choice. You are an excellent attorney, Mrs. Hunter. I've seen you twice in the courtroom. My first employer sent me to Helena to observe you. He thought it would help me to win cases. I remember telling him no one can argue a case like you. He told me I was wrong. Your father, Corbin Michaels, was the king of the courtroom."

All our eyes move to Pick. He rolls his eyes, tipping his chin to the phone.

I snicker, admiration from a dumbass doesn't mean much to Pick.

Hinkle sighs. "I received a call from Fantasyland. The owner has revoked Elizabeth's and my memberships. I'm assuming you have video footage of us there. I made Elizabeth aware you have enough evidence to get her cases thrown out of court. I also informed her I would not lie on the stand. I told her we may be looking at imprisonment, or at least restitution costs. She has withdrawn her lawsuits. I'm taking Jason and going back to Nebraska. I'll text you my address in case you should need my testimony in the future."

"Elizabeth?"

"I don't know her plans, Mrs. Hunter."

"Thank you for letting me know, Mr. Hinkle. Goodbye."

Flame hits the end call button. All of us stay still as statues, staring at Princess's cell, processing.

My father is the first to react. "Pick, should we be concerned Elizabeth will find another attorney and try again?"

"No, there is too much evidence against her. No attorney in their right mind would touch her case."

Cookie puts a hand to my cheek. "Tell me how you're feeling, Amour."

There aren't enough adjectives in the dictionary to describe how I'm feeling—from rage it happened, to overjoyed it's done.

"*Amour*"—Joker rolls his eyes—"is feeling fucking fine, Cook. The bitch is out of his life."

"Jesus, Joker," growls Beau.

"The bitch is gone," drawls Joker. "We have an engagement party going on downstairs. I, for one, would like to get my drunk on and dip my wick into a fine piece of ass."

"Plan your wedding, baby. We're getting hitched." I laugh, kissing Cookie's lips.

CHAPTER 30

WICKEDY OLD WITCH – COOKIE

Phone to my ear, I grab my hobo bag and guitar and throw them over my left shoulder. Then I head out the door. "I'm telling you, sister, if the wickedy old witch calls one more time, I'm going to have Maggie put a voodoo hex on her butt."

"Which wickedy old witch?" Jewel giggles. "Try saying that three times fast."

I move across the lawn as fast as my legs will carry me. "Why?" I furrow my brow. "Is that another American thing?"

"No, it's a tongue twister, babe. Which wickedy old witch, Fawn or Sylvie?"

"They're both wickedy old witches." I giggle. "Fawn."

My eyes hit the new two-story cabin High built us. It's beyond gorgeous: mammoth, with six bedrooms, eight baths, a great room, a playroom, a music room, a huge kitchen, and a man cave for him. The front and back have massive windows, allowing for spectacular views of the mountains and lake. Never did I, Chéri Fayette, dream I'd step inside such a grand home, let alone own it.

"Oh, I'm hitting the FaceTime button. You need to see my porch," I squeal.

A white-toothy handsome smiling faced blond comes onto my screen.

"Joker," I laugh. "You've already seen my porch. In fact, you built my rocking chairs." I tear up a bit. Maggie would say, "Freakin' pregnancy hormones." Not me; I love everything about having High's baby. "Thanks for painting them barn red, Joker."

"Anytime, little mama. How's my nephew treating you this morning?"

I put my hand to my pregnant belly. "Like a badass MMA fighter, using my bladder as his kicking bag."

Joker scrunches up his nose. "Christ, woman, TMI. Tell your old man the boys and I will be at the house in an hour to help him hang the mantel."

I giggle. Our mantel is a giant piece of oak. High and his dad worked on it for a solid month; it turned out beautiful.

"Here's Jewel." I give him an air kiss. He chuckles, giving me one back. Then, Jewel's smiling face comes onto my screen. I flip the camera, showing Jewel my six rustic red rocking chairs.

"Nice, babe. They make the cabin pop. Now tell me what Fawn has done to whip you up."

"The witch called me, saying crap like she wanted to talk mother-to-mother. Fawn had the nerve to ask me about my *will*."

"Your will?"

"Yup, my last will and testament," I confirm. "Megan shared with her mother that the property is in my name. If something happens to me, she'll get it. Seeing the new cabin, Fawn was all over that crap. Then Megan told her it would change when High and I make it legal this Saturday. The witch wanted to know if Megan would be included in the new will."

"What did you say?" bites out Jewel, her anger flaring.

"I told her she needed to speak with High."

Megan didn't come back after the holidays. She took a teaching job in Denver. Our FaceTime calls went from nightly to weekly. High told me he's good with that: "Megan's an adult, baby. It's her decision. But that decision has consequences." He didn't need to tell me those consequences meant she wouldn't be included in our will. Family takes care of family—that goes both ways.

Megan didn't share in the joy of her new brother; she didn't show for the Jack and Jill baby shower the girl posse threw for us, and she didn't become excited when I offered her a room in our new home. That didn't prevent her from showing Fawn the picture I'd sent her of her father, grandfather, and grandmother working on it. It was my way of trying to nudge her in the right direction. But Megan didn't take the hint, and she didn't make an effort to integrate herself into our family. Instead, she chose to live in the civilian world with Fawn and Ed. That didn't stop her from requesting money from her father. I kept my mouth shut. High has a relationship with his daughter. It isn't the relationship he wants, but still, they talk every week and always end with an "I love you."

"You need to tell High and let him handle the witch," grits out Jewel.

On the last day of November, we learned I was pregnant. Dana, Rene, and all the Sinners were thrilled for us. There are no words to express the joy High and I felt. From that day forward, every single morning, night, and between, High kisses my belly, telling his child how much he loves him.

After everything High has gone through, he is finally happy. I won't blow that up by telling him about Fawn. If Fawn has questions about their daughter, she's the one who needs to bring them to High. I'll support him with any decision he makes concerning Megan.

"*Non*. High doesn't need the stress. The inspector is coming the day after tomorrow. Keep your fingers crossed we pass. We want to be in and settled before the baby comes."

Jewel laughs. "The baby isn't due for another month. The cabin will pass inspection. Hey, on a good note, the twinkling firefly lights came yesterday. Joker is going to hang them along the deck. Everything is a go for your wedding on Saturday. Sly and Tank are getting the hog."

High and I will be married at dusk on the club's deck. It's where we shared our first kiss and fell in love. I didn't want a traditional wedding; we're Sinners. I wanted it casual: a hog roast, music, kids running around, and my badass bikers partying in their usual wild way. High invited all the Native Americans. I asked Margo, Willy, Al, and my band, along with their families.

"Okay, sister. I'll be at the club to help make the food."

"Nope, we're all over it. Concentrate on getting into the house."

I run up the steps, rushing to the door. "Thanks. I need to go. I'm late getting to Callaghan's. Love you."

"Stop running," laughs Jewel. "Love you more. Later, babe."

I push open the door and walk into our foyer. The odor of polyurethane assaults my nose. High, Dad, and Mom must be finishing the upstairs floors. *Oui*, I now call Dana "Mom" and Rene "Dad," because they are just as much my parents as they are High's.

Mercy, they need to open all the windows and doors. They'll be high as kites.

"Amour," I shout, moving into our country kitchen. It's gorgeous: oak cabinets, granite countertops, stainless steel appliances, and glossy hardwood floors. My favorite part of the room is the picture window over the farmer's sink; while I'm doing the dishes, I can see the deck, backyard, and lake. I unlock and push up the two smaller windows on each side of the picture window, letting the pine-scented fresh air in.

I've gotten over my need to hit flea markets, tent sales, and "oops" racks at big-box stores. I make *beaucoup* money gigging at Callaghan's, and we don't have the expense of Elizabeth or Fawn hanging over our heads. I still love a deal, but I'm not a penny-pincher anymore.

Elizabeth is entirely gone from our life. Bram Osterhout told Dad the Wheelers were foreclosed on, and Elizabeth was evicted from her apartment. According to Bram, the Wheelers had sold all their belongings to buy a used van. They moved to a small apartment in Helena. Elizabeth and her mother are working as cashiers at Wally World. Mr. Wheeler got a teaching job at Sacred Heart Elementary School.

Needless to say, High and I avoid going to Helena, and we'll never enter Wally World.

I was shocked when Beau told us Margo received a letter from Jason. Jason and Lewis are in therapy, getting the help they need to heal. He apologized for his mother and father's deceit. Jason also thanked her for supporting him, but he didn't want the money left in his trust fund. His dad, Lewis Hinkle, is a lawyer at a firm in Beatrice, Nebraska, advocating for farmers. Jason is working on his grandfather's small dairy farm. He's back in college, studying agriculture, and living with his dad.

Willy was correct: Margo does have a heart the size of Montana. She sent Jason a check for two hundred and fifty thousand dollars, along with a picture of Jason Sr. smiling down at a newborn baby he thought was his son.

My man said it was bullshit; Margo should have kept her money. Maggie agreed: "Tigers don't change their stripes, Cookie. Jason had an agenda for writing the letter." Jewel agreed with Maggie: "Hinkle, Elizabeth, and Jason were cohorts. Jason knew his parents were trying to rip off High and Margo." Jillian said, "Corrie showed me the kink video. Nasty. Hinkle and Elizabeth are two peas in a pod. Twenty-three years of getting their freak on, and then they suddenly stop? Bullshit. They're together, Cookie."

I don't know if Elizabeth, Jason, and Lewis turned over a new leaf. I'm just glad they're gone from our lives.

High comes to the top of the landing; a white mask is covering his nose and mouth. "Baby, get your ass outside, now!"

When the chemicals come out, I'm not allowed inside our new home.

My eyes are pinned to his bare chest, his muscles, and tatts. Lord, he is beautiful! High romanced me between the sheets this morning, but...*Non, there isn't time. I need to get my butt to Callaghan's.*

I smile up at my man like I'm his genius partner taking his back. "Amour, I opened the windows in the kitchen for you."

He chuckles, mirth dances in his sky-blue eyes. "Carry your ass outside. I'll be there in two seconds to take you to Callaghan's."

My man is beautiful, sexy, and bossy.

CHAPTER 31

BOUND BY LOVE – HIGH

"I'll be back," I yell over my shoulder to Mom and Dad. Then, I jog down the stairs, through our kitchen, and out the door. My cock goes solid seeing my woman in her pink halter top and low-rise short shorts, her tanned, pregnant belly on full display. Her long blonde hair is piled high atop her head.

In thirty days, Christian Rene Fontaine Jr. will be born. Cookie and I decided on a home birth—we've done the classes with Polly. Now it's all about getting our new cabin done in time.

Dad and I are working from sunrise well into the night, sanding, staining, and polying the wood. Mom jumped in to help when I kicked Cookie out. I don't give a shit if we're "partners" in all things—I don't want her breathing in goddamn chemicals.

Yesterday I found her in the backyard, her iPhone in one hand, a can of barn red spray paint in the other. She was trying to figure out where the posts needed to go for our son's fenced-in play yard. *Damn YouTube!* My woman smiled up at me so fucking proudly, I couldn't stay pissed. I took the spray paint away from her and lied. "JJ just called, baby. He wants you to make him éclairs." Cookie beat feet into our old cabin. When it comes to the Sinners' kids, no request is too large. Dad laughed. He knew JJ didn't call. Clue in, spray paint is a chemical.

I give Cookie a soft kiss. Then, I put my lips to her belly, knowing I'm going to feel my son's foot against my lips. "Love you, baby boy." As I predicted, my son gives me a light kick to my kisser. I choose to think of it as his "I love you back." It happens every time.

My relationship with Cookie and our unborn son is entirely opposite from what I had with Fawn. I can probably count on one hand the number of times I touched Fawn's pregnant belly. Sex was off-limits by Fawn's fourth month: she didn't enjoy it, and I didn't push. I was working at the logging camp when Megan was born. I am slightly screwed up over it: I feel more for my unborn son than I do my daughter. Parents are supposed to love their children equally.

Dad picked up on my mood; we talked. "Christian, you were in a different place in your life. Chéri loves you. Christ, son, she wrote a song about you being her religion...her light." Then he chuckled, "She's going with you when you die. It's not funny, but lord, she meant it."

Yeah, she did, and it's reciprocated. I won't live without my woman.

"Chéri feeling the way she does is a love that binds you, her, and your child." Then he laid it out: "From what you told me, Fawn didn't do anything to cultivate your love for Megan. Megan was ten when Fawn took her. She was old enough to decide whether she wanted a relationship with you. Megan chose to cut you out of her life. Then she pops back into it ten years later and expects you to forgive and forget." He sighed. "The love you have for your daughter is good enough. You have nothing to feel guilty over."

Dad was entirely correct: Fawn, Megan, and I were bound by obligation. Cookie, any babies we have, and I are bound by love.

"Bike or truck, baby?"

"Bike, Amour."

I didn't need to ask; Cookie loves riding bitch. I bungee cord Cookie's guitar to the saddlebags, swing my leg over, and hold out my arm. Cookie uses my forearm and shoulder to heft her body onto my bike. I chuckle. My woman is all baby and boobs. She snuggles her pregnant belly into my back, gripping the sides of my tee. My baby's foot thumps my lower spine. I reach around and pull her ass closer to me. Then, I pop the clutch, and we're off.

Twenty minutes later, we're pulling into Callaghan's parking lot. I catch sight of a slim guy parked across the street at Pony Market. He appears to be fiddling with the choke on his dirt bike, but that isn't what piques my curiosity. The guy has a skullcap on with a high-powered rifle slung over his shoulder. It's 9:00 a.m. and eighty degrees in the shade. Besides that, all the big game is out of season. If he's still there, I'll check him out after I drop off Cookie.

I flick two fingers at General, Pick, Godfather, and Kelley. They're working on the inside of Sinners Beauty Salon. Honeypot is scheduled to graduate from beauty school at the end of September. Wolfe has half his crew working on Sinners Biker Babe Boutique; the other half is at the Native American Village, finishing the Reservation School's replication.

I park in front of Callaghan's and clock the band's vehicles pulling in behind us. Cam leaps out of his truck. He struts over to us, giving me a fist bump.

"High," yells Guard Dog. He's with Maggie's father, Mac. "We're heading to your place to check the security feed and help hang the mantel."

"I'll be there after I settle Cookie."

Mac tips his chin up in acknowledgment. They swing their legs over their bikes. Their Harleys rumble, and then they're off, heading up the mountain.

"If you need to take off, I'll get Little Bit set up," says Cam.

I chuckle, helping Cookie off my bike. "Nope." I grab her guitar and walk her up the stairs. "Don't play the electric guitar, baby. I don't want the loud vibrations next to our kid's head."

"Okay, Amour."

Cam and the guys chuckle, following us inside.

"And no running or bouncing around the stage, babe. CJ doesn't need to be shaken up."

"All right, Amour."

Rex smiles. "Mornin'. What'll it be today, little mama? Decaf iced coffee or decaf iced tea?"

"You'd better ask High," laughs Lex. He takes Cookie's guitar from me and moves toward the stage.

"Fuck you, smart-ass." I grin. "Evian on the rocks with a twist of lemon, Rex."

"Yeah, that's what we thought," snickers Woody, following Lex.

"Evian is excellent water, dude," says Cam, heading back toward the stage. "A French nobleman discovered it during the Revolutionary War. The French thought it held curative and restorative powers."

"How in the hell do you know that shit?" asks Max on his heels.

"It's on the Evian website," snickers Cam.

"You're such a nerd," says Max. "Who the hell looks up a water's website?"

Cookie giggles.

I grin, walking her up the stage steps. Then I give her and her belly a chaste kiss. "I'll be back to pick you up at one. Don't push it, baby. Take a break between songs."

"I will, Amour."

"Cam, any problems, call my cell."

"I will, *Amour*." He laughs, air-kissing me.

"Smart-ass," I chuckle, heading out the door.

I glance over to where I saw the guy on the dirt bike. He's gone. I chalk it up to a hunter planning to hunt out of season. It's not unusual; people who need to feed their families don't give a shit about government regulations. I start my bike, pop the clutch, and ride back up the mountain.

CHAPTER 32

I WANT TO SEE THE STARS — COOKIE

Mic to my mouth, I try to belt out David Guetta, "Titanium." For some reason, I can't get enough air into my lungs to hold the notes. Frustrated, I throw up my arm, stopping the band.

I run my palms over my taut belly, blowing out a breath. *Lord, what is happening to me?* I've sung this song a thousand times; it should be a piece of cake.

I inhale a deep breath, hold it for the count of three, and exhale. Then, I do it again, trying to expand my lungs. The pain in my lower back intensifies—it started two hours ago, and it won't quit. I put my hands on my hips, bending side-to-side.

"Little Bit, are you all right?" asks Cam, all kinds of concerned. He struts over and puts a hand on my shoulder. "You're trying too hard."

Non, that's not it. My back is killing me from standing. This isn't just my bread and butter; it's the band's, too. I need to do my part—suck it up and sing the damn song.

"Cookie, we don't need to do this song," says Lex. "Big deal it was requested on Facebook. We'll choose another one from the list. The audience won't give a shit."

I put two fingers to my left temple and rub in circles. Good lord, my head is starting to throb. Fatigue washes over me. I'd love to go home, lay on our bed, and relax to one of High's body massages. So incredibly relaxing. *Buck up, rocker chick, and stop bellyaching. Get it done.* I inhale again and blow out another breath.

Rex jogs up the steps, handing me my water. "Cookie, this isn't a good idea. You've been at it for two hours, and you're whipped."

I take a sip of the water. "I'm okay." I smile at Rex. "I just need a minute. Rex, will you stretch out my lower back?"

He looks at Cam and then down at me. "What's wrong with your back?"

"I'm just tight," I assure. "I need to make room for my lungs to expand."

He puts his hands to my lower back, massaging, not stretching. "I think we should call it a wrap for today. I'll call High."

"*Non*, I'm fine, Rex." I take another sip of my water, handing him the glass. "Let's take it from the top."

"This is fucking bullshit, Cam," he barks, walking away.

I close my eyes and bob my head, swaying to the beat. *You can do this. Let the music take you on a ride.* I open my mouth and start singing. When I get to the hook, I take a deep breath, pushing out the lyrics."

POW!...SMASH! The picture window blows out, sending missiles of glass into the dining room.

A searing pain hits my neck; it's as if someone branded me with a hot poker. I grab the left side of my neck and sway on my feet, trying to stay upright. Warm, sticky blood seeps through my fingers, covering my hand, running down my forearm, dripping off my elbow. My stomach tightens; my pussy cramps. I retch and moan, going to my knees. Cam, Woody, Lex, Max, and Rex are screaming something at me. I have no clue what they're saying. *High...*I need to get to High. I let go of my neck. Blood drenches my halter top—metallic iron assaults my nose. I ignore it and get up on all fours, trying to crawl my way to the stairs.

POW!...POW!...POW!

From out of nowhere, Cam is on me, covering me with his body, his tee to my neck.

I fight him, slapping at him. My blood spatters across his face and chest.

"Let me go! Amour! Amour! Amour!" I screech. Then, pain rips through my stomach. Warm water gushes between my legs, soaking my shorts. I groan, digging my nails into Cam's back.

POW!...POW!...POW! Wood splinters, flying through the air in all directions, raining down on Cam's back and head. He covers me, protecting me with his body.

"She's been hit...left neck...too much blood!" screams Cam. "Her fucking water just broke. We need to get her out of here!"

Woody, Max, and Lex crawl to us on their bellies. They grab Cam and me. Slipping and sliding in my bodily fluids, they grunt and swear, dragging us behind one of the large speakers.

"Oh, my fucking god," shrieks Woody, his wide eyes pinned on me.

"Keep your shit tight, Woody," growls Cam. "Fucking help me!"

"Stay down! I count one asshole," bellows Rex.

Rad-da-tat-tat-tat...Rad-da-tat-tat-tat...Rad-da-tat-tat-tat!

The sound is deafening, my head is fuzzy, I can't think.

"Come on, you motherfucker, show yourself! You chickenshit bastard," yells Rex.

POW!...POW!...POW!

The cymbal makes a loud ting; it's a Frisbee, sailing above our heads.

"Rex, do you see any of the Sinners?" yells Cam.

I groan, my belly tightens, my pussy cramps.

"Time her goddamn contractions," Cam orders Max, and then he demands Lex's tee. "Woody, goddamnit, breathe with her."

Lex yanks off his tee and puts it against the saturated one covering my neck.

"Breathe with me, Cookie!" demands Woody. I stare up at him. Even with my brain hazy, I recognize Woody is basically hyperventilating; he's breathing so fast.

"General, the boys, and the Native Americans are shooting their way over here!" yells Rex back.

Repeated *Rad-da-tat-tat-tat!* *Rad-da-tat-tat-tat!* comes from outside. High…that's High's rifle. My mind clears a bit, and I fight to get free. "Amour! Amour! Amour, I'm here!"

"Little Bit, fucking stay still," shouts Cam into my face, putting more pressure on my neck. "Rex, the Sinners, and the Native Americans are trying to clear a path for us. High isn't out there, sweetheart."

I look up at Cam and furrow my brow; tears leak from my eyes, running down my temples. High has to be out there; I need him…our baby needs him. I turn my head and quit fighting. High is going to stay on earth with his parents and daughter, the way it should be. Our baby needs to stay with him. I close my eyes. The memory of me freezing to death on the grate filters into my mind. I think of the stars…so many beautiful, glittering stars.

"I want to see the stars before I go," I whisper to God.

"*No—no—no!* Goddamnit, Cam!" yells Max. "Cookie, don't you fucking give up. High is on his way."

A door bangs open; people are rushing into the bar. They're shouting things I can't understand. They need to calm down so I can hear them.

"Cookie, it's me, Pick. We're going to Urgent Care."

I force open my heavily lidded eyes and stare into his golden orbs. It's déjà vu. Pick and I have been here before. "I want to see the stars before I go."

Pick is running with me in his arms. I want to tell him to stop running; it hurts my stomach and neck. But I can't get my words out.

"I fucking told you once before, Cookie: God does not want you until you're old and gray. Do you hear me, Chéri?! There are no goddamn stars out, so you can't die!" shouts Pick, leaping into a truck.

All four doors of the truck slam shut simultaneously. Kelley is at the wheel.

General is sitting beside him, yelling at someone to lock down Pony, the Sinners Compound, and the Reservation. "Jewel, keep your eyes on the goddamn monitors, and find High! Get his ass to Urgent Care!"

Jewel is my beautiful best friend, my chosen sister. Her face comes into my mind, alight with happiness. She held me, laughing and crying. "I'm going to be an aunt," she squealed into the night. She held out her arm for High. His deep, rumbling laughter washes over me; he came to us, wrapping us up in his strong arms.

CJ needs to live for his father, his aunt, and his grandparents. He needs to experience all the joy and love the Sinners will bestow on him. He needs to live in our big house, go to school, and make lots of friends.

"Cookie, it's Godfather. Open your eyes, Cookie," he demands, running his hand down my hair.

I try, I really do, but my lids are too heavy.

I groan weakly; the pain tears through my stomach and pussy.

"It's a contraction, Cookie. Breathe with me, lass," commands Godfather. "In through your nose and out through your mouth."

I pray to High's light to give me the strength to birth our son, for him, Jewel, Mom, and Dad. Then I'll go to Heaven and wait for them to join me. I concentrate on High's beautiful face and draw in a breath. I blow it out and do it again.

"Good, lass, keep doing it," encourages Godfather.

My pain recedes, and the truck lurches to the left. It comes to a jarring halt. The back door is whipped open.

"Give her to me," demands Patriot. I feel my body being lifted, and then I'm cradled in strong arms. Someone is pressing hard against my neck.

I put my nose to Patriot's pit, inhaling. He smells like a weird combination of antiseptic, Downy, spice, and his unique maleness.

I find the strength to mumble in French, "Not Amour."

He says in French while running, "You'll smell your man's stink as soon as he gets here."

Pick growls, "Let her fucking smell you if it keeps her alive."

I keep my nose buried into him. It doesn't bring me the comfort High's scent does, but it keeps me connected to the living until High gets here. *Hurry, Amour!*

CHAPTER 33

COOKIE'S IN LABOR – HIGH

Joker, Guard Dog, Mac, Dad, and I heft the heavy-as-hell slab of oak. We're carrying it into the cabin when all of our cells start buzzing with texts and calls.

"Keep going," commands Mac, grunting. "Whoever it is needs to wait."

We shuffle our way over to the fireplace. "One, two, three, lift!" bellows Dad. We do; the mantel hits the mounts with a thud. "Anchor her down, Christian."

I quickly tighten down the bolts to the oak mantel. We all step back, blowing out our breath. It looks fantastic.

I pull my phone from my pocket: twenty missed calls, ten missed messages. I jab the message icon. I can't believe what I'm reading.

> General: Under attack... Sniper's hitting Callaghan's Bar. Lockdown Pony, Sinners Compound, and the Reservation. All brothers on their bikes!

General: Cookie's been wounded. In route to
Urgent Care. Find High!

Adrenaline speeds through my bloodstream. I sprint out the front door, shouting, "Get my parents to the compound!"

I leap onto my bike without a weapon, throat mic, or earpiece. *Get to your woman*, thunders through my brain. I peel out; dirt flies in my wake. When I get to Diva Mountain Road, I bring the bike up to 140 mph and lean low over the tank. Joker is riding next to me. His lips are moving, he has his earpiece in, he's talking to someone via his throat mic. Joker tilts his chin up and twists his throttle, pulling ahead of me.

Fuck! It's his way of telling me we need to go faster. I twist the throttle, bringing my bike up to 160 mph, heedless of the warm wind whipping my face, stinging my eyes. I beg God to save my woman and child, vowing to kill the motherfucker who did this to them.

We fly through the first roadblocks. Sinners, Cowboys, and Native Americans have locked down Pony. I lean to the left, needing to put my foot down so I don't wipe out. I lay my bike down in front of Urgent Care and sprint up the stairs.

"Cookie!" I shout, running through the waiting room. I clock the band standing outside a curtain; they're covered from head to toe in blood. All their faces are streaked with tears. It's a frenzy behind the curtain: Patriot is shouting orders to his grandfathers and Kelley. "Cut off her clothes, attach the monitor, take her vitals, start two IVs. Hang the saline and blood. Keep talking to her, Papa Pick!"

I whip back the curtain, taking in the scene. Kelley is cutting off Cookie's clothes. Pick has my woman in some sort of head embrace, speaking to her in French.

General is taking her vitals: "70/40, pulse 140 and irregular." He grabs a wand, running it over Cookie's baby bump. A fast *swish swish swish* fills the room. "Baby's heart rate is 240."

I want to ask where the hell Polly, Doc, and the nurses are. There's no time. Godfather is inserting a needle into the crook of Cookie's arm. Patriot is filling a syringe with a clear liquid. He has a sterile tray to his side, ready for suturing. They look as if they've been through a massacre: their faces, hands, and clothes are covered in blood...my woman's blood.

I skirt around everyone, getting to the head of the stretcher. No one notices me; they're working like madmen. I don't ask questions, and I can't see my woman's face. Pick's large chest is blocking my view. I lean down, whispering onto her crown, "I'm here, baby." It's the only part of her I can get to. Pick is covering her with his chest.

Pick's head jerks up. That's when I clock him holding pressure to Cookie's neck. The gauze is saturated crimson. "Take my place. I'll hook up the fetal monitor."

"Fuck, Pick, don't move," bellows Godfather. "Three, two, one, stick." Cookie groans as he jabs another needle into her arm.

"We have another contraction coming," warns Kelley.

Fuck, she's in labor a month early!

"Goddamnit," growls Godfather, quickly filling tubes with her blood.

"Time?!" asks Patriot.

"Five minutes apart," says Kelley, cutting off her shorts.

Cookie groans loudly, her belly ripples, becoming a solid mass. She tries to twist away from them. Blood drips from her neck, puddling onto the floor.

"Fucking hold her, Pick," yells Godfather. "I need to get these needles taped down."

Pick drops back over her, murmuring in French for her to stay still.

I put my arm around Pick's head. Temple-to-temple, I murmur into Cookie's ear. "Love you, baby. Breathe with me." I extend my arm, putting my palm onto her hard baby bump. Polly taught me I could judge her contractions by the feel of her belly—it's peaking. "Breathe in...one, two, three. And blow out...one, two, three." I rub gentle circles onto her baby bump. She calms at the sound of my voice and my touch. I take that as a sign she's aware I'm here with her. Cookie's belly softens. "Okay, baby, that one is over," I murmur, kissing her below her ear. The taste of her metallic blood hits my tongue. I lift my head a fraction; Godfather has the saline and blood dripping at a fast pace.

"I need to get in there," orders Patriot. "Cookie's jugular vein was nicked. I need to inject her with the snake venom. Turn her head, Pick, and hold her still."

Jesus Christ, snake venom!

"Baby, turn your head into Pick's chest," I murmur, helping her.

Patriot lifts Pick's hand; blood pours from her gaping wound. Patriot quickly swabs her neck with Betadine. Cookie moans, trying to move away. I hold her head tightly to Pick's chest, watching Patriot stick the needle into her wound. My woman screams weakly into Pick. Every goddamn nerve in my body buzzes, causing my hands to shake. *Fucking Christ!*

"Done," says Patriot, putting large pads of gauze over the wound. He moves Pick's hand. "Apply pressure."

Another contraction comes. Cookie groans louder this time; her breathing accelerates into short, rapid pants. She grunts and bears down, pushing.

Again I order her to breathe with me. I massage her belly, breathing a sigh of relief when the contraction ends. This one was stronger and longer in duration.

Pick straightens. I move my hand over his. He slides his hand out, and I apply pressure. We do a dance; he shifts to the right, I shuffle around the gurney, taking his place.

"Papa Sean, you're with me. Uncle Kelley, get someone to take her labs to Butte. Papa Pick, get the incubator ready just in case. Papa Gavin, we need to clean her up to see if she was hit anywhere else."

"She wasn't," yells Cam outside the curtain. "Only her neck."

"Her water broke," adds Woody in a shaky voice.

"They fucking figured that out, Woody," barks Max, irritated as hell.

The curtain whips open. Dad is standing beside Liam, looking shocked.

Liam has a phone to his ear, unfazed. He strolls over and grabs a sheet, snapping it open. Without missing a word of his phone call, he spreads it out over Cookie's naked body. Holding the cell between his shoulder and ear, he starts to untie my woman's blood-stained Chucks.

"Yeah, Lee. Cookie's breathing. She's in full-blown labor." He pauses. "No, Polly needs to go to the compound. Bluebird is already at the Reservation. Doc comes here as a precaution." Pause. "Nope, we sent the nurses home when the shooting started. They have kids. We didn't want them in the middle of a goddamn war." Another pause. "Yeah, Da, Uncle Kelley, and Uncle Sean are here with Tommy. I'll stay here and keep connected by phone." Pause. "Everything is under control. The boys are on their bikes. We'll have the fucker by nightfall." He massages Cookie's foot for a few beats and then leans down, kissing her toes. Liam moves to her other sneaker.

A tiny, weak giggle comes from my woman. The blood and saline have perked her up.

"Da, IV," growls Liam, tipping his head toward the almost-spent bags of saline and blood.

I kiss Cookie's lips. "You're going to be all right, baby. Bossy badass Liam is taking charge."

"Shite," breathes out Godfather, moving quickly to change out the bags.

"Yeah," Liam sighs. "Ten shell casings were found on the roof of the motel. The dirt bike was ditched on the side of the road ten miles outside of Pony. The fucker looks like he's heading toward Butte. Jewel's reviewing the security footage. Hold on, Lee." He looks at my woman's belly and then to me. "High, contraction. Rene, that fetal monitor isn't going to put itself on."

Dad picks up the belt, examining the small device attached to it. That gets another giggle from Cookie. He quickly attaches it to Cookie's belly. Fast *swish swish swish* emanates from a machine behind him.

She groans, "Oh, god, Amour," digging her nails into my arm. She pants into my ear, "My pussy hurts." Then she grunts, bearing down weakly.

I hold her tightly, keeping one hand on her neck. The other I put at the top of her baby bump, waiting to help my son down his mother's birth canal. "Deep breath and push CJ out, baby," I encourage. Cookie grunts, pushing. I push gently, hoping like hell it will work. Once again, the contraction recedes, and Cookie blows out a breath.

I kiss her lips. "You're doing great. Love you, baby."

A tear slips down her temple. "I thought I was going to Heaven without you."

I grin onto her lips. "No fucking way you or CJ are going anywhere without me."

"High, look and see where we're at down there," demands Patriot. "I need to button up her wound."

Jesus Christ, this isn't the birth Cookie and I had planned. We wanted it to be all about us and CJ.

"Amour," shrills Cookie, gripping my arm. "CJ's coming."

Patriot replaces his hand with mine at Cookie's neck. Dad takes my place, putting his arm beneath Cookie's shoulders, helping her to push. I sprint to the bottom of the stretcher. I'm just in time to catch my son's tiny head. I free his shoulders. Cookie grunts and screams as she gives one last big push: CJ slips into my arms. He scrunches up his tiny nose, furrows his brow, and wails.

I chuckle, putting my lips to his forehead. "Daddy has you, son. I will always have you and Mommy."

Cookie's chest is caked with dried blood. I don't give a shit; I lay our son on her chest. She puts her hand on his tiny butt, smiling up at me. The Sinners turn their backs to us, giving us a minute of privacy.

Tears drip down my cheeks. I kiss my woman's lips. "He's so fucking beautiful, baby."

"Of course he is, Amour." She says it as if she didn't have a doubt in the world. "CJ is a mini-me of you. Pure perfection."

Joker snorts and then breaks out in loud laughter from behind the curtain.

"Really, asshole?" I growl. "You ruined our goddamn moment."

"Get Cookie and the baby settled," orders Joker. "I need a moment with you, brother."

I kiss Cookie's lips, my baby's head, and get to work cleaning them up.

~

An hour later, I'm on the stretcher at Sinners Urgent Care, Cookie to my chest, our baby to her tit. My woman is passed out.

I smile down at my son. He has his tiny fingers wrapped around my pinky, sucking on his mother's nipple.

I can't relax; I'm strung tight over everything that happened this morning. Christ, I came close to losing them today. If it weren't for General, Godfather, Pick, Kelley, Rex, Cam, and the guys, my family wouldn't be breathing. I still can't believe Patriot used snake venom to seal up my woman's jugular. He learned about it after Godfather took a bullet in his chest, compliments of the Italian Mafia. The surgeon used snake venom to stop the bleeding. "It's great shit, brother. It works fucking fast," he laughed.

After I cut CJ's cord, Doc showed up and checked him over: six pounds, six ounces, and thirteen inches tall with a perfect Apgar score. "Hallelujah!" Cookie proclaimed proudly; she knew he was perfect. "He's Amour—his nose, his hair, his smile, and his eyes are all High's." Joker pretended to puke, and then he laughed. Dad chuckled, taking CJ. He swaddled him in his tee. "Go concentrate on Chéri, son. I have my grandson." Then he pulled out his phone, snapped a picture of CJ, and sent it to Mom.

Patriot put twenty-four sutures into Cookie's neck. Each stitch he made, I planned a new torture for the fucker who hurt her. Pick gave me his tee; I took off my boxers and dressed Cookie in them.

Cookie looked up at Pick, his tee to her nose. Her eyes brimmed with tears. "You don't smell like High. But I like it. I love you, Pick."

He chuckled, kissing her forehead. "I love you, too, Cookie."

"Hey, no love for me?" Patriot widened his eyes, pretending to be offended. His way of trying to lighten the mood. "You didn't like my odoriferous perfume."

Cookie scrunched up her nose. "I didn't like the antiseptic smell."

He rolled his eyes, bitching about how he's a doctor, antiseptic can't be helped. "I'll work out. After, you can stick your pretty little nose in my pit. You'll be a hummingbird smothering yourself in my sweet nectar."

Liam laughed. "Cookie, even Maggie's eyes water after he works out. The boy emits toxic fumes."

That got Cookie to giggle.

I kicked everyone out, settled Cookie against my chest, and helped CJ latch on to her nipple. "Rest, baby. I have you and CJ."

Entirely exhausted, she shut her eyes and fell asleep.

I look down at my son, happily feasting on his mother. "Baby boy, you need to burp and change tits." I remove my pinky from his tiny hand, using it to release his suction. Cookie doesn't even stir. "Mommy is out. We're on our own, son." I tip him up, rubbing his tiny back. He makes a loud belch.

Joker chuckles, separating the curtain. He struts in and drops down on the chair. Breastfeeding isn't a big deal to the Sinners. Our women whip out their tits just like they would a bottle.

I settle CJ on my forearm and pull down the tee. Then, I rub CJ's tiny lips over his mother's nipple. He latches on, sucking vigorously.

Joker's eyes go to Cookie. "Are you sure she's all right, brother? Cookie didn't move..."

"Yeah, Joke. She's just exhausted."

He nods, running a hand down his face. "I fucking hate this. I wanted to give you time to enjoy being a dad."

"I appreciate that, brother. But you didn't do this shit. I need to take out the asshole who hurt my woman."

"Yeah, I get that. Jewel called me tweaking. Fawn called Cookie this morning to talk 'mother-to-mother.'"

I furrow my brow. "What the hell? Mother-to-mother?"

"Yeah, she asked Cookie about her *will*. She wanted to know where Megan stood after the two of you got married. Cookie told her she'd need to speak with you."

My hand trembles against my son's tiny head. "That goddamn woman is dead," I say through gritted teeth. "Fawn hired a fucking hitman to take out my woman. The asshole I told you about, on the dirt bike."

"High, calm, brother. You have CJ to his mother's tit. We don't know if Fawn is involved. Cookie's mother, Sylvie, wrote her a threatening letter."

"Sylvie is a goddamn drug addict, brother. Where in the hell would she get the green to pay a hitman?"

"Drug addicts can be super creative," Joker reminds me. "Sylvie can't be discounted. Hinkle, Jason, Elizabeth, and the Wheelers need to be considered. And there is the possibility it was a crazy fan who got pissed off about something."

I grab my phone off the bedside stand. Then I jab Fawn's number, waving Joker to come closer. I can't put it on speaker; it'll awaken Cookie.

"Hello, High," says Fawn in her usual sarcastic way.

"Where the hell are you?" I murmur low.

"Where am I? In Denver, packing to move to our new townhouse. Not that it's any of your business. And why are you whispering?"

I ignore her question and ask one of my own: "Did you call Cookie this morning and ask her about her goddamn will?"

"Yes, High, I did. I meant to call you this afternoon but got busy. With the new baby coming, and your pending marriage, I needed to know if you'd considered Megan in your plans. We haven't been on the same page for a long time. I know you and Cookie were upset when she decided to come back to Denver. But Megan is still your daughter, High. Given the business you're in, it's important that Megan shares the assets equally with her brother."

Joker rolls his eyes, flipping off the phone.

"Fawn, a hitman tried to take out Cookie today."

"What?! Oh, my god, was she hurt? Is the baby all right, High? Megan…oh my god, Megan is going to go out of her mind."

I blow out a breath. Fawn is a bitch, but she's not faking her concern. Cross her off the list.

"Is Meg with you, Fawn?"

"No," she says in a wavery voice. "She's at Tarjay, shopping for baby clothes to send Cookie, from us. Meg was upset she missed the baby shower. High, you're not telling me something."

"Tell Megan I'll call her tomorrow, Fawn." I hit the end call button. "It's not them, brother."

"Yeah, I got that."

My phone buzzes. I look at the caller ID, showing Joker.

"Maggie?"

I hit the answer button. "Uncle High," whispers Keeley.

"Yeah, sweetheart, you have me."

"Aunt Jewel knows who hurt Aunt Cookie," sniffs Keeley. "She's crying. Papa Beau and Uncle Joker aren't here…"

"Keeley, give me the phone," whisper-yells JT in the background. "I told you not to call Uncle High. He's taking care of Aunt Cookie and the baby. I need to call Uncle Liam. He's in charge!"

My eyes go to Joker. He stands, jabbing a number into his phone. "Come on, fucking pick up, Jewel," he murmurs, walking away.

"Keeley, who hurt Aunt Cookie?" I coo, "Talk to me, sweetheart, tell me who hurt Aunt Cookie."

"Uncle High, we have a situation here. Nothing for you to worry about. I have it handled," assures JT in his four-year-old badass way.

Christ, no!

"JT," I growl. "Put Aunt Jewel on."

"Love you. Later." And the line goes dead.

Fuck me! I jab the button for Liam. My call goes to voicemail.

Two seconds later, he strolls into our bay, eyes on me, phone to his ear. Nodding, he says into the phone, "JT, I'll be at the club in an hour." Pause. "Love you, too, baby boy. Later."

"Who?!" I bark, my eyes pinned on him.

"I don't have all the intel yet, brother. Jewel is a goddamn mess. Dev, Sean, and AJ are working on it. Get Cookie and the baby ready to roll. We're taking them to the club until this shit is sorted out."

I nod, knowing whatever Jewel found out has everyone on full alert.

CHAPTER 34

SYLVIE'S SHOCKING INTEL – HIGH

The vibe in the war room is electric, zapping with the brothers' rage. An attack on one of our women is the ultimate offense, punishable by a painful death. Dad and I drop down onto our seats.

General's eyes move to me. "Are Cookie and the baby settled?"

"Yeah, Jewel and Mom are with them."

The last four hours have been a whirlwind of activity. Getting Cookie and the baby to Sinners' compound was a pain in the ass. We had no clue where the shooter was or if he had eyes on us. Adding to our misery, everything we purchased for the baby was still in boxes at our new cabin. Joker, General, Pick, Flame, and I went to our home to grab everything Cookie and the baby needed. Mom made a list, which turned out to be a goddamn nightmare: CJ's clothes, receiving blankets, diapers, wipes, butt cream, the Pack 'n Play, and the car seat. Then there was the shit for Cookie: peri-pads, breast pads, and... nipple cream? I felt like the biggest dunce that ever lived. I had a wife and child before Cookie, and I knew nothing. The reality of it: I am a new father and husband...almost-husband. I need to rectify that ASAP.

General chuckled, "Peri-pads are women's rags."

We didn't have any of those; we had tampons.

Pick looked at me like I had two heads. "Brother, you can't stick a tampon up your woman's pussy after she just pushed out a baby. Ouch."

Flame tossed his arm over my shoulder, examining the list. "We have rags leftover from the triplets. There are enough to get you through the next few days. Corrie has extra titty pads and a new jar of nipple cream. We're good, brother." I pointed to maternity panties and nursing bras. He smirked. "Period panties, brother. Nursing bras have flaps."

Right, we didn't have any of that shit either. I grabbed all my boxers, tees, and Cookie's bras; they would need to do. Once we got back to the club, we needed to rearrange our room to accommodate the crap—tiny people need a lot of shit.

Jewel was a sweetheart. "High, I'll take over so you can sleep." She appeared as tired as me. Emotional bullshit is a bitch; it'll wear you out quicker than any physical activity. "Nope, you can help me by staying with Cookie and my son when I go and take care of business." I sent her out of our room to rest. Then, I changed Cookie into one of my tees and a pair of my boxers. My woman was too tired to give a shit that I needed to use safety pins for the waistband. She was also too weak to spout her "we're partners" spiel.

CJ was next; I put him in a clean diaper and his footie pjs. I needed to call Polly for his umbilical care. Damned if I could remember what she taught us in our birthing classes. "Just turn down his diaper and keep it dry, High. It'll fall off in a week or two." *Right.* I helped Cookie breastfeed CJ, which took us forty minutes. By the time we were done, Cookie was exhausted. I wanted to sleep for a week. That wasn't going to happen; I had church, and a motherfucker to put to ground.

General brings the gavel down. "Church is in session. Mafia Man, you're up."

Mafia Man starts by lowering the large white screen. He clicks his computer several times, and four photos appear. Next to Virginia

Osterhout-Hinkle's image is a dark-haired, brown-eyed, tall, heavyset woman with track marks running up each of her arms, a fiftyish guy who looks as if he has one foot in the grave, and a twenty-something blond guy who could be the male version of Cookie.

"We don't have DNA proof, but it was confirmed by Sylvie Fayette: Van Styles is Cookie's biological father."

I furrow my brow. "The eighties rock star? How the hell did you learn that?"

"We didn't; Jewel did. She called Sylvie and told her what happened. Jewel offered Sylvie ten thousand dollars for information," explains Mafia Man.

"The fucking woman scrambled like a rat to cheese. Sylvie told Jewel that Styles had another kid, older than Cookie. His mother was a rich bitch from Butte, Montana. Virginia Osterhout."

I stare at the pictures, fucking stunned.

"Christ," bites out Dad. "Does Bram know?"

Mafia Man nods, circling the younger guy's picture. "This is Trevor Styles. He's the product of Virginia Osterhout-Hinkle and Van Styles's quick fuck backstage after one of his concerts. Bram Oster-hout came clean when Sean, AJ, and I paid him a visit. Virginia was sixteen at the time. Styles was topping the charts. Bram made arrangements with Styles's manager, Brian Stratton, for the baby to be adopted by his father."

"What the fuck?!"

"Yeah, High, it was all hush-hush. Trevor grew up watching his father shoot up and fuck around with working women." Mafia Man circles another picture, the heavyset woman with track marks. "This is Sylvie Fayette, Cookie's mother. Styles and Sylvie hooked up to 'party' when Van Styles had a gig in Quebec City."

"Fucking Jesus," I breathe out.

"I tracked down Van Styles," says Guard Dog. "He's dying of cirrhosis of the liver and needed to cleanse his soul." He rolls his eyes. "The man is a piece of shit. He knew about Cookie. He's the one who gave Sylvie the guitar to give to her. Years later, he arranged for Brian Stratton to sign Cookie to Stratton Records. Trevor didn't inherit his father's musical talent, and his father never let him forget it. He taunted the kid with Cookie."

Mafia Man clicks on another picture. It's of Trevor Styles at Blue Heaven, watching Cookie perform. The sneer on the bastard's face says it all: he recognized Cookie was his sister, and that she had their father's talent. Mafia Man clicks on another picture. It's blurry but recognizable. Trevor Styles is running behind Pony Motel—a Winchester Magnum with a high-powered scope is slung over his back.

"Trevor Styles is our shooter," confirms Mafia Man.

"Where the hell is he?!"

"We haven't a goddamn clue, High," says Rocky. "Given his bike was dumped on the side of the road, someone is helping him. But we have eyes everywhere. He can't hide forever."

Brainiac comes running up the stairs; a computer is in his hand. "Breaking news just came across the TV." His eyes go to me and then to his father. "Dad, a word in private," he says, tilting his head toward the corner of the room.

"Brainiac, spill it," I bark, irritated as hell Trevor Styles is in the wind. "No one is having a goddamn word in private."

"The Wheelers were found dead in their Helena apartment, Uncle High," he says gently, having care for me. "The cops were called to the scene after the neighbors heard gunshots. They haven't released names, but Scottie and I recognized their apartment number. Three body bags were being taken out. It's Elizabeth and her parents."

"Fucking Jesus," breathes out my father, running his hand down his face.

"Dad, I went on the dark web and accessed the street cams—"

"Timmy, we don't want you and your brothers involved in this," says Mafia Man.

Brainiac is a seventeen-year-old kid genius with a shitload of child abuse in his past. His adopted parents, Mafia Man and Maggie, want him to live a kid's life: free and easy, as do all the Sinners. He fights against us, wanting to protect his family.

"Brainiac," I say, holding out my hand, "come to me."

He puts his computer in front of me. I hook him around the neck, bringing him to my eye level. "Love you, nephew. I respect you for wanting to help me. I'm with your dad…"

"I'm a Sinner, Uncle High. We take care of our family."

"Yeah, we do," I concede, kissing his forehead. "Show me the footage."

He plops his bony ass in my lap. Christ, he's six-foot-two and weighs a buck sixty. It doesn't make a difference to him. I'm his uncle; showing me PDA comes naturally to him.

"The image is dark and grainy," he explains, his fingers flying over the keys. "But I'm sure it's Virginia Osterhout-Hinkle and Trevor Styles who put the Wheelers to ground." A black BMW SUV pops onto the screen. "Look." He points to a person sitting in the driver's seat. "She's wearing the same jacket as in that picture." He points to the big white screen. "Not many women can afford to wear a Saint Laurent original."

I furrow my brow, staring at the image. "How the hell do you know it's a Saint Laurent original?"

He snorts. "Uncle High, we're from New York City, and my mom is Maggie. She knows fashion." He sweeps his hands down his body to make his point. "My tees aren't fucking Fruit of the Loom."

I chuckle, "Right."

Brainiac clicks a button, moving to the next frame. "This is Trevor Styles running to his mother's SUV."

I'm not sure about that. The guy has the same build, but his face is too dark to make out his features.

Mafia Man reaches over, pulling the computer in front of him. Now his fingers are flying across the keyboard. He homes in on the guy's face. Bingo. Trevor Styles's image is as clear as day.

Brainiac grins down at me. "My dad is superfly on a computer."

I smirk. "Agreed."

"Do the three of you want to let us in on what you're looking at?" asks General, irritation lacing his voice. No matter how hard General tries to keep our women and children out of Sinners' business, they always get involved. It frustrates the hell out of him.

"Sorry, Papa."

"Your work is done, grandson," says General. "Take off, go play your video games."

Brainiac leaps up, gives General a smooch on his cheek, and runs down the stairs.

Tristen watches him go. "His love runs deep, Dad."

"Aye, as does all of ours for him," sighs General.

"Yeah, Dad, it does," grins Tristen.

Mafia Man plugs in Brainiac's computer, showing all the brothers the images.

Godfather agrees, "That's Virginia Osterhout-Hinkle and her son, Trevor."

"I get that Trevor was jealous of Cookie, and that's why he tried to put her to ground. But why kill the Wheelers?" asks Tank. "Yeah, I know Virginia and Elizabeth were besties. The Wheelers were disgraced. They moved on."

"They're a few cards short of a full deck," snorts General.

"Who the hell knows why crazy people do what they do. They're fucking crazy," explains Sly.

"Great explanation, Einstein. That doesn't help us figure out where the fuckers are, or their next move," barks Horse.

Horse is an older Native American, pragmatic, and hates any kind of drama. He has been General's friend and lieutenant for over forty years. He lives by the Sinners' beliefs: family and club are one entity, then God, and country. Someone screwed with his family; he's going to screw with them tenfold.

"If they follow their pattern, they'll hit Hinkle and Jason next," says Flame. "The assholes think they took out Cookie. Trevor had a high-powered scope on his rifle. I'm sure the cunt saw her fall. We're just lucky the bastard is a shitty shot, or his scope isn't calibrated correctly. I'm leaning toward the latter, seeing's how he missed all our men."

"Agreed," says Liam. "I think we need to fly to Hinkle. It's a seven-teen-hour drive from Helena to Beatrice, Nebraska. The assholes don't appear the hearty type. They'll probably stop at a motel for the night. That puts them in Beatrice before nightfall."

Christ, I'll need to leave Cookie and the baby. There's no help for it. Virginia and Trevor need to be taken out, and I need to be the one who does it.

I nod. "We'll leave at first light."

CHAPTER 35

YOU REAP WHAT YOU SOW – HIGH

It's before dawn; Cookie is lying across my chest, stoically listening while I explain what went down in church. I've prepared myself for angry tears or a hysterical outburst of rage about her father being Van Styles, giving her the guitar, and setting her up with Stratton Records. I expected a reaction over her brother trying to put her to ground. I anticipated at least a look of surprise over Virginia and Trevor going on a killing spree. Nope, nothing but her fingers tapping out a tune on my chest.

"Baby, you need to tell me how you're feeling," I murmur onto her crown.

She tilts her head to look at me. "About Van and Trevor Styles, Virginia Osterhout-Hinkle, or the Wheelers being murdered?"

"All of the above, babe."

"I feel nothing for Van Styles, other than gratitude for my voice, the guitar, and setting me up with Stratton Records."

Gratitude for Stratton Records. Jesus, the fucker raped her.

"That's bullshit, baby."

"If I hadn't gone through everything in my past, I wouldn't have you, CJ, Mom, Dad, and my Sinners family," she explains. "Having all of you is worth anything, Amour."

"Babe," I drawl.

"Van is a drug addict like my mother. They're selfish, sick people who don't know the meaning of love and loyalty. I'm certain if things worked out, Van would have shown up wanting something from me. Trevor and Virginia are rabid dogs that need to be put down." She looks up at me again. "Sane people don't try to kill an unborn child because of a singing voice. I have no thoughts on the Wheelers, other than what Maggie said: you reap what you sow." She furrows her brow. "I really don't know what that means. It's an American saying."

I grin; she's so cute. In Cookie's mind, everything she doesn't understand is an American idiom.

"It's from the Bible, baby. It means you get what you deserve—do bad things, bad things will happen to you."

"Amour, are you going to try and save Lewis and Jason? They did bad things."

"Hinkle and Jason are trying to redeem themselves, baby. They pose no threat to us. So if the opportunity arises, then yes, I will save them."

Cookie squeezes me. *"Bien."* Her blues meet mine. "Don't take chances, Amour. Put Virginia and Trevor to ground and get out of there. No torture, no MMA fighting, no hesitation—two bullets—*pop, pop*—and then you're gone. CJ and I will be here waiting for you. Promise me, Amour, two shots, and it's over," she says, bossy as hell.

Christ, *pop, pop*. She's been taking lessons from the other biker babes.

"Baby," I drawl.

"Promise, Amour!" My feisty Frenchwoman, Chéri, is coming out to play.

I kiss the crown of her head. "Shh, you're getting worked up. I promise I'll do what needs to be done. Now, give me your lips. I need to get ready. Mom, Dad, and Jewel will help you with CJ."

Our kiss is hot, wet, hungry, and long. She fists my hair, holding me to her. I deepen our kiss; my cock becomes hard as granite against her thigh.

"Amour," she moans into my mouth.

"Your pussy is off-limits." I breathe onto her lips, "Four weeks, baby. Patriot's orders." Then I give her a nip and pull away.

"Four weeks," she says incredulously. "*Non*, I will expire from need."

I chuckle, giving her a chaste kiss. Too cute. Then I roll out of bed, lean down, give my son a kiss on his tiny forehead, and make a beeline to the shower.

CHAPTER 36

TWO POPS — HIGH

Our research told us Hinkle and Jason are living with Hinkle's parents on their small dairy farm. Mafia Man and Rocky flew Joker, Flame, Liam, Sly, and me to Lincoln Airport. From there, we needed to rent a van and drive forty minutes to Beatrice, and then another thirty minutes to Hinkle's farm.

There's a reason Nebraska is one of the Plains states: all we saw for miles is flatland, tall prairie grass, barbwire fences, cows, cows, and more cows.

"Nebraska is part of Tornado Alley." Sly rattles off the statistics of Nebraska's tornadoes: they happen more in the spring and summer. "June is the height of the storm season. Interestingly, they touch down more often in the late afternoon to early evening."

Interesting to whom? I don't give a shit about Nebraska's tornadoes.

Flame rolls his eyes, clearly not giving a shit about Nebraska's weather either. "Hinkle's farm should be coming up on the right."

I pull the van over onto the side of the road and grab the binoculars: I get eyes on Hinkle's tiny farm. The two-story farmhouse is old, in need of a few coats of paint. The two red barns, silo, and fencing appear to be well-kept. I furrow my brow, homing in on the black sedan parked in front of the house. It's a rental. Then, I catch sight of a dead border collie lying to the right of the porch.

"Shit," I breathe out, handing Flame the binoculars. "The dog has been shot in the head."

He takes the binoculars and peers through them. "Christ, we're late to the party. There's a piece of Virginia's Saint Laurent original in the dog's mouth." He hands me back the binoculars.

I hold back my laughter. None of this is funny, but Christ, the way he said 'Saint Laurent original' in his sarcastic badass way...yeah, it's fucking funny.

"Car's coming," says Guard Dog.

We all slouch down and wait for the yellow taxi to pass.

I sit up and watch the driver make a right into Hinkle's driveway. "What the fuck?" I put the binoculars to my eyes and watch Bram Osterhout pay the driver. He waits for the taxi to leave, then runs up the porch steps.

"What the hell is going on, High?" asks Liam, irritated as hell he doesn't have a set of binoculars.

"Bram Osterhout is banging on the Hinkles' front door."

"Jesus, is he a part of this shit?" asks Rocky.

Trevor swings open the door, pointing his rifle at Bram. He jerks his head, commanding Bram to step inside.

"Nope," I declare. "His grandson just put a gun in his face."

"We need to get a look inside that house," growls Joker.

I agree by grabbing my M4A1 and hopping out of the van. My Sinners brothers follow my lead.

"High, I'm aware you want to torture Trevor and Virginia." Liam checks his Glock, then tucks it into the front waistband of his jeans. "God knows the bastards deserve it, but we need to rethink the plan." He peers through the scope of his rifle aimed at the farmhouse. "If Hinkle's parents are home—and I believe they are, given their truck is parked by the barn." In one smooth move, he swings the weapon to his back, continuing, "We'd need to put seven people to ground to avoid any witnesses. Hinkle's parents and Bram are innocent."

That's Liam: a badass ex-Irish Mafia boss, now a Sinner. He kills without remorse if it's justified—Hinkle's parents and Bram would be unnecessary kills.

Cookie's words come into my mind: *"No torture, no MMA fighting, no hesitation—two bullets—pop, pop—and then you're gone."*

I blow out a breath, nodding my agreement. Then I sprint for the barbwire fence, plowing my way through the waist-high prairie grass, my brothers at my side. A warm easterly wind blows over me; the intense odor of cow shit hits my nose. There is over one hundred head of dairy cattle behind the fence. I leap over the barbwire, pointing to the fly-covered, steaming piles of dung. Mafia Man isn't known for his grace. If there is a cow pie, he'll slip in it.

"Fuck you, brother." Mafia Man bitches through my earpiece, "A man slips twice: once on unforeseen ice and the other in his woman's blood. He never lives it down."

I chuckle, using the cows as cover. They moo their greeting, probably hoping it's dinnertime. We get to the barn with the herd following us. Opening the gate without the goddamn animals' escaping will take an act of God. And the ladies love Joker.

"What do you have in your fucking pocket?" I growl, knowing he has some kind of snack. My best friend loves to eat.

"Skittles," he whispers, trying to push the thousand-pound, overly friendly cows away from him.

"Give them the fucking Skittles," grits out Flame.

Joker moans, "Keeley gave them to me, for energy to fight the bad guys." He pulls the bag from his pocket and tosses it to the opposite side of the barn. Like dogs, the cows trot toward the Skittles bag. We hastily move through the wooden gate, quickly slipping the looped chain back over the post.

I leap over the porch rail and duckwalk to the open window. Jesus Christ, Virginia and Trevor have two silver-haired, thin, wrinkled older persons zip-tied to dining room chairs. Lewis, Jason, and Bram are all in a line, also zip-tied to chairs. Trevor is pointing his rifle at them, taunting them with eeny, meeny, miny, moe.

"Virginia, why are you doing this?!" shouts Bram, shaking the chair. "The Sinners know about Trevor. They know he shot Christian's pregnant woman. They won't stop hunting him until he's dead, Virginia!"

"Why am I doing this, Daddy?" sneers Virginia, baring her straight white teeth at him. She looks like the rabid dog Cookie referred to her as. "I did everything you asked of me. You said giving Trevor to his father would be for the best. Do you know what Van Styles did"—She pounds a fist onto her chest—"to my son? That alcoholic, drug-addicted loser kept him a secret. The bastard made Trevor feel like he was nothing because he didn't inherit his father's talent for music. Van Styles taunted Trevor with a daughter he made with a heroin-addicted, disease-ridden, prostitute, Daddy! Cookie was the spawn of the devil!"

I growl. Rage burns through me, triggering my every nerve with the need to kill the bitch.

Joker puts a hand on my shoulder. "Keep it cool and look for the shot, brother."

It's impossible to shoot Virginia or Trevor without killing one or more of their hostages. Unnecessary collateral damage will get me twenty-five to life. That isn't happening; Cookie and CJ are waiting for me at home.

Virginia continues her rant: "Lewis Hinkle is a pervert, a predator, an adulterer, and a con man, but yet he got it all, Daddy!"

"Virginia," drawls Hinkle, trying to soothe the beast.

She backhands Hinkle across his mouth; her diamond slits his bottom lip. Hinkle's mother screams, watching her son's head snap to the side. Hinkle spits a stream of blood onto the hardwood floor.

"I'm going to fucking kill you!" screeches Jason, his eyes pinned to Trevor.

Trevor tosses his head back, laughing demonically. Then he leans forward, mocking, "How are you going to do that, *Jaaassson?* You're zip-tied to a fucking chair."

Jason spits a loogie into Trevor's face.

"Fuck!" roars Trevor, wiping the spitball onto his tee. He points the rifle at Jason, ready to pull the trigger.

"Virginia, I did it," yells Hinkle, shaking his chair. "You have me. Let my parents, my son, and your father go. They have nothing to do with this. Goddamnit, Virginia, they're innocent!"

"Sorry, Lewis, you're all going to die," says Virginia, gently moving the barrel of the rifle away from Jason. "But first, your parents and son need to know what a sick, disgusting, deceitful person you are." Her face twists. She spews her venom about Hinkle and Elizabeth's kink, the Fantasyland club, and how they deceived Jason Cooper. "You, Elizabeth, and her despicable parents ripped off Margo, Christian, and me for millions. The Wheelers needed to pay"—She leans forward—"with their lives. Cookie needed to die for her father and mother's sins."

"Virginia, Chéri Fayette didn't die…"

Trevor whips around, staring at Bram. His mouth is open, his eyes blazing with fury.

Go to hell, motherfucker! I squeeze the trigger. *Pop!* Trevor hits the floor with a thud; a gaping, baseball-sized hole is in the back of his head. Virginia screams, staring down at her son. I quickly rotate. *Pop!* Virginia falls on top of her son; she too is missing part of her skull.

"Nooo!" bellows Bram, his wide eyes on his daughter's body.

Jason moves his eyes to the open window. "Christian! Oh, god, Christian! They killed Mom, Grandma, and Grandpa," he cries. A river of tears stream down his cheeks. "I left them…"

"Nope, you came here for a better life. Your mother was screwed up, but she loved you, Jason," I say, telling him what he needs to hear. He's just a confused kid; his mother used him as a pawn in her deceit. I climb through the window and yank my hunting knife from my left boot. I slice through the zip ties at Hinkle's wrists and ankles.

"Give me the gun, Christian," demands Hinkle, holding out his hand. "We'll tell the police it was a home invasion. I killed them in self-defense."

"We'll testify to it," agrees Hinkle's father.

The old woman nods, staring daggers at the blood pooling on her hardwood floor.

I hand Hinkle my unregistered Glock. He wipes my prints clean with his tee. "Go! You and the Sinners get the fuck out of here. I'll call the police in thirty minutes."

Bram jerks his head up. "I will never lie for you, Christian Fontaine. You killed my daughter in cold blood," he spits at me. "I'll put you behind bars for the rest of your life."

Pop! Bram's body slumps; the zip ties keep him in the chair. A trickle of crimson runs down the bridge of his nose. The room fills with the offensive odor of piss and shit.

Mafia Man moans, stepping away from the window. The man is as badass as his blood brothers. Blood, brains, bone, and burnt bodies are no problem—but the noxious smell of bodies evacuating their contents makes his stomach turn sour.

Hinkle looks at me, letting his arm fall to his side. "Go!"

Christ, Hinkle put a slug right between his father-in-law's eyes.

Joker grabs my tee, pulling me back. "Brother, it's done. We need to make tracks."

Two bullets—pop, pop—and then you're gone. CJ and I will be here waiting for you. I turn, leap out of the window, and run beside my brothers. I'm finally free from my past, clear of all the screwed up self-imposed obligations I felt for Elizabeth and Jason. It feels fucking fantastic!

EPILOGUE ONE

WEDDING DAY – COOKIE

The last six months have been a wild ride. After High came home from Nebraska, High, Mom, Dad, CJ, and I moved into our new cabin. I wasn't a girl who dreamed of a handsome husband, a big house, or having a humongous, wonderful family until High came into my life. He is my religion, my light, and I worship at the altar of his body every morning and night. We are partners, all in, bound by love.

A week after we had settled into our new home, High, Mom, Dad, and I had a housewarming party. All the Sinners came, including Megan, Al, Margo, and Willy. Megan fell head over heels in love with her little brother. She still lives in Denver with Fawn and Ed, but FaceTime's High every night before she goes to bed. Megan talks, her dad listens—they have a good relationship.

While Margo was here, she informed us Mrs. Osterhout didn't have a funeral for Virginia or Bram. She felt disgraced by the police and the news media: Virginia, Bram, and Trevor were criminals who Lewis Hinkle killed in self-defense. Al said Mrs. Osterhout closed Bram's business, put their home on the market, and left Butte a broken woman. I wanted to feel sorry for Bram Osterhout; he didn't have anything to do with his daughter and grandson's murderous rampage. But I couldn't. He threatened to nark on my man. *Merci* to God, Lewis Hinkle put him to ground.

No one has heard from Jason, Lewis, or his parents. My guess, they're like us and want to put it all behind them and move on.

Four months ago, I found out Sylvie had passed: complications stemming from pneumonia. To my astonishment, Van Styles died on the same day. It wasn't Van's death that surprised me—it was that he named me as his next of kin. It didn't shock me the hospital's social workers told me they both died indigent. My biological parents' parting gift to me was their cremation bills. High paid them, flew Van's ashes to Quebec, and had the crematorium bury them together in Quebec's cemetery with a simple headstone. It was his way of giving Sylvie and Van a bit of respect for making me for him.

High worried I was messed up over Sylvie and Van's deaths. I didn't cry, express any anger, or want to visit their graves. "Baby, talk to me. I know they were shitty parents, but they were your parents." I shook my head. "*Non*, your parents are my parents. You, Megan, CJ, Mom, Dad, and the Sinners are my family. Van was a stranger I'd never met. My love for Sylvie died long ago. They were tortured by their addiction. I hope Sylvie and Van find peace together in the after-life." That satisfied him, and he moved on to other important business: romancing me between the sheets.

I smile, looking at myself in the full-length mirror. Jewel comes up behind me and hugs my middle. "You are the most beautiful bride I've ever seen," she squeals, swaying us from side to side.

I giggle, not disagreeing. Jewel made my wedding dress—entirely badass biker babe in an outlandish, sexy way. It's made out of white gossamer with metallic silver and baby blue stars that shimmer in the light. It's mega-short with an empire waist, a halter top, and a long, detachable train. The empire waist has a thin baby blue leather belt studded with tiny silver Harley buttons. She also made me a short baby blue leather jacket embroidered with the Sinner's patch on the back, seeing's how High and I decided our precession would be riding the bike to the club with his brothers at our sides. We'll be married on the deck at twilight. After, we'll party as only the Sinners can do: wild and free!

I lift my foot, showing Jewel the perfect, kick-butt, four-inch high-heeled, glittery baby blue wedding booties.

"Those are the freakin' bomb, sister! Don't let Brie see them," she giggles. "They'll be on her little tootsies in a flash."

Our eldest niece, Brie, is totally into fashion, makeup, and jewelry; she needed me to wear a tiara. She reasoned that I looked like a biker princess, and all princesses wear tiaras. I belly-laughed when she held out her hand for Uncle High's credit card. "Uncle High, I found Aunt Cookie a mega-super-fantabulously gorgeous star tiara. Aunt Jewel is going to attach a veil to it."

My man is smart, and he knows our niece. Money is no object to Brie when it comes to her fashion ideas. "Show me," he chuckled, not wanting a ten-thousand-dollar bill at the end of the month. She did, getting her uncle to purchase one for me; one for her besties, Blossom and Willow; and one for herself. After all, they're princesses, too.

Jewel lets my waist go and pins the sparkling tiara into my long curly hair. "We'll attach the veil when we get to the club."

Knock knock knock. "It's us," sings Maggie. "We're coming in."

Maggie is holding a bottle of champagne and a tray of chocolate-covered strawberries. Her eyes widen. "OMG, sister, you're fantabulously, mega-mega, off-the-friggin'-charts, sexy-gorgeous."

Jewel and I glance at each other, giggling. Brie is a mini-me of her mom.

"Babe, that dress is…well…just wow," says Jillian. "Love the lacy baby blue bra and panty set." She tilts her head, staring at me. "Is that La Perla?"

"It most certainly is," grins Princess. "Gossamer is sheer, and our sister has magnificent boobs. They need to be showcased while we're stargazing. Now pour us a glass of bubbly. The grandparents have our kids, our men are driving, and we need to get our buzz on."

Raine pops the cork and pours our champagne. The girl posse gets down to business: getting our biker babe buzz on.

Dad struts into the room; CJ's on his hip. He does a slow blink and clears his throat. "You are..." He blinks again. "That is..."

"Gorgeous, sexy, beautiful, stunning, ravishing, Papa," laughs Megan from behind him. She shrugs, smiling at me. "He needed a bit of help finding his words."

"Yeah, if my son sees you, we're going to be late for the wedding."

Mom whizzes into the room, a jewelry box in her hand. "No-no-no, we can't be late for the wedding: Father Darling loves his Jameson. We need him standing for the nuptials. Meg, take CJ from Papa. He needs to be dressed in his wedding attire. I laid out his jeans, long-sleeved tee, and cut on our bed. Rene, pour us a flute of champagne."

"Da, Da, Da, Da! Ma, Ma, Ma, Ma! Pa, Pa, Pa, Pa! Mé, Mé, Mé, Mé!" sings CJ.

I smile at my son. At six months, CJ has a beautiful musical tone to his voice. And he is a little mini-me of his father. He's also bossy like his father: CJ is announcing who he wants, and it's not his big sister.

Mom looks at CJ, melting into a puddle of love. She is *Mémé*, his grandmother. She reaches for CJ. "Mémé will change you." She kisses me on the cheek. "We love you more than all the stars in the sky. You have something borrowed," she laughs, taking her champagne from Dad. She takes a big sip and then tips the glass to my bed. "My clutch, which also counts as something old. It was my mother's." She whispers, taking another sip. "I'll give it to you next week."

Dad rolls his eyes at her need for something traditional.

I giggle, taking a drink of my delicious champagne.

"You have something blue: your underwear and booties." She hands Dad the jewelry box. "Dad has something new for you."

Dad raises his glass. "A toast to my daughter on her wedding day. *À ta santé!*" He translates: "To your health."

Jewel, Maggie, and Princess say in unison, "*À la vôtre!*"

Maggie giggles, winking at Dad. "To yours."

Dad chuckles, "Good to know, *mon chéri*, the three of you speak French."

He opens the jewelry box. Good lord, there is a set of white gold diamond hoops that could work as bangle bracelets. And the freakin' diamonds are not small.

Dad puts his hand on my cheek. "Mom and I know how you feel about gifts. But, just like you got used to taking them from Christian, you will get used to taking them from us." He holds up an earring. "The circle is unbroken. It has no beginning and no end. Infinity. Mom's and my love is endless for you."

Mercy, tears spill from my eyes, running down my cheeks. Rene and Dana are my parents in every way, and they love me to infinity. It's not because I can sing, it's not because I'm a meal ticket; they love me just for me. Unconditional love.

"Oh, my god, she's crying. Tissues, quick!" demands Jewel. She rips several out of the box and dabs at my face. "Sister, stop crying. Your makeup."

"*Merci beaucoup*, Dad. They are very, very beautiful." I put my hand over my heart. "Your words touched my soul. There are no words to describe my love for you and Mom. You made Christian in your likeness: protective, caring, loving, nurturing…"

"For someone who doesn't normally talk much, she has a lot to say," whispers Jillian, before taking a gulp of her champagne.

"Shh, they're having a moment, Jill," whispers Princess.

Dad and I look over at Princess.

She flashes us a toothy white smile, waving us on. "Don't mind us, keep talking." She sips her champagne. "If you need input, Cookie, I'd add, sexy, bossy, tremendously handsome, and, of course, badass. Not that I'm looking at High or Rene. Those are words that describe all of our men."

"You forgot muscled. Dev has lots and lots of muscles. He's mega-hot," says Maggie, as if everyone feels the same way about her husband.

"Stamina. Our men have loads of *stam-in-a*," adds Jillian. She gives us big eyes with a slow nod. "You know, to get the job done *right*." Then she tips her flute to Rene, taking a huge gulp.

Megan scrunches up her face. "Ew, god, it's gross to think of Papa and my father having stamina."

A low, rumbling chuckle comes from Dad. I giggle, looking up at him. He grins wide, shaking his head. *Oui*, he's amused.

"Baby," yells High up the stairs. "Shake your ass. We need to get a move on!"

"I'll reiterate: bossy," says Princess, downing the rest of her champagne.

I laugh, tip back my glass. I guzzle down my champagne and shake my ass.

EPILOGUE TWO

THE WEDDING – HIGH

I watch my woman sway her fine ass down the stairs. Our son's bebopping on her hip, enjoying the ride. Seeing Cookie, my cock becomes a thick iron rod. It's twitching like a goddamn teenage boy's dick, wanting the smoking hot chick.

My woman is beyond gorgeous all the time, but she is a sexy goddess in that dress and those boots. There is no hiding the bulge in my jeans. *Christ, I'll be hard for hours.* I shift, moving my cock away from my button-down fly. I know from experience: rubbing a quick one out won't help. After CJ's birth, during our four-week no-go period, I tried that several times; I just became erect within minutes. Nothing relieved my hard-on except my woman. Thanks to all that's goddamn holy, my woman partnered up: I did a lot of titty fucking and received more than my share of blow jobs. Without a doubt, I'm fucking my woman in those boots.

"Da, Da, Da, Da," sings my son, his little legs kicking excitedly against his mother's side.

I move to the bottom of the stairs, taking CJ from Cookie. Then I put my lips against hers. She opens as she always does, wanting my fevered kisses. Our tongues duel. I moan; she answers with a groan. My cock throbs painfully from the taste of her—champagne and strawberries, mixed with her unique sweetness. I put my hand on her ass, pulling her closer into my body.

"Dad, your kids are in the room," reminds Megan. "CJ and I don't need to witness you getting your *groove* on with Mama Cookie."

Joker chuckles, "CJ's been getting an eyeful of his old man's PG foreplay since the day he was born. It isn't going to rattle his cage."

Joker can hold a grudge longer than anyone I know. He'll stick a hot poker into a wound without a moment's hesitation...and do it while smiling. Forgiveness doesn't come easy for my best friend. In his mind, Megan hasn't earned redemption for treating me shitty. He's letting Meg know she doesn't know her little brother, or us. She moved to Denver.

Cookie runs her fingers over my lips, her hazy blues staring into mine. "Do you think you can wait until after we say I do?"

I let out a low chuckle. My woman's eyes are dilated, heavily lidded; her breaths are coming out in tiny pants. And the way she's angled herself, cock-to-pussy, they're all indications she is wet for me. She is hoping I say no and tell everyone we need ten minutes of alone time.

I glance at the clock on the stove—4:30. Sunset is in one hour. We're lucky the temp is holding at sixty-five; it's unusual being this late in the day at the end of March. A ten-minute quickie would take the edge off, but we can't; time's ticking.

I kiss her nose. "We need to wait. Let's get a move on."

I chuckle again, hearing her sighed French expletive.

I smack her ass, grabbing a handful. "Snowsuit, baby. It'll be cold on the bike."

Cookie snatches up CJ's snowsuit and tosses it to me. "*Oui*, CJ won't ride between us." She says it as if our six-month-old son has a say. In her beautiful mind, he does.

As soon as CJ was old enough to express himself, he let it be known I'm his number one. Our son likes to ride front and center, attached to me. If it's sunny, above forty degrees, and not raining, Cookie and I are on the bike with CJ strapped to my chest.

I hand off CJ and the snowsuit to Dad. "I need to grab his helmet and harness."

CJ goes into a fit of wiggles, trying to get down on all fours to follow me.

"We need to put gates at the top and bottom of the stairs ASAP, son."

"Yeah, Dad," I agree, grabbing the helmet and harness from CJ's room. I hurry back, aware CJ is giving his grandfather a hard time. My son dislikes clothes of any kind...he loathes the snowsuit. He hates being trapped in the damn thing.

Cookie is down on the floor, head bent, with CJ's hands wrapped into her hair. He's giggling wildly as she blows raspberries onto his neck. Quick as lightning, she zips; he's trapped. She kisses his sock-covered foot. "Biker boots, baby boy."

Cookie doesn't give a shit about her dress, her hair, or her makeup. It's all about our son and making him happy.

I drop to a knee, kissing Cookie's temple. "Go fix your tiara before Brie sees it. I've got CJ."

She laughs, righting the tiara. "Our little fashionista will turn into a mini bridezilla."

I smirk, putting on CJ's biker boots. *Bridezillas* is a TV show Brie loves to watch. It's a bunch of bitches losing their shit over their wedding. I laughed my ass off watching Cookie's facial expressions go from confused to horrified.

I slip on my cut and then strap the harness to my chest. Cookie puts CJ's helmet on his head, leaving the visor up. CJ likes the wind in his face when we ride. My woman is a wonderful mom, but she's a pushover. I'm the voice of reason where our son is concerned.

"Baby, visor down. He can't wear his shades." I look at my brothers, trying to decide who Megan should ride with.

In church I had requested the brothers ride by my side in a procession to the club. They were all in. The brothers showed at our house five hours early, their women in tow. They didn't bring the younger

Sinners' kids. "We need a little adult time," said Flame, carrying in a case of Killian's. "Running Bear, Merrill, and the Native Americans are at the club babysitting."

I snickered. Eleven-year-old, bossy Brie would be running their asses ragged, making sure party central meets her expectations. She deemed herself our "wedding coordinator." Cookie loves Brie, so she played along, giving her free reign.

I kicked back, drinking beer with my brothers in my man cave. The girls took over the upstairs, helping Cookie to get ready in biker babe fashion: wine, champagne, strawberries, and lots of giggling chatter. Even Cookie's best friend, Jewel, showed on the back of Joker's bike. "It's time to live in the real world again, High," she said, giving me a peck on the cheek. She had pushed her fears aside for Cookie.

"Saddle up." General chuckles, "Megan, you're with Cue Ball."

Cue Ball smirks. "Have you ever rode bitch on a bike, Megan?"

"Um, no. I rode in front of Dad a few times when I was a kid."

"She'll be fine," assures Raven. "Just hold on and lean with Cue Ball."

When the Sinners ride together, we have a formation—president and vice president take the lead. Everyone else rides behind them, two abreast, according to rank. Today it has changed; we'll use the entire road. Cookie and I will be riding behind General and Raven, Pick and Hialeah, and Dad and Mom. The front row signifies the parents of the bride and groom. Cookie asked General and Pick to ride beside Mom and Dad. They were the closest she came to having a dad before my father came into her life.

Joker and Jewel, Tank and Jillian will ride on our right. Flame and Princess, Mafia Man and Maggie on our left. Everyone else will ride behind us.

It takes ten minutes for everyone to saddle up, ready to ride.

"Wait," shrieks Hialeah, leaping off the back of Pick's bike. "We need a wedding picture!"

I chuckle. Hialeah has been running around all afternoon, snapping pictures. She knows my woman loves them.

"Hialeah, get back on the bike," orders Robbie. "I'll take the picture."

She hands him the camera and runs back to Pick's bike.

Robbie points the camera at us. "Everyone say, Robbie's the bee's knees!"

There are groans from the brothers and bursts of giggles from the girls.

I twist my neck, grinning. "Bee's knees," I murmur onto Cookie's lips. The picture is snap with my woman and me in a heated kiss. I nip her bottom lip. "Call it, baby!"

Cookie raises her arms over her head, letting out a loud, wild whoop. Harleys come to life, rumbling and vibrating the ground. Then we're off, cool wind in our hair, the scent of pine filling our lungs, riding free in brotherhood.

Fifteen minutes later, we're riding up Sinners Road. CJ's arms and legs start dancing. I look up and moan. *Goddamnit, the four amigos snuck out without anyone noticing.*

Keeley, JT, and JJ are eight feet in the air, hanging onto the chain-link fence like monkeys. Anna is less daring; she's on the hip of a prospect. The prospect has his cell to his ear, his eyes pinned to the kids. The other recruit has his arms held high above his head, ready to catch them if they fall.

"Fuck," bellows General, pouring on the gas.

On the opposite side of the fence, Harleys are racing toward the gate—Blade, president of the Whitefish chapter, and Geronimo, president of the Red Devils. My best guess, they're who the prospect called for help.

Without a mind to her Uncle Blade, Uncle Geronimo, or us, Keeley waves her little arm to and fro. "Hi, Aunt Cookie!"

"Aunt Cookie, we have a surprise for you," shouts JJ, grinning as if he doesn't have a care in the world.

JT has a phone to his ear, jabbering to someone. God only knows whose cell he's confiscated.

Cookie waves back, telling them to hang on tight, not to fall.

"Get your little asses down from there," shouts Mafia Man, leaping off his bike, Flame on his heels.

The problem with that order: Mafia Man didn't clarify *how* he wanted them to get down. Keeley scrambles over the barbwire and does a swan dive toward her dad.

"Oh, my god!" cries Megan.

Our women stay calm; for them, this is just another day with the Sinners' kids.

Mafia Man grunts on impact, catching all twenty-five pounds of Keeley against his chest. Keeley, being Keeley, giggles, telling Mafia Man, "I love you, Daddy."

Flame is up and over the fence before anyone can blink. But it's too late—the boys make a flying leap. Geronimo and Blade catch them in midair.

The drama is over. I chuckle, looking at our kids. They're covered in dirt from head-to-toe—they've been rolling in the mud. Keeley has her dress off; it's lying in a heap on the other side of the gate. Lord knows where her sneakers ended up.

Our kids were born to be wild and free; it's in their DNA. No punishment will change them. That said, they will be punished by their fathers, or their Uncle Liam. But they'll hold off until tomorrow; today, it's all about the wedding.

Keeley cartwheels over to my bike, holding her little arms up. "Happy bridezilla day," she giggles.

I shake my head, grin, and lift her onto the tank in front of CJ and me. CJ reaches out and grabs a fistful of Keeley's curly brown hair, giggling. She doesn't mind; she loves her little cousin. Her back bows, her head tilts, she puckers for CJ's drooly kiss. I quickly put my hand on CJ's helmet so she doesn't take a hard thunk to the face. Keeley laughs, giving CJ a smooch, and then she rights herself, ready to ride.

Cookie scoots closer into my body, trying to grab hold of Keeley.

"I've got her, baby." I put my arm around Keeley, pop the clutch, and ride slowly behind Blade and Geronimo.

It's funny as shit; Liam needs to stop three times, swiping up Keeley's dress and sneakers. "Fuck the bow. She won't wear it," he mumbles, passing it by.

JJ and JT are riding with Blade and Geronimo. They're getting lectured all the way back to the clubhouse. The kids are respectful; they listen, but neither promises never to do it again. That would be a broken promise—the ultimate no-no.

I park in front of the porch. A huge banner is strung across the beam: CONGRATULATIONS, UNCLE HIGH AND AUNT COOKIE, the letters scrolling and glittery. Hundreds of multicolored star balloons are attached to the rails. We're a one percent bikers' club: all the brothers are badass. That said, every single one of them would climb a ladder to hang that shit for Brie.

The music is pumping, laughter is flowing from the clubhouse. The smell of the hog roasting over the pit infuses the air.

Burt and Herb are sitting on the porch, beers in hand. They chuckle at Keeley, aware their chosen granddaughter will probably grow up more badass than their chosen grandsons.

Liam lifts Keeley off my tank, kissing her forehead. He has JT on his hip. "Love you two, and I want you both in one piece. Tomorrow morning we'll talk, and then both of you will be in timeout for thirty minutes."

Keeley wraps herself around him, hugging him tightly. Unlike Brie, who would have argued with Liam to the death, Keeley and JT accept it. Then Liam hands Keeley off to Mafia Man and carries JT inside.

I remove CJ's helmet. He tips his head back, giving me a four-tooth smile. I chuckle, wipe the drool from his chin, and give him what he wants—a kiss from his old man. Then, I hold out my hand, helping my woman off the bike.

She sighs. "So beautiful."

I follow her eyes over to Mafia Man; he's redressed Keeley. Now, he has his forehead to hers, his large hand's cupping her entire neck. He's talking to her low and gentle. Keeley has her tiny hands on the sides of his face—wolf eyes to emerald eyes.

"Right there is unconditional love. I want my children to have it," says Cookie wistfully.

"Baby, CJ has *it*. All our kids will have *it* because we have *it* for each other. In a few minutes, we are going to pledge *it* in front of our friends and family. Then, we're going to fuck, consummating *it*." I kiss her lips, moving her up the steps. "*It's* a done deal."

"Ewww, Dad. Good lord, stop," whines Megan, coming up beside us.

Dad chuckles, "Meg, there's no stopping *it*."

Mom and Cookie giggle.

I swing open the door, stepping inside with Cookie.

Cookie puts her hand over her heart. Wide-eyed she breathes out, "Mercy."

Yeah, fucking mercy. It appears as if the night sky puked stars—the place is covered in shimmering silver stars, hanging from the ceiling and walls, even coming up from the floor. There are star candles, star plates, star napkins, and star glasses—even our wedding cake is a goddamn gigantic glimmering silver star.

"Brie, Willow, and Blossom have been busy," chuckles Guard Dog, moving to the bar.

I catch sight of our wedding coordinator and her besties holding court with the Sinners, Red Devils, and Native Americans. Flutes of sparkling apple juice are in their hands. I snort. They're dressed like princesses: full makeup, tons of jewelry, and star tiaras atop their heads.

I cast my eyes down on Cookie; she has her blues pinned on the girls, entirely amused.

Maggie strolls up beside us, beaming with pride. "Brie said, as your wedding coordinator, she was going to give you the stars." Maggie giggles. "I had no idea she'd create the entire galaxy. It's freakin' mega-super-fantabulously rad!"

Maggie would think that; she's the grandmaster of over-the-top party decor.

She moves away, smiling proudly as she heads to the bar. No one would ever guess Maggie didn't birth Brie; mother and daughter beat to the same drum.

Joker whips out his shades and slips them on CJ. "You'll be blinded by the aurora borealis, nephew," quips Joker, then blows a raspberry onto his neck.

CJ giggles wildly at his uncle's antics.

Tables are groaning with a variety of Cherokee, Irish, and American foods. Wolfe and William Bull are manning the bar.

Everyone has a drink in their hand, greeting us with congrats, backslaps, bro-hugs, and kisses on our cheeks.

Out of the corner of my eye, I clock Running Bear. He has Flame and Princess's triplets, Meadow, Cass, and Joey, in a carrier attached to his chest, bringing out more food. Merrill is running around with Mafia Man and Maggie's baby, Gee, riding on his hip.

"Merrill, where are the older kids?" I ask as he whizzes by us.

It isn't like Jonas, Abel, Johnathon, Jacob, Conan, Conor, Scout, or Runner to leave the little ones.

He backtracks, stopping in front of us. "Brie has them out back, tending the hog and decorating the deck with Running Deer, Mouse, Rabbit, and Eagle. Faith, Bluebird, and Cottonwood have commandeered my kitchen. Mable and Bess are getting their drunk on with Mrs. Fitzpatrick and Alroy." He gives Cookie a kiss on her cheek. "You're a vision among the stars. Glowing!"

Brie, Blossom, and Willow come running up to us. Brie is holding a massive bouquet of heather and lavender with a sprig of shamrock. A piece of broadcloth is tied in a trinity knot, holding the bouquet together.

Brie holds it out to Cookie. "You're not Irish, Aunt Cookie. I didn't find too much on the French tradition, other than a Catholic ceremony in Latin. So, I made you a bouquet according to Irish tradition."

Cookie smiles, taking the bouquet. "Do you know the meaning of the flowers, Brie?"

We live with full-blooded Irish and Scots; therefore, all Sinners know every Irish tradition has a specific meaning.

Brie waves General over to us. "Aunt Cookie wants to know what the bouquet means."

He chuckles, coming over. In a deep brogue, General explains,

"White heather brings good luck to the marriage. The shamrock is also for luck, and the lavender is an ancient symbol of love, loyalty, and devotion. It helps to ensure a happy and long-lasting union." He runs his finger over the knot. "The trinity knot symbolizes and honors the maiden, mother, and crone—the three life cycles of a woman."

Cookie leans down, kissing Brie's cheek. "Beautiful. *Merci*, Brie, for giving me a piece of your heritage."

Blossom and Willow hold up two small bags, one for Cookie, the other for me.

General smiles, running his hand down each of the girls' heads.

"The bags contain sage, corn, tobacco, and sweetgrass," he says, his eyes pinned to the girls. "It's part of the Native American Fire Wedding Ceremony. Kernels of corn represent fertility and growth. The tobacco is an offering to our creator. Sage and sweetgrass are sacred herbs with healing power."

"They won't have their fires," whispers Willow up to General.

I know the Fire Wedding Ceremony, having been to a few. Fawn and I were married at the Justice of the Peace in Butte. I didn't feel we qualified for such a sacred ceremony. It's beautiful and spiritual, meant for two people who love each other. Cookie and I don't qualify; neither of us has Native American blood.

I drop to one knee. "How about Cookie and I sprinkle them into the bonfire and have Running Bear say a prayer?"

Willow breaks out into a huge grin. "That will work."

A loud drum roll sounds beside the dance floor.

Brie grabs Willow and Blossom's hands. "It's time!' They're off like a shot.

Everyone turns; the Heartbreakers are standing, their instruments at the ready. Cam is at the mic. He chuckles, "I'm told by our wedding coordinator's mother, it's time for the nuptials." He reads, "High, Dana, and Rene, your presence is being requested out on the deck with the brothers and"—he chuckles—"the girl posse. I need Patriot, Brainiac, JT, and JJ up here with us." He smiles over at Cookie. "Little Bit isn't a traditional woman. She wanted a biker babe wedding."

Laughter comes from our family and friends.

"Brie wanted to give her aunt and uncle a wedding they'd never forget." He smirks, looking around the room. "This fits the bill. I know I won't forget it."

Another round of laughter comes from our family and friends.

"Let's get High and Little Bit hitched so we can party our asses off!"

That gets a roar of approval.

Jewel has a baby bottle in her hand. She takes CJ from me, cradling him in her arms. CJ takes the bottle, looking at it as if to say, "What the hell is this?" Then, he moves his sky-blue eyes to me.

I grin down at him. On occasion, CJ drinks from a bottle, but never when his mother is close—it's mommy's tit or a sippy cup. In the morning and at night, the three of us snuggle while he breastfeeds. I put the nipple into his mouth, "Mommy's milk. Suck."

He does, snuggling into his Aunt Jewel.

Joker tosses his arm over my shoulder. "Let's make tracks, or your woman's going to beat you to the deck."

On our way out, Flame cracks open a bottle of Jameson. He tips it to me. "Groom first."

I chuckle, take the bottle, guzzle down several swallows, and pass it on.

JJ and JT run by us, beating feet to Cam and the Heartbreakers. We make it to the deck; it's filled with more of our family and friends, laughing, drinking, and eating—loving life.

The deck has a thousand twinkly firefly lights strung along the rails. Father Darling is waiting at the other end, appearing disgruntled with Running Deer. The bottle of Jameson makes its way around. Maggie tips it back, taking a sip, and then she passes it to Running Deer. He takes a swig and bypasses Father Darling, handing it to Princess.

I chuckle to myself; I'm sure Running Deer is making sure the priest stays sober long enough to marry us. My eyes go to the millions of stars in the sky. The first time I kissed Cookie, it was right here, under the stars. I had no idea a tiny woman with huge blue eyes and a gorgeous rack would change my life. She barely said two words to me that night. It didn't matter; she had marked me like no other woman had. I was hers, and she was mine.

There's a massive bonfire burning, its wood snapping and crackling. From the smell of the smoke, I know the Native Americans built it with seven different kinds of wood. They're giving Cookie and me another piece of their culture.

Mable, Bess, Mrs. Fitzpatrick, Alroy, Herb, and Bert are sitting around the fire in lawn chairs, keeping warm. They're drinking and conversing, probably about the old days. DJ is sound asleep, snuggled against Alroy's thin chest.

The fat dripping from the hog hits the hot coals, making a sizzling sound. It's not lost on me, as old and crotchety as Mrs. Fitzpatrick is, she has one eye on the kids by the pit. If one of them gets too close, she'll order them to step back. If they don't move fast enough for her, she'll send one of us to make them step back.

The beginning bars of Cookie's song starts playing. Patriot, Brainiac, JT, and JJ's voices filter out onto the deck:

"My Religion"
Take me to church with the beat of your heart,
Let me rejoice in the warmth of your skin,
Let me bask in the glory of your passion,
Your body is the absolution of my sins,
Amen...Amen...Amen...
Your light is my religion,
Your body is the church of my salvation,
My soul is yours to keep,
I worship at the altar of you,
Amen...Amen...Amen....

Fuck me, she dirtied it up. Tears burn in the backs of my eyes. My father puts his arm around me, giving me a quick squeeze. Joker just about busts a nut holding back his laughter at my mother offering me one of her soggy tissues. Then Cookie comes through the door, her arms linked in General and Pick's arms.

My feet move without my permission; my cock is hard as steel. Pick chuckles and drops his arm, kissing Cookie's forehead. "We almost made it."

General snorts, kisses her cheek, and hands her off to me. I lift her into my arms. Cookie wraps her arms around my neck, her legs around my waist. My hands go under her ass, my fingers kneading into her globes.

"We should have taken those ten minutes," I murmur onto her lips. "I need to romance you between the sheets, baby. I'm hard as granite."

Cookie stares into my eyes. Forehead-to-forehead, she thinks for a few beats. "I could tell them I need to pee."

Christ, that's it; I throw my head back, laughing. Any other woman would tell me to suck it up and wait. Not my woman, she's going to announce to three hundred people she needs to take a piss so she can get me off in the bathroom."

I slip my tongue between her lips, taking the time to love my woman's mouth—hot, wet, and wild.

"God, Dad, we're all here!" chastises Megan.

"Megan, they're showing their love," explains Brie. "It's nothing to be ashamed of or embarrassed about. Uncle High and Aunt Cookie enjoy each other's bodies." Brie goes on to educate Megan on the facts of life. "Doing the dirty is entirely natural and mega-beautiful between two consenting people. It can be Donkey-Kong physical, super loud, or soft and sweet. You need to talk to your mom about that when you're ready....Oh, and it's not polite to listen. It's private."

The brothers are chuckling, snorting, and snickering. The girl posse is giggling.

Joker is next to us, bent over, hands on his knees, fighting for breath. "Jesus Christ," he drawls, laughing.

Rocky tips his head way back, face to the stars, muttering, "Tell me she did not just fucking go there."

Guard Dog guffaws, "Oh, she went there, big brother."

Cookie and I laugh against each other's lips at Mafia Man's moaning. Yup, there's going to be another sex conversation in his future.

Cookie smiles. "Maggie and Mafia Man had 'The Talk' with Brie. She's eleven. She'll get her period soon. Maggie's totally open and honest with her kids."

"Christ, baby, thank god we have a boy," I chuckle. Then I glance at Megan. She's speechless. "Megan?"

She tosses up her hands and bursts out laughing. "I'm twenty-one," she reminds everyone. Yeah, Meg is an adult. Her values have been molded by her mother. I need to accept she is a civilian; she has chosen her path.

I carry Cookie over to Father Darling. He's found the bottle of Jameson; he's already barely standing. Damn!

Running Bear steps forward, wiping the tears from his cheeks. "Brie keeps it real," he chuckles. The babies are asleep against his chest, undisturbed by his laughter.

Pick and Flame come forward, divesting him of the kids.

Running Bear looks at Father Darling and then to General.

General says in Cherokee, "Preform the ceremony, *Edoda*."

Cookie and I face each other, front-to-front, holding each other tightly. She's smiling up at me, tears glittery in her blues. I give her a lip touch, keeping my eyes pinned to hers.

Running Bear launches into the Cherokee wedding prayer. When he's done, he chuckles, "Cookie has said multiple times she and High are partners in all things." He gives a short talk on love, commitment, and partnership. "Their scale is balanced by what they give of themselves to each other. A song, 'My Religion,' Cookie wrote honoring her love for High. Cookie reuniting High, Dana, and Rene. High holding his son to Cookie's breast, allowing her to sleep without worry. High explaining how to hook a plow to a truck in terms Cookie can understand."

Joker snorts, trying to hold back a laugh. That gets a giggle out of Jewel and a chuckle from my father.

Running Bear laughs lightly. "Cookie plowing the driveway for High."

That gets a loud giggle from my mother.

Running Bear smiles at us. "Love is not an obligation. It's a selfless commitment—a partnership bound by love. Follow me to the fire. We will sprinkle your corn, sage, tobacco, and sweetgrass. Our creator will bless your union."

I lift Cookie into my arms, carrying her to the bonfire. Setting her onto her feet, I take her bouquet and hand it to Joker. He looks at it as if it's a snake ready to strike, then quickly hands it off to Mafia Man. Then, he does something out of character: threads his arm around Jewel, his muscled forearm under her thin one, supporting CJ's sleeping body. Where Jewel is concerned, his words and actions don't jibe.

Running Bear asks us to repeat after him as we sprinkle the contents of our bags into the fire. The kids giggle as we repeat the words onto each other's lips, dumping our tobacco, corn, sage, and sweetgrass into the fire.

We don't hear Running Bear pronouncing us married. I swoop up my woman, lips fused. Then I stalk inside, through the game room, and up the stairs to our room. I've been hard for hours. The ceremony intensified my need to fuck my woman...my wife. I set Cookie on the bed; she looks up at me with all-consuming love. She shimmies up her dress, spreading her knees wide. Her breaths are coming out in pants. She runs a finger down her soaked panties, her heated gaze on the bulge in my jeans. My woman's tits are engorged from not feeding our son. If they fill much more, she'll be in pain. That will entail warm compresses before I can suck them dry. I strip, slipping onto the bed.

"Baby, I need to get you out of your dress and take care of your tits."

She whimpers her frustration. I chuckle, undoing the Harley buttons. Then I grunt when her hand finds my balls. She rolls and squeezes them, sending a lightning bolt to my cock. Her small hand moves to my shaft, stroking me from root to tip.

"Running Bear asked our creator to make your seed plentiful and my womb fertile."

"Yeah," I agree, removing her dress and then her bra. I run my hand over her tits, pinching her nipples gently. My woman has gorgeous globes: massive, firm, and round. Her areolas are a duskier rose color than before she was pregnant—her pretty pink, hard buds are pointed, begging to be sucked.

My wife trembles at my touch. She moans, pushing her chest up.

I remove her panties and put them to my nose. I inhale, filling my lungs with her pussy perfume. Then I release them; they flutter to the floor. I feather the pad of my finger around her clit and through her fold. She moans; her hips surge up. *Fuck, so wet for me.* I put my mouth to her clit, sucking lightly.

She threads her fingers through my hair, holding me to her. I kiss between her lips, down her cleft, tonguing her sacred hole.

"Oh, god!" she cries out, clamping her thighs around me.

I run my hand over her belly, up her sides, to her tits. I cup them in my palms. Resting my chin on her mound, I ask, "Are you still set on breastfeeding CJ until he's two?"

She jerks up her head, staring down at me in disbelief.

I chuckle, kissing her mound. My cock is goddamn granite, throbbing against the mattress. My wife is wired; her entire body hums with sexual need. Her scent is in my nose, her sweet taste on my tongue. I know I need to slow my ass down; teasing her will make her squirt. My wife loves full-body orgasms, and I intend for her to have one on her wedding night.

"Answer, baby," I demand, licking around her naval.

"Um...*oui*, or three," she says breathily.

A trickle of milk runs down each of her breasts. I slide up her body, my tip at her pussy entrance. She wiggles, trying to get me to glide in.

I steady my breathing. "Just my head while I empty your tits."

"I'm going to die, Christian!"

I chuckle again. Christian is the name she uses when she's annoyed with me. "You won't," I assure.

I latch on to her right nipple, giving my cock a tiny push. My head pops into her warm, wet, sweet hole. I groan. *So fucking good.*

Cookie cries out, *"Plus s'il vous plait!"* More, please.

245

I knead her breast and add to my suction, swallowing down her milk. It's sweeter than cow's milk, silky on my tongue. Delicious.

My wife writhes beneath me. I give her two more inches of my cock, forcing myself to stay still. It's fucking torture. I switch tits, sucking aggressively. The sound of my audible swallows fills the room.

"Amour, I can't...impossible, Amour," she mewls, thrashing her head against the mattress. She fists my hair, begging for me to fill her.

I give her another inch, rocking my hip slowly—her wet runs down my shaft onto my balls. I moan with the need to bury myself to the root. My body shakes from the effort of holding back—sweat beads pop out across my brow. My cock lengthens, thickens, becoming painfully hard.

We're both riding the razor's edge of ecstasy.

I drain her tit dry, licking the remnants of her milk off my swollen lips. I place a soft kiss onto each of her nipples.

"Wrap your legs around me, baby."

I cover my mouth with hers and slam my cock forward, impaling my woman.

She screams my name, digging her heels into my lower back. A gush of wetness comes from her pussy. My wife trembles from head to toe, her pussy clenching around me like a vise.

Jesus, so goddamn good!

I send my hips flying, fucking like a bull in heat. My balls slap against her beautiful ass. The squishing sound of her taking me, the smell of her sex, heightens my euphoria. Sweat pours from my temples, black spots dance behind my lids. I growl and snap my love for her against her lips. Tingling hits my lower spine, shooting straight to my balls. My sack draws up, my cock lengthens, thickens, and twitches.

"*Goddamnit!*" I shout, needing to be deeper within her.

I grip my woman's ass, anchoring her to take my powerful thrusts.

My wife's body tightens around me. She mumbles feverishly in French how much she loves me. Her words rocket me over the edge. I hump wildly, my cock jetting out my seed.

"Jesus Christ," I murmur between ragged breaths.

Cookie's pussy is still milking me. I stay deep, languishing in the feel of her. I push her long blonde curls from her face with a shaky hand. Her blues are clouded, her mind muddled in a euphoric haze. I cover her sweat-soaked body, wrapping my arms around her head, holding her close. Our heartbeats are fast; our mingled breaths are erratic. I murmur softly to her until our breathing settles and her pussy relaxes.

I turn us to our sides, face-to-face. Cookie's leg is hooked over my hip, her head resting on my bicep, her nose tucked into my pit.

"Totally worth the wait," she mumbles against my skin.

I chuckle, "Yeah, baby, it was."

We lay silent, wrapped up in each other, enjoying our closeness. The silence is broken by the loud sounds of sex coming from the other side of our wall. Joker and Jewel.

Cookie giggles, "It's not polite to listen."

"Christ," I laugh, kissing the crown of my woman's head.

"Da, Da, Da, Da," sings CJ from the other side of our door.

"Grandson, you're with *Mémé* and me tonight. Daddy's romancing Mommy between the sheets," says my father. "Consummating *it.*"

My mother giggles, "You're bad, Rene."

Dad's rumbling laugh filters into our room.

"Goodnight, Uncle High, Aunt Cookie, Uncle Joker, Aunt Jewel. Love you," yells Keeley up the stairs.

"Keeley, they're *mega-busy*," chastises Brie in her bossy way.

She's correct about Joker and Jewel; they're at their crescendo.

I chuckle, answering for all of us: "Night, sweethearts. Loved our wedding, and we love you both more."

Two sets of giggles fade away.

My wife kisses me just below my pit. "We have the best family in the whole wide world."

"Yeah, baby, we do. Lips."

I'm ready for round two, this time loving my wife, soft... and...sweet.

A HUGE THANKS FROM ME TO YOU!

I hope you enjoyed *Bound by Love: Sinners Series Book – 2.*

For more information about Susan Liberty's books please visit www. susanliberty.com

Kick back, relax, and enjoy the read!

Gratitude,
Susan

ABOUT THE AUTHOR

Susan Liberty grew up in Central New York. She obtained a Bachelor's Degree from Chamberlain College of Nursing with a minor in English. She furthered her education at the New York State University at Albany, focusing on American Literature and Creative Writing.

CREDIT TO THE LEGENDS

Adele, "Set Fire to the Rain," by Adele and Fraser T. Smith, 2010, XL Columbia, *21*, 2011.

Aerosmith, "Dream On," by Steven Tyler, 1972, Intermedia, *Aerosmith*, 1973.

Alicia Keys, "Girl on Fire," by Alicia Keys, Salaam Remi, Jeff Bhasker, and Billy Squier, 2012, RCA, *Girl on Fire*, 2012.

The Beatles, "In My Life," by Lennon–McCartney,1965, EMI, *Rubber Soul*, 1965.

Celine Dion, "I'm Alive," by Kristian Lundin and Andreas Carlsson, 2002, Columbia, *A New Day Has Come*, 2002.

Creed, "What's This Life For," by Scott Stapp and Mark Tremonti, 1995, Wind-Up, *My Own Prison*, 1998.

David Guetta ft. Sia, "Titanium," by Sia Furler, David Guetta, Giorgio Tuinfort, and Nick van de Wall, 2011, Virgin/Capitol US, *Nothing but the Beat*, 2011.

Fleetwood Mac, "Landslide," by Stevie Nicks, 1975, Reprise, *Fleetwood Mac*, 1975.

Guns N' Roses, "Knockin' on Heaven's Door," by Bob Dylan, 1990, Geffen, *Use Your Illusion II*, 1992.

Guns N' Roses, "November Rain," by Axl Rose, 1990–1991, Geffen, *Use Your Illusion I*, 1991.

Imagine Dragons, "Radioactive," by Alexander Grant, Ben McKee, Josh Mosser, Daniel Platzman, Dan Reynolds, and Wayne Sermon, 2012, KidinaKorner/Intersope, Night Visions, 2012.

Journey, "Open Arms," by Steve Perry and Jonathan Cain, 1981, Columbia, *Escape*, 1981.

Kings of Leon, "Beautiful War," by Caleb Followill, Nathan Followill, Jared Followill, and Matthew Followill, 2013, RCA Records, *Mechanical Bull*, 2013.

Lady Gaga, "The Edge of Glory," by Stefani Germanotta, Fernando Garibay, and Paul Blair, 2010, Streamline/Kon Live/Interscope, *Born This Way*, 2011.

Miranda Lambert, "The House That Built Me," by Tom Douglas and Allen Shamblin, 2009, Columbia Nashville, *Revolution*, 2010.

Lynyrd Skynyrd, "Free Bird," by Allen Collins and Ronnie Van Zant, 1973, MCA, *Lynyrd Skynyrd (Pronounced 'Lĕh-'nérd 'Skin-'nérd)*, 1973.

Madonna, "Like a Prayer," by Madonna and Patrick Leonard, 1988, Sire/Warner Bros., *Like a Prayer*, 1989.

Nirvana, "The Man Who Sold the World," by David Bowie, 1993, DGC, *MTV Unplugged in New York*, 1995.

Pink Floyd, "Comfortably Numb," by David Gilmour and Roger Waters, 1979, Harvest, *The Wall*, 1980.

Queen, "We Will Rock You," by Brian May, 1977, EMI, *News of the World*, 1977.

R.E.M., "Everybody Hurts," by Bill Berry, Peter Buck, Mike Mills, and Michael Stipe, 1992, Warner Bros., *Automatic for the People*, 1993.

The Rolling Stones, "Wild Horses," by Jagger/Richards, 1969–1970, Rolling Stones, *Sticky Fingers*, 1971.

Scorpions, "When You Came into My Life," by Klaus Meine, Rudolf Schenker, Titiek Puspa, and James F. Sundah, 1996, East West, *Pure Instinct*, 1996.

Steppenwolf, "Born to Be Wild," by Mars Bonfire, 1968, Dunhill/RCA, *Steppenwolf*, 1968.

Tina Turner, "Proud Mary," by John Fogerty, 1970, Liberty Records, *Workin' Together*, 1971.

Whitney Houston, "I'm Every Woman," by Nickolas Ashford and Valerie Simpson, 1992, Arista, *The Bodyguard: Original Soundtrack Album*, 1993.

ALSO BY SUSAN LIBERTY

The Promise Series:

Broken Promises

A Vow to Love and Protect

A Pledge for Eternity

The Sinners Series:

Hearts that Burn

Bound by Love

Forever Mine

Ties that Bind

Blood of Our Blood

Boundless Love

Scandalous Series:

The Untamable Lizzy Brown